"BIG MONEY, DIRTY SECRETS AND THE ULTIMATE IN BLACKMAIL!"
Best Sellers

Against the opulent background of the world's richest financial capital and the international playgrounds of the wealthy, one man battles to stop the most daring, most sophisticated blackmail caper ever attempted.

The demand: a fortune in uncut diamonds . . . or else a prestigious Swiss bank and five of its major depositors, each with a secret numbered bank account full of someone else's money, will have the lid blown off their secrets.

For the five, disclosure means certain disaster. For the bank, it means a breach of security threatening the world's most notorious financial system. For David Christopher, the one man smart and tough enough to stop the plot, it means following a cold trail through a sizzling jungle of lust, greed, treachery, and daring.

THE BLOCKBUSTER NOVEL OF INTERNATIONAL SPLENDOR AND KNIFE-EDGED SUSPENSE!

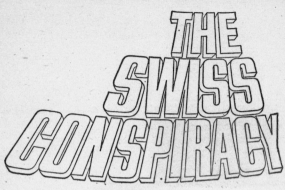

THE SWISS CONSPIRACY

Michael Stanley

Based on the screenplay by Norman Klenman, Philip Saltz-man and Michael Stanley. Story by Norman Klenman, Howard Merrill and Norman Sedawie.

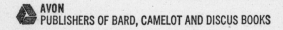

AVON
PUBLISHERS OF BARD, CAMELOT AND DISCUS BOOKS

THE SWISS CONSPIRACY is an original publication of Avon Books.

AVON BOOKS
A division of
The Hearst Corporation
959 Eighth Avenue
New York, New York 10019

Copyright © 1976 by Avon Books
Published by arrangement with the author.
ISBN: 0-380-00492-5

First Avon Printing, February, 1976
Fourth Printing

AVON TRADEMARK REG. U.S. PAT. OFF. AND
FOREIGN COUNTRIES, REGISTERED TRADEMARK—
MARCA REGISTRADA, HECHO EN CHICAGO, U.S.A.

Printed in the U.S.A.

I

Guard Otto Brunnen was dreaming about Wurst. Not just the Kalbsbratwurst of Zurich, although he often thought that veal sausage was his favorite. Today his imagination ran riot in a pork-butcher's shop and he was surrounded by sausages of such odoriferous variety that his stomach gurgled in response. There were Klopfen from Basle, Schublig from St. Gallen, longeole from Geneva, Salsiz from Engadine, boutefas from Payerne . . .

"Excuse me," the voice interrupted timidly. Irritated in the extreme at this intrusion on his fantasy Guard Brunnen snapped, "What is it?" His eyes focused on the intruder. Just as he would have guessed. A little old woman with a black scarf tied around her mousy gray hair, a gray knitted shawl over her shoulders and a worn black handbag hanging from her left arm.

"Madam," Guard Brunnen told her sternly, "the tellers are straight ahead, the deposit and with-

1

drawal forms are on those counters over there. We have no bathroom and no telephone."

She looked at him with beady black eyes. "It was just that I thought you should know about the letter."

"What letter, madam?" Guard Brunnen was reaching the end of his patience. He wanted to get back to his Wurst. He wondered how much a Wurst shop would cost. Perhaps one day he could save enough to make a down payment on one of his own.

"The one on the floor. By your feet."

A thrill of anxiety shot through Guard Brunnen's nervous system and there was a singing sound in his head. When he managed to turn his head downward, sure enough, there it was. On the polished marble floor the envelope was an eyesore. Guard Brunnen blinked in disbelief. It was not possible. An envelope. On the floor of his bank. Hurtilbank. One of the premier banks of the Bahnhofstrasse. Of Zurich. Of Switzerland itself. Guard Brunnen waved the old lady aside and bent down to retrieve the envelope, straining the brass buttons of his dark serge uniform. As he straightened up, his overweight body pumping air, Brunnen had a feeling of trouble and resented it. Trouble was not befitting a fresh sunny spring morning when there were only a few customers in the bank, going about their own business and leaving him free to dream of sausages. Until now. The guard looked the envelope over. It was sealed and ready for posting. On the front the writer had scripted with some kind of glo-red felt pen the address:

URGENT

Brunnen looked around hoping that somebody had dropped the envelope by mistake and would come to him to claim it. There were three customers at the teller windows, a plump elderly man standing at a courtesy desk laboriously filling in a deposit form. Nobody else except the little old woman. The guard vented some of his exasperation on her.

"Thank you, madam," he informed her in his loftiest tones, "I shall now deal with this letter and dispose of it. Good morning."

Holding the envelope away from his body as if it were beneath his rank in the bank to deal with an envelope from the floor of the lobby, Brunnen strode away from the little old woman with all the dignity he could muster. He mounted the broad marble staircase whose majestic proportions were the pride of Hurtilbank, going over his account of the incident. No matter what he said the Gorgon would find a way to blame him. She always did. Footsteps clacking on the marble slabs, Brunnen took the staircase to the first floor and let himself into a large office where busy clerks fed information into computer terminals against paneled walls. The clerks did not look up, but the four secretaries noticed him from their electric typewriters without more than a momentary break in their typing rhythm and wondered why Brunnen was looking even more ill at ease than usual. They understood how he felt. The Gorgon had that effect on everybody.

Then Brunnen was face-to-face with the Gorgon

3

herself. "The Gorgon" was the staff nickname for Madame Florelle, the tyrannous Chief Accountant of Hurtilbank. Chunky, severe and elderly, Madame Florelle heard the guard's explanation without changing expression. Her nod of dismissal convinced Brunnen that he was in deep trouble, and he returned to his post in the lobby, a doomed man.

Florelle looked over her domain. Her toilers, without missing the exchange between her and Brunnen, had already anticipated this move. Every computer was active, every typewriter was typing busily. Florelle returned two file trays to a file box and locked the box. Then she took the papers on her desk and folded them into a legal-size manila folder which she placed carefully in a deep drawer of her desk. She selected one of a formidable bunch of keys from a ring attached to a belt around her waist and locked the desk. She tested the drawers to make sure that the lock was holding. Only then did she pick up the white envelope from her desk and, all businesslike efficiency, march from her kingdom into the adjacent office.

Madame Florelle was in the ledger room of Hurtilbank although she might have stepped through the looking glass into the nineteenth century. Many of the bookkeepers still preferred their traditional standup Hong Kong desks where they wrote industriously in heavy ledgers with leather-bound corners. The room had dark walls of polished wood, tall, narrow windows and window boxes with flowering petunias. The results of the figuring done in this Dickensian setting would end up on computer cards, but Madame Florelle did not deem it likely.

Florelle disdained elevators. After leaving the

4

ledger-room, she climbed the stairs to the executive floor of the bank. She opened a door marked:

F. BENNINGER, VICE-PRESIDENT

and went inside. A secretary looked up inquiringly as Florelle entered, then blushed as she realized who it was.

"Is he free, Maria?" Florelle asked.

"Yes—yes, of course. I'll let him know ..." The secretary pressed an intercom switch. "Madame Florelle to see you, Herr Benninger."

A muffled voice came back over the speaker. "Send her in, Maria—and bring us two coffees."

Maria looked up at Florelle, trying to hold on to a nervous smile, but the older woman was already on her way to Benninger's office. As the door closed behind her, the second secretary, a timid sparrow of a girl whose typewriter had raced at breakneck speed from the moment Florelle entered the room, stopped typing and looked over at Maria.

"What do you think, M.?" she asked.

Maria was busy matching two cups with saucers and spoons and didn't answer.

"I mean," the sparrow went on, "it has to be something pretty important to bring the Gorgon out of her cave at this hour, don't you think?"

Her full attention on the spout of the electric coffeepot, Maria measured out two demitasses, put two lumps of sugar into each saucer and picked up the cups.

"The Gorgon doesn't take sugar," said the second secretary.

"I know, Suzanne," Maria answered, "but she'll

give me hell if they aren't there." Maria gestured to the door and Suzanne got up to open it for her.

"So what do you think, M.?" Suzanne insisted.

"Let you know when I come out," Maria told her. "Now open the door before the Gorgon turns me into stone."

Franz Benninger, the cruder Hurtilbank clerks used to joke over their fourth Lowenbrau, could only reach climax if he made love in a morning suit. The Executive Vice-President of Hurtilbank came from a family that had been with Hurtilbank for a century, and he wore his position in the bank as if he were a bishop presiding over the liturgy in his home cathedral.

Benninger was in his office a half-hour earlier than any of his staff, knew every detail of the bank's procedures from personal experience and had a phenomenal memory for the balances in individual customer accounts. Not that he was given to proving his knowledge. Franz was too discreet, too good a banker for that. It was just that his staff knew that Benninger knew more about their specialized tasks than they did, and their respect for his authority was tempered with fear.

Despite all this, despite his conservative manner, his apparent lack of humor, his fastidious manner of dressing, his impatience with imperfection, there was something about Benninger that attracted women. It was hard to say exactly what it was. Slim, in his forties, on the dark side, he was not a handsome man. Still it was there. Some kind of banked fire inside him that a woman sensed.

This spring morning, Benninger was elegant in a charcoal-gray silk suit with a white carnation boutonnière. Sipping his coffee, he looked at the white envelope on his desk, the clear firm script, the distinctive red of the felt pen.

"What do you think, Franz?" Florelle asked him. Benninger put down his coffee and ran the sensitive tips of his fingers over the vellum of the envelope.

"Curious," he told her. "Very curious."

"What does that mean? Is it a joke?" Madame Florelle had no time for subtleties.

Benninger went on stroking the envelope as if he were attempting to read its contents with his hands. "Possibly," he told her finally. He stood, picked up the letter from his desk and said, "I have a feeling about you, my friend!" A smile touched his face as he met the granitelike earnestness of Florelle. "But feelings are idiotic, aren't they?"

"Not always," she answered unexpectedly. Florelle finished her coffee and preceded Benninger to the door, where she waited for him to open it for her. "I'd like to know if it is a joke, Franz. After you've been to Herr Hurtil. Will you give me a call?"

"Don't worry, Elsa. It's probably nothing at all." Benninger wished he believed it.

The distinguished President of Hurtilbank, Herr Johann Hurtil, had a beaked nose that made him look like an eagle. The impression was bolstered by his broad, slightly hunched shoulders and a way he had of cocking his head to one side, the better to listen to somebody addressing him.

However, even those who were irritated by his aquiline appearance and mannerisms admitted that he was the ideal president for a Swiss bank. His great-grandfather had founded Hurtilbank. His grandfather and father had been presidents before him. His English was Oxford, his French Parisian, his German, Italian and Spanish fluent, natural. If his intelligence was something less than genius-level, he had a quality more valuable to a bank president: instinct.

Hurtil had a feeling for the directions a bank should take. When other banks were still strong on Eurodollars, Hurtil was already into marks and yen. As larger banks were diversifying into marks and yen, Hurtil was already investing in gold and silver. When gold and silver became the universal goal, Hurtil was already using petrodollars to corner futures in sugar, wheat, rice and other grains.

The source of Hurtilbank's fiscal strength was its president's willingness to take on new money in secret accounts from whatever source. Contrary to popular impression, the volume of funds in secret accounts in the average Swiss Bank is a relatively small proportion of the bank's total deposits. Estimates indicate that secret bank accounts may contain approximately ten percent of a Swiss bank's gross turnover. Not that this is insignificant. Ten percent of a bank's gross turnover can mean the difference between a healthy profit and near-bankruptcy.

But Johann Hurtil, despite his aristocratic financial lineage, believed in the stability of funds in the account of the secret investor. It did not matter to him whether the investor was a Latin American military dictator, an African general, Emperor Haile Selassie, the deposed monarch of Ethiopia, a new-rich American PX sergeant in Germany or Vietnam, an English real-estate dealer, a Japanese manufacturer, an Australian mining king, a Burmese opium trader, a Las Vegas gambler: Turks, Greeks, Italians, Germans, French, Americans or Third World plunderers—they were all one to Johann Hurtil.

And for a very good reason. This kind of money tended to stay put. It was being saved for a rainy day. Frequently it stayed forever. It was never collected because the dictator was assassinated or the gambler was murdered or the businessman was jailed. And in each of these events the winner was Hurtilbank.

Not even Hurtil knew what proportion of Hurtilbank resources came from secret bank accounts. He left that to Benninger. This was another quality that made Hurtil a successful president. He knew the men he could trust to run his bank while he wined and dined the bankers and investors who needed to be wined and dined, or he represented Hurtilbank at important meetings of the Swiss or international financial community.

Benninger knew that secret bank account funds represented 39.87 percent of Hurtilbank resources, and for some reason this figure surfaced in his mind as he entered the luxurious office of his president and shook hands with Hurtil across the dark blue leather top of the vast desk.

Hurtil waved Benninger to an easy chair, then chose a pipe from a Dunhill stand and began a deliberate ritual of filling it. The aroma of the special mix filled the office and Benninger, a nonsmoker, realized that he enjoyed tobacco as long as it was not burning.

"Beautiful morning," Hurtil said easily.

"Yes—yes, it is that." Benninger was anxious to get down to business but knew better than to try until Hurtil was ready.

"Let's hope we've had the last of winter."

"Probably too much to hope for, at the end of

April. Always the chance of a fog or two, don't you think?"

Hurtil finished tamping the threads of tobacco into the bowl of his pipe and looked around for a lighter. The lighter, a squat silver Ronson galleon, was nearer to Benninger who stood up and handed it across to Hurtil. Then he dropped the letter in front of Hurtil.

In the act of pressing the button of the lighter, Hurtil paused and looked up at Benninger.

"Something urgent?" Hurtil was slightly caustic. He liked to control a conversation totally, especially with his brilliant vice-president.

"Perhaps," Benninger answered.

Hurtil failed to get the Ronson going—Benninger could swear it was intentional—then opened a drawer in his desk, extracted matches. He lit one, then a second and a third, while Benninger watched him in dread fascination. Finally the pipe began to draw smoothly and Hurtil was ready to talk business.

"Why is it urgent?" he asked Benninger.

"I don't know that it is. The foyer guard found it this morning on the floor inside the main entrance. Seeing that it was addressed to you, he brought it to Madame Florelle who passed it on to me."

"Curious." Hurtil was finally involved.

"That's what I thought," Benninger replied.

Hurtil reached for a gold letter opener on his desk and slit open the envelope neatly at the top fold. He peered inside, then asked Benninger to give his opinion.

"I don't know much about letter-bombs," Benninger admitted, "but if it was, I think it would have gone off already."

"Comforting thought," Hurtil remarked.

The bank president extracted a sheet of vellum paper that matched the envelope and unfolded it.

"Preposterous," he said, tossing the sheet of paper across the desk to Benninger.

Benninger reached for it and looked over the single sheet carefully, before reading the message. The writing matched the address on the envelope. The same script. The same felt pen. The same glo-red color. The message read:

> YOU WILL PAY US
> FIVE MILLION FRANCS
> FOR OUR SILENCE .
> WAIT FOR INSTRUCTIONS

Benninger leaned over and passed the page carefully back to Hurtil. If Hurtil was nervous the only sign of it was another series of matches in a renewed effort to light his already dead pipe.

"What do you make of it?" Hurtil asked.

"A threat . . . and a demand for ransom, I suppose," Benninger answered.

"Well, of course it's a demand for money—but ransom? You pay ransom to buy back something you own from somebody who has stolen it from you. Isn't that correct?"

"That is correct."

Hurtil waved his pipe, sure that his logic was irresistible. "Tell me, what do they have that is so important that we would be forced to pay out five million francs to get it back?"

Benninger spread his hands helplessly. "I don't know—I really couldn't begin to guess . . ."

"Of course you couldn't. Because they have nothing. That's the whole thing. In a nutshell. After all, what could they have?"

11

Benninger stood up. The man became the machine again. "I'll run a routine check over the vaults, the safes, the safety deposit boxes—but I'm sure you're right."

"I appreciate your bringing it to my attention all the same, Benninger." Hurtil waved his pipe generously. "We can't be too careful, can we?"

Then Hurtil rose, and smiled dismissal at his vice-president. It was simple courtesy. It also gave Hurtil a chance to remind the five-foot-seven Benninger that his president was a shade over six feet tall.

Benninger was at the door of Hurtil's office when the intercom phone on the president's desk buzzed urgently.

"Just a moment, Benninger," Hurtil said, "it might have something to do with this letter." Hurtil picked up the phone. "Yes, Anna? . . . Miss Denise Abbott? Did she say why? Yes . . . A personal matter . . . I see. Well, how about two-thirty this afternoon? I should be back from lunch by then. Confirm that for me, will you?"

Hurtil cradled the phone thoughtfully and then seemed to realize that Benninger was still with him. "Oh, sorry, Benninger. Just a routine bank matter by the sound of it." His smile this time was genuine. "I'm becoming an alarmist in my old age."

There was a surge of sympathy between the two men, as if they had a sudden realization that their personal rivalries were picayune compared to the Loch Ness monsters brooding beneath the surface of the future.

II

Mr. Robert Hayes of Chicago was no Adonis. He was only five feet four, disliked exercise and ran to pudginess. His taste in dress seemed to have been formed on a diet of Prohibition movies, even including the broad-brimmed felt hat. A noticeable squint in his left eye had only one thing in its favor: It had relieved Hayes of the onus of serving his country during the Second World War.

It might have been the combination of these repelling qualities that led to Hayes's selection as chief courier for Luigi Valente Associates of Chicago. Or else it was Luigi's macabre sense of humor. He figured that Hayes was the least likely of his men to be afflicted with the vice of personal ambition. And the least likely to attract the smooth, well-dressed, well-educated predators of Europe.

Robert Hayes was the first step in the long process by which Luigi Valente Associates, better known as Big Lug's Mob, laundered its money.

Once or twice a month, Hayes picked up a steel,
leather-covered attaché case from Valente, boarded
a TWA 707 at O'Hare International Airport
connecting with a TWA 747 at John F. Kennedy,
New York, that flew him to Zurich via Geneva. The
attaché case held cash, usually a round million
dollars, creamed off from Big Lug's gambling casinos, numbers games, prostitution rings, drug sales,
union payoffs and the freight ripoffs at the airport,
the docks, the rail and the trucking terminals.
Hayes's regular trips to Switzerland removed the
cash from the inquisitive scrutiny of the agencies
of the State of Illinois and of the United States
Federal Government.

But Zurich was only the first step on the tortuous
journey. From there the funds fed into a Lichtenstein or a Bahamanian company. These companies
built luxury hotels in Mexico and gambling casinos
around the Caribbean. The gambling casinos were
attached to elegant hotels on beaches that were
never used. The Mexican and Caribbean hotels and
casinos were theoretically owned by enterprising
indigenes who liked to cross-pollinate with more
diversified American companies. These in turn had
a penchant for hotels in Florida, transportation
companies in California and huge real estate and
construction empires in New York and Chicago.
And so finally home again to Big Lug as the vigor-
ous president of Luigi Valente Associates.

Robert Hayes had never quite accustomed
himself to the thought of carrying around a million
dollars in cash in a nondescript briefcase—even one
with a combination lock. When the big rubber
wheels skidded on to the runway at Zurich airport
there was no more relieved passenger on the 747
than Hayes. Between him and the security of the

14

vaults of Hurtilbank was only a short limousine ride to the city. And that was a pushover. The Swiss had a quaint old-fashioned respect for other people's money, even when it was as accessible as a very portable briefcase carried by a very small man.

Normally Hayes left the first-class section of the 747 with a jaunty smile at the stewardesses, a strutting little peacock of a man ready to take over Zurich. Except for today. Except for this brisk fresh inviting sunshiny day waiting to embrace the jaded traveler from the Windy City.

Dwight McGowan was the first to notice the tension in Hayes. The big paunchy Texan was attending to a very important piece of business. He was retrieving his genuine Texas pale fawn-colored Stetson hat from the overhead locker when some idiot bumped into him. Hard. McGowan almost dropped the hat. The big man recovered his balance and swung around, angry, to protest—only to find that Hayes seemed oblivious of what he had done and was moving toward the exit door with the anxiety of a man who considers being first off the plane a matter of life and death.

McGowan shrugged his shoulders and let Hayes go. It takes all types, he muttered to himself, and why disturb my ulcer? Besides, McGowan had another important task at hand. The overhead locker also held a longish canvas bag in which McGowan had stashed his bourbon. Armed with his canvas bag, McGowan was like a camel in the desert. He could go fourteen days, if necessary, without water.

McGowan took his time, eased the canvas bag safely to his seat, struggled into a light-tan spring topcoat that matched his cowboy hat and was

15

ready to go. McGowan could see Hayes at the head of the line, moving impatiently like a dog waiting for an elevator door to open. On a whim, he decided to keep Hayes in sight. Was it sheer cussedness or did the man really have a deadline to meet?

There were half a dozen other passengers between Hayes and McGowan, and the Texan let it stay that way—past the tired smiles of the steward and the hostesses, through the long flexible snout into the terminal, along echoing aseptic corridors between lavishly lit signs advertising banks and watches and chocolate and hotels and such typical Swiss companies as the Zurich Hilton and Hertz Rent-a-Car. Hayes still remained intent, locked inside himself, on the fast-moving walkway, against the excited chirruping of eager boarding passengers, gliding by in clouds of French and German and Schwyzerdutsch.

What puzzled McGowan was that Hayes did not look like a man given to self-absorption. Yet Hayes seemed to miss completely the quick start of the immigration officer who examined his passport. Even from where he was, back down the line, McGowan saw the officer double-check the name of Hayes against a card or notebook in front of him.

Then after Hayes grunted his thanks for his passport and headed for the customs officers who may or may not question incoming passengers, McGowan could have sworn that the immigration officer passed some kind of signal across the terminal. The vibration from the immigration officer seemed to end up at a stocky muscular civilian with a short moustache. The civilian was wearing a navy-blue topcoat and a narrow-brimmed dark-blue felt hat with a small peacock feather in the band. McGowan knew that he might have been mistaken because the civilian was intently reading a German newspaper and the signal, if it was a signal, had no visible effect.

By the time McGowan had completed his own brief session with the passport officer the man with the moustache had disappeared but a customs officer was making an unwonted spot check of Hayes's briefcase, despite his insistence that he had nothing to declare. McGowan could see Hayes muttering obscenities as he fiddled with the combination lock on his case, then used a key attached to a money belt and finally flipped open the lid of the case for the inspector.

McGowan's eyes bulged at the sight of the tightly packed bundles of American one-hundred-dollar bills. Hundreds of thousands. Maybe a million. Even the *sangfroid* of the Swiss immigration official suffered a ripple of reaction.

"The purpose of your visit, m'sieur?" the officer asked Hayes.

"Business. What else?" Hayes snapped back. Whatever the reason for Hayes's tension, it was not the money. He had done this trip dozens of times. To the Swiss his money was manna. Why should their customs officers make trouble? The inspector examining Hayes's briefcase snapped it shut and handed it back to Hayes with a bland, "Enjoy your stay in Switzerland, m'sieur."

This time Hayes did not even bother to grunt. He twisted the dial of the combination lock, picked up the briefcase and, almost at a run, headed for the luggage delivery where a feeder-mouth was spewing the 747 baggage on to a perpetual oval track. McGowan was so busy watching Hayes that the customs officer had to repeat his question.

"Do you have anything to declare, m'sieur?" McGowan came back to reality.

"Well, no, sir. That is, I don't plan to stay all that long. Just a li'l old business trip is all." McGowan tried to give the impression that he, like Hayes, was about to give the people of Switzerland the benefits of a million or two of his money for fruitful investment.

The thorough inspector, as if it was important to prove that no visitor was immune from a spot check, looked doubtfully at the size of McGowan's duffel bag and then demanded to see inside it. Sorrowfully McGowan opened the bag and pulled back the sides. Exposed to the curious gaze of the inspector were ten bottles of Southern Comfort bourbon, still in their original cartons.

"You import liquor, m'sieur?" the inspector asked.

"No, sir," McGowan replied.

"They are for gifts, perhaps?"

"No, sir. That's all mine. Got me a thirsty ulcer, I have. Feeds on bourbon." McGowan had the forced heartiness of a man defending a practice his primitive training had branded as evil.

The inspector looked severe. "For more than two bottles, m'sieur, there is an import duty."

"That's O.K. by me, mister. Just you tell me where I pay. Southern Comfort's mother's milk to me. Got to have my ulcer-milk right with me."

McGowan chattered on in relief while the inspector assessed the import duty on eight bottles of bourbon. To McGowan his bourbon was more than alcohol. It was a kind of gauge of how things were with him. Now he could admit it to himself. Some

18

time in his dreams the thought had come to him: If he got the bourbon through then the problem would go away. It would be all right. Now he was sure of it.

A medley of taxis back from a black Mercedes 600 limousine, the stocky man with the moustache, still devouring his newspaper, leaned against a green Peugeot. Inside the Peugeot, another man sat at the wheel, quiet, waiting. The driver had the engine running and his eyes were on the man with the moustache.

Up ahead Hayes climbed into the Mercedes 600. The chauffeur closed the door on Hayes, lifted his valise into the front passenger seat, then went smartly around the car and got in behind the wheel. The man with the moustache folded his newspaper and looked at his watch. Then, as if tired of waiting for a friend who had failed to show, he got into the Peugeot beside the driver. Neither man spoke.

When the Mercedes 600 left the curbside and headed for the airport exit, the Peugeot was following it.

In the United States, among the people Robert Hayes worked with, common sense dictated endless precautions. A man did not have a daily routine. He used different drivers in constantly changing cars and varied his routes to meeting places which themselves were used only once or twice.

Part of the joy of coming to Switzerland for Hayes was that he did not feel the need of taking such precautions. Hayes liked to be met at the airport by his favorite driver and invariably insisted that the driver take him to Hurtilbank by the same route. Into the north of the city, across the Bahnhof bridge to the massive Hauptbahnhof and finally into the Bahnhofstrasse itself.

Drivers who tried to convince Hayes that it was much faster to reach Hurtilbank by the Seiler-Graven or the Limmat Quai, never drove for him again. Hayes liked that slow drive between the lime trees down the Bahnhofstrasse to the small Hurtilbank building. He liked the prosperous, well-dressed shoppers and businessmen. He liked the *mélange* of fiercely modern towers and solid stone or brick buildings centuries old. He liked the thought that more money flowed through more banks in this single street than in any comparable street in the world. It gave this plain little man a feeling of power. He might be only a bagman. A small cog in the machine. But each time he visited Zurich, each time he drove down the Bahnhof-strasse, Hayes felt more at home. By God, he would show them all one day.

When the limousine drew up outside Hurtilbank and the chauffeur let Hayes out onto the sidewalk, Hayes almost forgot the tension that was eating away at him. He drew in his first conscious breath of Swiss spring air. He looked across the promenade at the Burkliplatz where the deciduous trees were shadowed with a transparent green of young leaves. The lawns, already rich and thick with grass, framed beds of flowering tulips and a profusion of spring flowers. At the end of the street was the Zurichsee, a sparkling blue expanse of inland lake which helped to explain why the Swiss did not seem to miss the ocean. Hayes thought that after the interview at the bank he might even take a drive around. Just look at the place for a change.

Might do him a lot of good as a matter of fact.

Hayes told the chauffeur to wait. He thought he would be maybe half an hour. Then he took his briefcase and turned toward Hurtilbank. Hayes sighed. The geraniums were in red flower in the windowbox. The small brass plaque engraved with the words

HURTIL ET CIE

was, if possible, polished even more brightly than usual. Through a glass display window to the left of the small double-doored entrance Hayes could see the bank's come-on—gold coins and medallions for sale.

Hayes was so busy savoring the familiar or perhaps sweating about the interview to come that he did not notice the green Peugeot parked at a discreet interval back from his limousine or the stocky man with the moustache who watched him enter Hurtilbank.

"I forgot to ask you, M.," said the sparrow to Maria, "how was the date with Fritz?"

"Youck!" Maria grimaced, looking critically at a torn fingernail.

"How come?" the sparrow wanted to know.

"No chemistry," Maria told her matter-of-factly, searching for a nail file in the drawer of her typing desk. "Like kissing a dead fish."

Suzanne was still giggling when the telephone rang. Maria took the call without a pause in her futile search for a nail file.

"Herr Benninger's office . . . just a moment." She put the call on hold and buzzed the inner office. Benninger's voice came through on the intercom.

"Yes, Maria."

"A Mr. Hayes to see you, sir."

"Mr. Hayes?"

"Yes, sir. Mr. Robert Hayes. From Chicago."

"Oh, certainly, Maria. Have him come up right away." Maria returned to the telephone.

"Brunnen? ... Yes, that's O.K. Herr Benninger can see Mr. Hayes immediately. Put him on the elevator and I'll meet him here."

Maria put down the phone, looked at her nail again and said, "Damn!" Then she got up, straightened her dress, and was about to go to the door, but changed her mind. She quickly took a compact from her handbag, checked her face, decided to add a dash of lipstick and fled—all under the hypnotized stare of the sparrow.

When the doors of the elevator parted Maria was there with a warm welcoming smile for the little man from Chicago.

"Good morning, Mr. Hayes," Maria greeted him. "Did you have a nice flight this time?"

"It was O.K.," Hayes said.

Hayes was couched in gloom again, abstracted, uneasy, shoulders slightly hunched under the weight of his anxiety. Maria was female enough to feel his mood. She did not speak again until the door closed behind Hayes and Benninger.

"Who's he?" asked the sparrow.

"Investor from the States," Maria told her. "Dated me once. He was O.K. A lot of chemistry. But wow, has he got something on his mind today? I'd love to be a fly on the wall."

Maria went back to her search for a nail file.

Herr Franz Benninger came around his desk,

suave, composed, the epitome of the gracious official receiving a distinguished client.

"Mr. Hayes, welcome to Zurich. We are delighted to have you ..."

"Cut the crap, Benninger. I want some answers."

Benninger blushed as Hayes ignored his
proffered hand, dropped his briefcase carelessly on
an easy chair and took some papers from his
pocket.

"Won't you at least sit down, Mr. Hayes? Try to
compose yourself? A drink perhaps?"

"I'll sit down when I'm ready to sit down,"
Hayes snapped back at him. "Here, take a look at
this."

Hayes shoved a sheet of paper at Benninger,
who took it, looked again at Hayes, and then decided to retire behind the protection of his desk.
Benninger studied the sheet of paper, then looked
across at Hayes, bewildered.

"I fail to see why you are so disturbed, Mr.
Hayes." Benninger was even more precise than
usual. "This is a statement of your account issued
by our bank. It is identified only by number—in the
usual way. I must presume that it was hand-deliv-
ered satisfactorily, since you have it in your possession. Really, Mr. Hayes, I see no problem ..."

"Then how about this?"

Angrily Hayes shoved a second sheet of paper
across the desk to Benninger. It was a photocopy
of the original bank statement, with one difference.
And the sight of that difference made Benninger's
stomach churn and his legs weak. Carefully Benninger drew in his chair and sat down. He hoped
that Hayes would not notice that his hands were
trembling and a fine sweat had broken out on his
upper lip.

With a tremendous internal effort Benninger ordered his hands to pick up the sheet of paper and his eyes to read it. Beyond any doubt it was the same felt pen. The same glo-red ink. The same clear bold rounded script. And the message itself had a dreadful familiarity.

> MR. ROBERT HAYES
> UNLESS YOU PAY US
> ONE MILLION SWISS FRANCS
> TO BE SILENT
> YOUR SECRET BANK STATEMENT
> WILL BE REVEALED
> TO YOUR BUSINESS ASSOCIATES

Fighting for time, Benninger asked, "How did you receive this?"

"Who cares?" Hayes answered him. "I got it." Hayes flopped into an armchair. The pseudo-anger gave way to terror and his voice almost squeaked. "You know what they can do to me?" Hayes took a folded tissue from his pocket and began to mop up the perspiration from his face. The fight had gone out of him. "I trusted you and your damned bank. You told me nobody would ever know and I believed you."

"Just a moment, Mr. Hayes ... just one moment. I sympathize deeply with your problem. Hurtilbank will do everything in its power to assist you, but any breach of security—that has to have occurred back in your own country. It is your own security which must be at fault."

The terrified rag doll which had been Hayes turned snarling animal.

"Don't be goddam stupid, Benninger. Anybody sees my statement, I'm dead. It goes right from here," Hayes tapped his right breast pocket, "into a safe deposit box . . . nobody but nobody . . ."

Hayes jumped up in a tantrum.

"Listen, you dummy. Don't you have any idea of the kind of people I work for? They kill a guy just for looking sideways at somebody they don't like. If they knew about this bank statement, they'd throw me into a sausage-making machine and eat the sausages—personally."

Unnerved anew by this thought, Hayes leaned across the desk and snatched the original of his bank statement out of Benninger's hand, folded it with jerky movements and put it back inside his coat pocket. Fear gave his eyes a mad gleam as he glared across the desk at Benninger.

"If there's a leak, it's right here, Benninger. In this super-secret unbreakable bank of yours." Hayes banged the desk with his fist. "I want to know who? and how? . . . right now."

"Please try to calm yourself, Mr. Hayes. We will never get anywhere if you keep on shouting like this." Benninger came around his desk to Hayes and took him by the arm. "Now please sit down, Mr. Hayes, and let us try to deal with this unfortunate incident rationally."

Reluctantly Hayes turned to the soft black leather armchair where he had thrown his briefcase, picked up the case and sat down to nurse the case in his lap. He had the beginnings of a rigor and Benninger was afraid Hayes was in for a heart attack.

The banker went to a wall cabinet beside his desk, opened the door, took down a bottle of Chivas Regal and poured two fingers into an amber-colored glass. He brought the glass back to Hayes.

"Here, drink this, Mr. Hayes." When Hayes made no move to accept the drink, Benninger pleaded, "Please, Mr. Hayes. You've had a serious shock. Take it."

Slowly Hayes reached for the scotch, held it with two hands and began to gulp it down. Benninger watched Hayes until he seemed calmer and then returned to his chair. The Swiss leaned on his desk and looked again at the ransom demand.

"Mr. Hayes, I want you to try to see this from my point of view. Our Swiss bank secrecy is a—well, sacred tradition. It is supported by Swiss Federal and Cantonal law. It is protected by extreme measures. There is no record, no instance that I know of, where it has ever been violated . . ."

Hayes began to mutter to himself.

"Speak up, Mr. Hayes. I can't hear you."

"I said somebody's squealed my goddam number to somebody . . . if it wasn't me—and it sure as hell wasn't—then it was somebody in Hurtilbank . . . and I want to know what Hurtilbank's going to do about it. Now. Today."

"Mr. Hayes . . ."

Hayes stood up. For him the conversation was obviously finished. The ball was in Benninger's court.

"Don't 'Mr. Hayes' me. I'm a dead man if I don't come up with a million Swiss francs in . . . who the hell knows how long I've got?"

While Hayes was talking he was fiddling with the combination lock of his attaché case across the desk from Benninger. His jittery fingers drew the banker's eyes.

"I don't have a million francs," Hayes went on, "and even if I did have, I'm damned if I'm going to put up for a leak that came from some shit in your goddam bank."

Hayes's ultimatum coincided with his unexpected success in opening the lid of the attaché case to reveal the cache of dollars inside.

"There's a million there," Hayes said carelessly. Now he was back on his own territory. "It's for the Valente account. Corporation account. O.K.?"

Benninger nodded that it was O.K.

"You count it," Hayes told him. "I'm too bushed. I'll pick up the bag later. And you can tell me what you're going to do . . . about that." Hayes pointed to the bank statement in front of Benninger.

Then before Benninger could react, Hayes was at the door of the office.

"I'm at the St. Gallen like always," Hayes said. Then he was gone.

Half to his feet, Benninger suddenly sank back into his chair. He looked at the glo-red script. So neat. So composed. So confident. With a deep sigh he reached for his phone, pressed the intercom button and dialed Hurtil's extention.

A fourth-generation banker is inured to the usual shocks of international banking: plunges in exchange rates, the vagaries of futures, the precipitate devaluations of nervous nations. But the photocopy of the bank statement of Mr. Robert Hayes, or rather of No. 406901 secret account at Hurtilbank, did not belong in any of the usual crisis categories. President Johann Hurtil was pale, not at all his poised self as he studied the sheet from Benninger and realized its implications.

"It must—it simply has to be some—some carelessness on his part. At the Chicago end. Don't you think?"

"Exactly what I said to him, Hurtil."

"And what—that is, how did he respond?"

"Do you recall the circumstances?"

"Vaguely. Doesn't he represent one of those gambling groups or some such?"

"Indeed. But this account . . ."

Hurtil looked at the statement. "You mean 406901?"

"Right. This account is a private account of his own. He has been borrowing from the syndicate account, speculating with the group funds in an effort to make profits for himself—quite unknown to the people he represents."

Hurtil did not like this at all.

"But, for heaven's sake, why did you allow this to happen? It's quite . . ."

"He has power-of-attorney for the group. He deposits and transfers millions of dollars. Hurtilbank has absolutely no control over him . . . but the point I'm making is this: If his people learn of this account Hayes will be executed. Immediately. Without compunction. These people are like that. If Hayes let so much as a whisper of this account slip out he would be signing his own death warrant. That's what he told me. I believe him."

The intercom on Hurtil's desk buzzed and the president vented some of his frustration over the speaker.

"Absolutely no calls, Anna. Understand?"

His secretary's voice came back respectful but firm. "I know that, sir, but Herr Helmut Rascher is calling you from Bonn. He insists that it is a matter of extreme urgency. He refuses to get off the line, sir."

"All right," Hurtil growled, with unaccustomed gruffness. "Put him through." Hurtil picked up the receiver of his telephone and pressed the lighted button. "This is Johann Hurtil," he said.

The voice at the other end of the phone launched into an hysterical flood of German. As the gist of it penetrated Hurtil's understanding he became very still and seemed to shrink in size as Benninger watched him. Finally he agreed to something and with careful precision placed the receiver back in its cradle.

Benninger did not need to ask Hurtil what the story was. Instinctively he knew. He waited while Hurtil stood up, walked over to his long French windows, drew aside the filmy lace drapes and looked out over the Burkliplatz as if this was a pleasure that he might not enjoy much longer. His voice seemed to come from a long distance when he spoke.

"That was one of our German investors. Herr Helmut Rascher. Bonn. He's flying in this afternoon. I think you can guess his—the nature of his particular problem."

"Oh, no," Benninger groaned. "Not another one."

"Oh, yes," Hurtil said. "Another one."

Hurtil came back from the windows. "It's just occurred to me," he said, like a man who sees and accepts the worst. "Mlle. Denise Abbott is coming to see me at two-thirty this afternoon with a personal problem. Do you think her personal problem might be the same as the problem of Mr. Hayes and of Herr Rascher?"

"God forbid," Benninger answered.

"God does not seem to be on the side of Hurtilbank at this moment," Hurtil answered abstract-

edly, crossing the room. "I think I shall break a
custom and have a drink. How about you?"

"I can't recall when I needed one so desperately." Hurtil's bar was a fine antique set into one
corner of his office beside a library of leather-
bound classics. The interior of the Louis XV piece
was mirrored to add luster to the cut crystal glasses
and decanters lining the shelves. A silver ice
bucket and tongs had already been prepared for
immediate use. Hurtil looked inquiringly at Benninger.

"A vodka, I think," Benninger said. "With ice."
Hurtil selected a Stolichnaya, put two ice cubes
into a crystal glass and covered them with three
fingers of vodka.

"I believe I'll join you," Hurtil told Benninger,
handing him his drink. "Now that I've made it." He
returned to the bar, mixed a second generous
vodka and raised his glass.

"To Hurtilbank, Benninger. May we have the
wisdom we need in this hour."

Benninger raised his glass in response. "Amen to
that."

Both men drank. Simultaneously they turned
away from the desk and looked for an easy chair.
Each man sat down, sipped his drink, and let the
alcohol fortify his sagging spirits.

"Do you think there will be others?" Hurtil
asked.

"It's impossible to tell," answered Benninger.
"Why should there be one or two or three? On
the other hand, if there is one, why not a dozen?"

"Ghastly thought. Well, at least we know what
that ransom note to the bank means."

"Presumably the five million francs will buy us

their silence about the identities of Hayes and Rascher and whomever else is known to them."

Hurtil was cynical. "We have only their word for that."

"You're right," Benninger agreed. "I understand statistics show a blackmailer never lets go. Once a payment is made, he keeps on demanding more."

"That is exactly the problem confronting us, Benninger," said Hurtil, waving his glass. "How do we defend ourselves? We are at bay, Benninger. How do we raise the drawbridge? Settle in for the siege?"

The vodka was getting to Hurtil. Restoring some of his courage. Or else, now that he had faced the worst, Hurtil was recovering his confidence. Some atavistic warrior instinct was asserting itself. He drained his glass, stood up and returned to the bar. "Finish that off, Benninger, and bring your glass here."

Benninger obliged and Hurtil poured two more stiff drinks, adding only a single cube of ice to each glass. This time the bank president did not sit down but walked across the room, away from Benninger.

"Listen to me, Benninger. My great-grandfather didn't found this bank for unprincipled desperadoes to undermine it. I don't know how these criminals got their information. Whether they bribed one of our clerks or—or—"

"Impossible," Benninger protested.

"What do you mean, impossible?"

"I mean that none of the clerks or bookkeepers would have . . . I mean, we've known them . . ."

"Ha ha! You're beginning to see the possibilities. Now that's what I want, Benninger. We have to be ruthless with ourselves. Suspect you, me, Florelle—

31

the whole bank. If we go down, we're going to go down fighting. You've got a good mind, Benninger. Put it to work. Tell me, how do we fight? What's our plan of campaign?"

Benninger was flattered. This was what he had always dreamed of. He and Hurtil side by side. Allies. Turning Hurtilbank into one of the leading financial institutions of the world. His vodka-loosened tongue was already speaking. The rationalist. The logician. The mathematician laying out the steps of his proof.

"Our weakness is that the information they have is dynamite. If it is published, a man like Hayes will die. Almost any secret-account holder will be damaged. Therefore the account-holders will be terrified, as Hayes and Rascher are. They will not fight. They will demand that the ransom be paid. And they will demand that Hurtilbank pay it. Hayes, as a matter of fact, has already insisted that the ransom is our responsibility."

"Go on," Hurtil told him.

"From our viewpoint, that is the bank's viewpoint, this information is even more dangerous. Once it is even suspected that Hurtilbank has lost control of the secrecy of its numbered accounts . . ."

"Hurtilbank will follow Sindona's Banque de Financement. The government will close us down."

"Exactly. There will be panic among our other account-holders. They will transfer accounts to other banks or to other countries that seem safer. Beirut. Singapore. Hong Kong. The Bahamas."

"So what do we do?" Hurtil asked. "Go to the police? The Federal Police have a bank detail. It's done some good things too."

"Never," Benninger answered vehemently.

"Why not?"

"Twenty-four hours after the police have the case, the press will have it. It will be headlines around the world. You can say good-bye to Hurtilbank."

"Aren't you being a little dramatic? The police have solved some very difficult cases, after all."

"Yes, and the newspaper headlines are one or two days behind. Look at the case of that American who wrote the so-called autobiography of Howard Hughes."

"Didn't he have a Swiss wife?"

"That's the one. Do you want that kind of publicity about Hurtilbank?"

Hurtil shook his head and took a brief turn on the thick cream wool carpet. "Can you handle it as an internal matter then? Put some people on to it from inside the bank?"

Benninger sipped his vodka before replying. "I've been wondering that," he admitted. "While we were speaking about the police. On the whole, I think not."

Hurtil was plainly disappointed. "Why not?"

"Too dangerous. It means that we must take these people into our confidence—tell them the problem. That immediately increases the danger of spreading the story. Somebody will say something in a bar. A reporter will hear of it." Benninger took a sip of his drink. "In any case," he added, "we simply do not have anybody qualified for this kind of investigation."

This time the bank president looked crushed. He gestured with his glass. "You mean that we can do nothing? That we must sit here passively and let those scoundrels take away our bank?"

"I didn't say that."

"What is your alternative?"

"David Christopher."

Hurtil choked on a swallow of vodka and spluttered. "Who?"

"David Christopher."

"That fellow in Geneva?"

"That's the one."

"But—well, he's an American."

"That could be an advantage in keeping the story from Swiss reporters."

Still dubious, Hurtil protested, "But what do we know about him? How do we know we can trust him? To invite the wrong person into our confidence would be tantamount to suicide."

"Christopher, if I may say so, Hurtil, is exactly the man we need in this kind of situation. First I was most impressed . . ."

"You've met him?"

"Several times in recent months when he was working for Swiss National Assurance and for Crédit Suisse. If you want confirmation call Reichert at Crédit Suisse—or Linden if you prefer at SNA . . ."

"I'm not doubting your word, Benninger. If you say he's a good man, he's a good man. What's his background?"

"The United States Department of Justice. Left them with an excellent reputation to go into private practice as an investigator. Apparently enjoys Switzerland and settled here."

"What does he . . . I mean how . . . his appearance? That kind of thing? We have to safeguard the image of Hurtilbank, you know."

Benninger gave the question serious consideration before he answered. "He is not a conservative businessman, if that is what you are asking. Neither does he look like an investigator. What can I say? His standards of style are those of our sons. People will probably think he is a rich American client of the bank. He drives a Lamborghini."

Hurtil walked across to his desk and put down his glass carefully on the writing-pad blotter. "I don't know why I am putting these objections, to be honest with you. I must be unnerved by the whole situation. I asked you for a plan and you gave me one. What other choice do we have?" He reached for his telephone. "How do we get in touch with this American?"

"He has an office in Geneva. Under his own name. David Christopher."

Hurtil switched on his intercom. "Anna?"

"Yes, sir?" the disembodied voice answered him.

"I want to talk to a Mr. David Christopher in Geneva. If he is not in his office ask if there is a number where we can contact him. It's urgent."

Hurtil walked back to the bar and glanced toward Benninger, who brought across his glass. The bank president topped up both drinks, gave one to Benninger and proposed another toast.

"Here's to David Christopher. May he prove the right man for Hurtilbank's hour of need!"

III

———◆———

David Christopher was tired. Or depressed. He
wondered if it was the girl. Probably it was the
girl.

He slipped the Lamborghini into second and
flickered his lights at the white Mercedes ahead.
His personal radar played over the driver of the
Mercedes, weighing her possible reactions. Fast-
lane drivers were invariably surprised when another driver overtook them. Their usual instinct
was to speed up—to try to shake off the intruder on
their territory. The girl with the Lanvin scarf and
the dark glasses at the wheel of the Mercedes was
an exception. Activating her right-hand signal she
put the Mercedes smoothly over into the middle
lane ahead of a blue Citroën and allowed Christopher to pass.

David had an impression of platinum blond hair
under the scarf and of a youthful, strong, good-
looking face behind the dark glasses. It could almost have been Lisa. He swore softly to himself,

guided the automatic floor gear back into Over-
drive and felt the surge of exhilaration as the
wheels bit into the concrete autobahn linking Bern
with Olten and Aarau and Zurich.

Christopher let the speedometer needle settle
back to a 185-kmh cruising speed, felt for a cigarette and his lighter and began to think about Lisa.
These Swiss girls had something. They really did.
An air. A way of moving their bodies. It was so—
so—so feminine, damn it. The way they moved you
knew that they knew they had a vagina. And tits.
And wasn't that what it was all about? Basically,
anyhow.

Not that he meant to knock American girls. He
could think of one or two from his own immediate
past who could stand up in any company. Diane
for one. And Helen and ... but that wasn't the
point. You had to admit that a girl like Lisa was
different.

Take just the languages, for example. You were
brought up in the States, right? Your English was
O.K. You could maybe stumble along in fair Spanish. Or maybe not. But these European babies.
Wow! They answered the phone in French, spoke
to their bosses in English, talked German to their
girlfriends, Italian to their grandmothers and Spanish to the maître d' without so much as batting an
eye. And talking of eyes. David thought about
Lisa's eyes and decided that he had been a damn
fool. Why the hell did he have to fight with her?
Over nothing. Well, to him it was nothing but
she'd made such a goddam fuss over it.

David could see the trouble developing before it
happened. A Mercedes diesel semi-trailer was in
the middle lane struggling to pass a Volkswagen
Home-Mobile, a Simca 1100 and a Deux Chevaux

ambling along in the slow lane. As David came into the scene, the driver of a Fiat semi-trailer following the Mercedes decided to make a bid for first position and pulled out in front of the Lamborghini at a bare ninety kilometers.

Christopher used the big engine to slow his speed, dropping back into third, then into second, fuming at the delay. He'd promised to meet Hurtil and Benninger at the bank by six for an initial briefing. He'd like to check into a hotel first and wash up. Be cool. This could be the big one. If these damn trucks held him up much longer, the rush-hour cars would be belching out of Olten and Aarau and that would be it for him.

David dropped back to look over the situation in the light of the road ahead. The autobahn was climbing slightly and the three lanes of traffic were locked in mortal combat at the ferocious speed of 75 kmh. This was ridiculous.

Christopher switched the Lamborghini to the middle lane, where he could see both sides of the highway. The break came. The slow lane was widening out into a long paved turnoff to a truck-resting zone on top of the crest. The resting zone was parallel with the autobahn and David thought he might be able to make it.

He gave his engine full power and shot to the inside of the slow lane and away from the autobahn into the rest zone. The Deux Chevaux hiccuped in audible surprise and the driver of the Simca bleated his horn to register his indignation. Two semi-trailers were parked in the resting zone, and the drivers, chatting over thermos coffee beside their halted trucks, looked up in astonishment as the golden Lamborghini shot past them spraying gravel.

David could hear the semi-trailers on the autobahn changing gears as the drivers reached the
crest and prepared to continue their battle on the
downward slope. He propelled the Lamborghini
back onto the freeway, inches ahead of the sway-
ing Home-Mobile. David had a glimpse of scared
eyes in a blubbery face before he gave the big engine its head and was away and clear again on the
final leg to Zurich.

Christopher laughed. An image came into his
mind of Lisa that night in the restaurant on Lac
Leman. La Perle du Lac, it was. Must have been
something special. It was Lisa's birthday, come to
think of it, and he'd invited half a dozen friends to
join them. One of the guys had made a crack about
Lisa's cleavage. Something like that. Instead of
blushing modestly and pretending she hadn't really
noticed that she had a cleavage, Lisa looked him
straight in the eye and said, cool as a cucumber,
"You prefer me topless?" She put up her hand,
touched her shoulder strap and out popped a cute
little breast, creamy, rounded, the nipple pert and
eager, staring the guy down until he was the one
who blushed. Then Lisa wiggled her shoulders
somehow and the breast was back inside her dress
and she was sipping her drink, calm as all getout.
God, he was sorry about that fight.

And there was that other time he had a love-
lunch date with her in his apartment on the Quai
Gustave Ador. When he let himself into the apartment, quietly, to surprise her with a gift of perfume or chocolates or whatever, he could hear this
motor buzzing. He followed the noise and found
her lying on a towel on his enormous divan, stark
naked, drying her hair with a little portable blower
she had thoughtfully brought along with her. As if

it was the most natural thing in the world. David chuckled at the recollection. A girl like that could drive a man crazy. They had spent a lot of time making love and very little eating lunch. No wonder she kept her figure.

He thought to himself that Switzerland was O.K. With girls like Lisa. And with times like now. Every bit of tillable land under pasture or crops. Herds of milk-cattle or goats. Red-tiled farm villages like an extended family, hardly changed since the original VIII Cantons won their independence from the Hapsburgs of Austria in the fourteenth century, despite the heavy mounted cavalry of the High German Nobles. And these goddam great Juras spreading their folds and valleys and plateaux, pools of blue lakes surrounded by shaggy cliffs, then the sudden burgeoning of fertile farmland—and all this sheer across the country from Italy to Austria. It was something. It really was.

Not that he didn't miss the States. Sometimes David asked himself if he had done the right thing leaving the U.S. Justice Department. He had been a damned good man for old Justice, even if he said so himself. The roaring days under Bobby Kennedy when they mounted their white chargers and followed Bobby to get the bad guys of organized crime. They'd shaken them up some too. And Dave Christopher had done his bit. There were a few of the big guys in New York and Vegas and Chi and Miami who'd sworn to—what was it that ugly ape in New York had threatened? No, it wasn't New York, come to think of it, it was Chicago. One of Big Lug's captains. Said he was going to fix David Christopher for good. He was going to pull out his tongue through his asshole.

Well, it was all a long way off now. Along with

the camaraderie of Justice. That's what he missed most. The backup. Knowing you had an organization of thousands of people behind you. And an automatic hookup with the FBI and National Security. What was it they used to joke? You could get a dossier on a Bedouin at a Sahara oasis in five minutes. His camel took a minute longer.

It was not too bad, though, when you went private. If you had the background, that is. The Federal Police in Switzerland or wherever. Interpol. The U.S. consulates. A few friends in the CIA. You could run down most of the stuff you needed to do the job. It might take a little longer but ...

ZURICH 40KM the autobahn sign told him. That was O.K. A good run, really. And he'd have time for a shower. Before the meeting. Sounded like a new angle. A mysterious threat to the bank. What could you threaten to do to a bank? Blow it up?

David yawned and stretched his tired body. Maybe when this was all over, maybe when he got back to Geneva, he would call her up again. But would she talk to him? Damn you, Lisa. Damn you.

At 5:15 P.M. David Christopher picked up the phone in his hotel room, dialed 9 for an outside line and then dialed Hurtil's private number at the bank. The bank president answered immediately.

"Hurtil."

"David Christopher, Herr Hurtil."

"Ah, good. You are here? In Zurich?"

"At the Regina. Six o'clock still O.K.?"

"Indeed."

"I'll be there."

"Ah, Herr Christopher?"

David stopped toweling his head and listened.

There was some anxiety in Hurtil's voice. "I'm still here, Herr Hurtil."

"Yes, we suggest, for this first visit—er, since you have a—shall we say, a rather distinctive automobile, that you leave the car at the hotel."

Christopher smiled. Sometimes he regretted the mad extravagance of the Lamborghini. But only sometimes. "Anything you say, Herr Hurtil."

"Come to the Bahnhofstrasse by taxi. Get off at Number 12A. It is an office building. From the lobby there is a private walkway which leads to Hurtilbank. The side entrance. Ring there and my executive vice-president, Herr Franz Benninger, will be waiting for you. He will bring you to my office."

"Very good, sir. I'll be there at six."

David put down the phone carefully and went back to drying his hair. He was wearing a white terry-cloth bathrobe which cooled and dried his body at the same time. David thought to himself that Hurtil and Company were very uptight. Whatever this thing was, they were scared stiff. Sounded interesting. As a matter of fact, a gut feeling told him it was more than that. This was the big one.

The private walkway was more like a tunnel and David surmised that Hurtilbank did everything possible to encourage the business of clients who liked to bank with discretion. The bell, when he pressed the button, rang with a hollow sound as if it were in some vast empty space. Christopher could hear quick footsteps on a marble floor. A heavy lock turned. The door opened cautiously and a small dark man looked at him carefully.

"Mr. Christopher?"

43

"Herr Benninger. Good to see you. It's David Christopher."

Benninger allowed himself the trace of a smile, shook hands with David, drew him inside the bank and then locked the door behind him.

"I apologize for these precautions, Mr. Christopher . . ."

"Not at all," David reassured him. "Don't apologize for anything that gives me twenty-four or forty-eight hours of peace before the word gets around that I'm in town and working for Hurtilbank. Didn't we meet in Gus Reichert's office?"

Benninger was relieved at David's ready recall. "That is correct. Also when you were . . ."

"Don't tell me. I've got it. Jack Linden. SNA. Mid-January, wasn't it?"

"The fourteenth."

"That's right. It was the fourteenth."

David walked beside Benninger through a lobby with a tall squared ceiling supported by fluted Ionic columns of chocolate and white marble.

"Would I be justified in concluding that you were the one who suggested me for this job?" David asked Benninger as the vice-president showed him into an elevator.

"Let us say rather that our president still must be convinced that you are the right person to help us."

David shot a grateful look at Benninger. "Advice noted with thanks," he replied.

It was the kind of honesty he liked and David warmed to this reserved banker.

"If you will pardon me," Benninger said, leading the way across the corridor to the president's suite. The outer secretarial office was empty. Benninger knocked on Hurtil's door, waited for the distant,

"Come in," and then opened the door for David Christopher.

Hurtil came forward, tall, dignified, his silver-gray hair carefully groomed, the jacket of his navy-blue three-piece suit closed on the middle of its three buttons, the epitome of the gracious host.

"I'm Johann Hurtil, Mr. Christopher," he said over the handshake. "I believe that you and Herr Benninger are already acquainted."

Aware that he still had something of a selling job to do on President Hurtil, David wondered if he had dressed correctly for the occasion. His navy-blue slacks, royal-blue shirt, blood-red cravat, pale-blue jacket and russet Gucci slip-ons were in marked contrast to the austere business suits of Hurtil and Benninger. However, it seemed to be what Hurtil expected because he waved David to a cream leather armchair without any cooling of his courtesy.

"Now what would you like to drink?" Hurtil asked him. "I believe we can accommodate you in a modest variety of liquors, sherries, wines, apéritifs ..."

"A small scotch on the rocks would be fine," David answered.

"Any preference?" Hurtil asked. "We have Chivas Regal, Johnny Walker, Pinch, J&B, Glen Livet ..."

"Glen Livet?" David asked. "I don't believe that I'm familiar with that one."

Hurtil was flattered when David rose from his chair and went across to the bar to look at the bottle of Glen Livet which Hurtil showed him.

"It's an unblended whisky," Hurtil said, "and of course most people prefer a blended whisky but it has its select circle of admirers."

45

"Let me try it," David said. "Nothing like a new experience."

Hurtil selected a Baccarat crystal glass from the mirrored shelf and looked for the ice tongs.

"I'll tell you a small story," he told David. "It was one of your countrymen who actually introduced me to this whisky. One of our Hurtilbank clients. His name was Albert Lewin ..."

"The film producer?" David asked in surprise.

"That's the fellow," Hurtil answered. "You knew him?"

"Afraid not," David confessed, "but every film buff is a fan of the great Albert Lewin. Famous in his day. *Dorian Gray. Flying Dutchman. The Moon and Sixpence.* You name it. He made it."

"So I understood," Hurtil beamed, handing David his drink. "A charming little man, I must say. A scholar in many fields. Now then, Benninger?"

While Benninger agreed to a soupçon of vodka and Hurtil mixed the same for himself, David settled back in his armchair. He felt better. The ice had been broken with Hurtil over a brand of whisky and an old friend. Well, was there any better way?

Hurtil raised his glass. "Here's to a fruitful partnership," he said.

"And a quick solution," David added.

The three men drank and then the silence hung heavy on the air while Benninger settled himself in an armchair which was a twin to David's and Hurtil sought the familiar comfort of his desk. David broke the silence.

"By the way," he suggested. "Since we are planning to be partners I wish you would call me David or Christopher, instead of Mr. Christopher."

"It will doubtless come out all three ways," Hurtil told him with a smile.

The bank president leaned back in his chair, tapped the tips of his fingers together, looked to his library for inspiration, then spoke abruptly.

"There is no easy way to put into words what has happened, Mr. Christopher. This morning we received this—this demand."

He passed the ransom note across the desk to David. Christopher put down his drink on a low table beside his chair and got up to receive the white vellum ransom notes.

"It was dropped in the foyer," Benninger explained. "The guard found it lying there on the floor."

"At first we thought it was a practical joke or one of those lunatics . . ." Hurtil looked depressed.

"So what happened?" David asked.

Hurtil sighed heavily. "You tell him, Franz."

Benninger was now his self-possessed, seemingly emotionless public persona.

"Since we received this first demand," he told David, "we have had personal visits or telephoned demands for interviews from five of our clients . . ."

"What kind of clients?"

"They have only one thing in common," Benninger replied primly. "They are holders of numbered accounts. Secret accounts."

"Where do they come into this?" David wanted to know.

"The blackmailers are threatening to make these accounts public, unless each of these clients pays one million francs in ransom."

"One million francs?" David was impressed.

"Five million francs for the five of them. Plus another five million francs from the bank. These days

47

that's about four million dollars they're going for. They must think they have you over a barrel." Christopher thought a moment. "You seem to be taking it for granted that whoever is trying to blackmail the bank, is also trying to blackmail these numbered accounts. Are you certain of that?"

Hurtil passed three sheets of paper across his desk to David. Each page was a photocopy of a secret bank statement. Each statement contained a threat in glo-red script demanding one million francs. No. 406901 identified Mr. Robert Hayes. No. 514628 identified Mlle. Denise Abbott. No. 637404 identified Mr. Dwight McGowan.

"There are two more clients who have telephoned. We are quite certain that the modus operandi will be the same." Benninger was as grave as Hurtil. He sat stiffly upright in his armchair as if it were a precarious perch.

David compared the depositors' letters with the bank's ransom note. It was obvious that the glo-red felt pen was intended to be the identifying symbol of the individual or gang at work. The irrelevant thought came to David that it was like a bunch of kids playing pirates. Drawing a skull and crossbones with their own blood.

"Let me be terribly naïve," David said. "Suppose these accounts were made public ... would it be such a great tragedy, really?"

Benninger was about to answer, then looked up to see that Hurtil was taking the question.

"David, this person or these persons, whoever they are, are fiendishly clever. Of all the clients Hurtilbank has, of all our numbered accounts—and there are many, numbered accounts being a specialty of Hurtilbank—these five are possibly, probably the five who can least afford publicity of any kind whatsoever."

"You've got to be kidding?" David said.

Benninger broke in with a touch of animation. "Believe me, Mr. Christopher. This is so. I know those accounts. By deliberate bank policy not even our president involves himself in the specifics. I can tell you truly, Mr. Christopher, that if I, with my twenty years' intimate experience of the persons and groups behind those numbers, if I wanted to choose the five most vulnerable to blackmail, I would pick at least four of these five."

Christopher, a specialist in the devious ways of the criminal classes, was impressed. "Tell me about these five people," he said. David put his hand inside his jacket and took out a Parker ball-point pen. From his left pocket he drew a small red-covered notebook. "I'll need to take a few notes," he said.

Christopher looked up as he realized that this idea was received with frowning silence by Hurtil and Benninger. "You can relax," David reassured them. "No names and I use my own coded shorthand."

Hurtil nodded to Benninger. The vice-president drew himself tight as if he believed he could not marshal his thoughts while his body was the slightest bit relaxed.

"Let us begin with the two who have not yet reached Zurich ..."

"If I may interrupt just one second," Hurtil put in. "Rascher is probably in the city. He will tell me the worst at my home at seven-thirty this evening. And Villegas is flying in tomorrow."

"Just so, just so," Benninger answered, impatient

with the interruption. "As I was saying, Mr. Christopher, we begin with Herr Helmut Rascher."

"Who's he when he's at home?"

"Rascher seems to be based in Bonn, Germany, although he is constantly on the move. He is an arms dealer. To African revolutionary movements."

"Why is his secret account so secret?"

"I really cannot tell you, Mr. Christopher," Benninger answered in his precise voice. "It is only that Herr Rascher insists that he has many enemies. Every time he comes to Zurich he seems more fearful that 'they' will find out about this account."

"Who are 'they'?" David inquired.

"That I cannot tell you."

"Should not be too difficult to check him out," David said. "All right, who's this Villegas? The name seems to ring a bell."

"Señor Carlos Villegas," Benninger said, "is the nephew of the former president of Santacosta."

"The guy who was assassinated?" David asked.

"That is the one. He was deposed by an army coup, put under guard and then killed."

"Is this account the president's slush fund?"

Benninger spread his hands as if the question was a difficult one to answer. "The former president did start the account," he admitted, "giving power of attorney to his nephew."

"This guy Carlos?"

"That is correct. While his uncle was alive it is true that young Carlos was the typical playboy. The Riviera, St. Moritz, Sardinia, Palm Springs. Expensive girlfriends, fast cars ..."

"Don't knock it," David grinned.

"Oh—er I'm sorry, Mr. Christopher, I didn't intend ..."

"Just kidding," David said. He realized that

50

Benninger was a very serious man. "So what is the clear and present danger if the account becomes known?"

Benninger paused and looked helplessly at Hurtil.

"David," Hurtil said, "we would only be guessing and we would prefer ..."

"Fair enough," David answered, slightly ruffled. "At least tell me what you know. The facts."

"Ah, that is different," Hurtil answered. "The facts are simple. Young Carlos has completely changed. He has given up his playboy life. He is saving money instead of spending it. He has become very serious ... and he has cautioned us that there could be dire consequences if the existence of this account and his connection with it became known."

"Thanks," David observed curtly. "We'll run a make on young Carlos too." Christopher looked up, ready to proceed.

Benninger asked Hurtil, "Do you want to tell him about Mlle. Abbott?"

Hurtil cleared his throat. "Very well. Yes, why not? You see Mlle. Abbott came to see me this afternoon. You have the copy of her statement with the blackmailer's threat in those papers." Hurtil waited while David pulled Account No. 514628 and the demand for one million francs from Mlle. Denise Abbott.

"O.K." David said.

Hurtil shrugged his shoulders. "It's the same story all over again. Mlle. Abbott was somewhat hysterical. She keeps talking about somebody called Jamey who is going to be terribly hurt if the blackmailers publish her account."

51

"I see there are regular deposits here," David said. "Where do they originate?"

"From an English bank," Benninger answered.

"They seem quite substantial payments," Christopher observed.

"She seems to have a very well-to-do, uh—er, friend in London . . ." Hurtil stammered.

"Off the top of my head," David said, rescuing Hurtil from his misery, "it seems as if it could be the classic English scandal situation. Wealthy man, could be a politician, running a girfriend besides a wife and family . . . it's not difficult to guess what the little lady is worried about. Not to mention losing a meal ticket. O.K., who's next?"

"Account No. 637404, Mr. Dwight McGowan," Benninger took over the explanations.

David looked at McGowan's statement. "More withdrawals than deposits on this one," he said.

"Mr. McGowan is a businessman from Houston, Texas," Benninger told David. "I believe he has interests in Los Angeles also."

"What's his problem?" asked David.

"What you have there is the pattern of his account over the last two years. His balance at one point was well over one million dollars, closer to two million on today's values . . ."

David's lips formed a noiseless whistle. "Now it's down to two hundred thousand francs."

"Exactly."

"What happens to friend McGowan if the little birdie tells all?"

Benninger looked puzzled. "I'm afraid I don't . . ."

"Oh, sorry," David apologized. "I mean what hold do the blackmailers have on him?"

"Oh, that." Benninger was thoughtful. "For myself, I don't know. He is here in Zurich. He came to see me this afternoon. He is one of those hearty blustering men. Yet, somehow, I had the feeling that if pure fear could kill, McGowan will be the first to die."

"Strange." Christopher replied. He was taking Benninger very seriously.

Hurtil was listening to this exchange and sipping his coffee. Suddenly he broke in, "How stupid of me. We have a picture of Mlle. Abbott."

The bank president stood up and crossed to the coffee table on which there were copies of *Newsweek, The Economist,* a Hurtilbank annual report and *Elle* magazine. He picked up the copy of *Elle* and showed it to David. On the cover was a picture of a beautiful girl, on skis at St. Moritz. The girl was a classic blonde beauty, wearing jewel-rimmed diablo dark glasses. She had a figure that even ski clothes could not disguise.

"That's Denise Abbott?" David was incredulous.

"That is Mlle. Abbott." Hurtil answered, returning to his desk.

"Well, I'll be ... her picture's been in *Vogue, Paris-Match,* you name it."

"She is quite in demand, I understand," Hurtil said carefully. He seemed to have a kind of paternal pride in his illustrious client.

David put down the magazine reluctantly and turned to Benninger. "I think we have one more of these." David held up Account No. 406901's bank statement for the month of March with the threat to Mr. Robert Hayes.

"Who's Hayes?" David asked.

"Mr. Robert Hayes," Benninger stated primly, "is an investor from Chicago."

"Anything else?"

"He represents a corporation called Luigi Valente Associates—"

"Oh, no," David moaned. "Oh, no. It can't be . . ."

"Some problem?" Hurtil asked anxiously.

David stood up, putting his papers down on the low end table beside his chair.

"You know my background?" he inquired of the bankers.

Hurtil looked smug. "We know it very well, Mr. Christopher, or you would not be here with us now. The United States Department of Justice. Since you became an independent investigator you have done work for Crédit Suisse, Swiss National Assurance and a number of multinationals . . . all of whom speak highly of you."

David waved a deprecating hand. "Very kind of you. When I was with Justice, I was an operative of the Department collecting evidence for its case against a Chicago mobster called Big Lug. Nowadays he is trying to go legit and finds it better to operate under the name of Luigi Valente Associates."

Hurtil and Benninger did not say anything. There was not much dignified bankers could say to the revelation that one of their clients rejoiced in the name of Big Lug.

David picked up the bank statement. "Mr. Robert Hayes," he mused. "I'll bet Bobby Hayes hasn't been called Mr. Robert Hayes since he was last up before a judge."

"You know him?" Benninger asked in disbelief.

"Thought everybody did," David replied. "He's a syndicate bagman. Delivery boy for Big Lug. Mainly cream from the Las Vegas take. What's Bobby up to?"

Benninger looked uncomfortable. It was not easy for him to overcome a lifetime of caution.

"Go on, Benninger," Hurtil prompted his associate.

"He brings over funds for the Luigi Valente Associates corporate account. He has been borrowing from the group account. He invests the funds and puts the profits into a second account. His own. That's the one you have there. At present he is heavily overextended."

David shook his head. "This is unbelievable," he said. "I mean Hayes is no beginner. He knows what they'll do to him."

Benninger shivered as he recalled that Hayes had used the almost identical words that morning. He watched while David, for the first time despondent, went back to his chair. Hurtil and Benninger did not dare to look at each other. If there was any lingering doubt in their minds about the gravity of their plight, David's reaction dispelled it.

David sat down heavily in his armchair. After a while he broke the awkward silence. "I think the police have to come in on this," he said abruptly.

"I don't see . . ." Hurtil began.

"I mean I know these characters," David said savagely. "This Big Lug, Luigi Valente—he's a monster. One whisper of this stuff and he's liable to charter a jet and send over a small army of his own killers. That's what he's like. You could have a miniwar on your hands here in Zurich."

Johann Hurtil stood up, and for the first time David saw in the beaked profile and the hunched shoulders the likeness to an eagle. For the first time also David realized that Hurtil was not just another suave cultured figurehead of the bank. There was an eagle's toughness inside him. Maybe even an eagle's aggressiveness.

"Before we called you, David, at midday, Benninger and I did some very deep soul-searching. We did our best to weigh up the—shall we say, greatest good of the greatest number in this emergency. I myself recommended the Federal Police Bank Detail be contacted. Benninger was against it. His reasons persuaded me."

"Could I hear the reasons?"

"If you wish," Hurtil answered. "They boil down to one very simple reason. Or instinct if you will."

"Which is?"

"Self-preservation."

"Meaning?"

"One of the prices we pay for living in a democracy, David, is that the police mean the press. You're an American. I don't have to tell you."

"How would that harm Hurtilbank?"

"How? I thought—surely that must be obvious. People invest in Switzerland because of two things we guarantee: Their money is safe and their money is secret. It is almost a cliché that our Swiss system is built on secrecy. From all eyes. Even courts. Even tax authorities. If this matter goes to the police and the press get a hold of it, there will be headlines around the world. Swiss bank security has been broken. A secret bank account in Switzerland is no longer secret. What do you think that will do to public confidence? The Bank Herstatt collapse in Germany, Franklin National in the United States ... these will be fleabites to the crisis in public confidence if this unfortunate incident is discovered. Personally I think the Swiss economy itself will be endangered. Be that as it may, it would be the end of Hurtilbank. Rather than risk that disaster we will pay the ransom and take our chances."

"I hope you realize, Mr. Christopher," Benninger added softly, "you are our one slim thread of hope in this dilemma. Even if we pay the ransom that will not be the end of it. We are only buying a respite until they make new demands against other depositors."

Christopher put up his hands in surrender. "Gentlemen, you've sold me. I'll be glad to take the case."

Smiles from Hurtil and Benninger. Manifest relief as they all stood and shook hands on the agreement.

"Don't thank me," David said. "Frankly I would have taken the case anyway. I need the money."

"Let's drink to that," Hurtil said.

The president offered to freshen his drink, but David declined. "A long night ahead," he apologized. The three men touched glasses and drank.

"Where do we go from here?" Hurtil asked.

"Contact the five victims," David said, "and let them know I am representing you and will be doing my best to protect them. We need their full cooperation."

"That's as good as done," Hurtil said. "Anything else?"

The telephone jangled and Hurtil frowned. He picked up the receiver, pressed the flashing button, and answered.

"*Ja?*" He listened intently. "Just a moment, Mr. Hayes." Hurtil covered the receiver with his hand and looked at Christopher and Benninger. "It's Hayes from Chicago. He wants to collect his briefcase and to find out what steps we are taking."

"I'll talk to him," said Benninger.

"Please hold, Mr. Hayes," Hurtil spoke into the telephone. "Herr Benninger is in the bank still. I shall transfer you."

Hurtil put the call on hold while Benninger crossed the room.

"If he is close by," David said softly, "have him come in right away. He might as well know now that I'm on the case. Not that he'll like it."

Benninger took the receiver from Hurtil. "Mr. Hayes? Benninger . . . I have your bag waiting for you. Would you like to collect it immediately? At the same time I can give you more information on the other matter . . . The side door, Mr. Hayes, if you please. Good-bye."

"Excellent," David said. He turned to Hurtil. "There is something else. It's almost seven now. Do you think Herr Benninger could spare me a few moments for the abbreviated tour of the bank? I need a quick feel of the system. Your security. Who has access to your files? The works."

"I would be glad to take you myself, David," Hurtil told him, "but I have my appointment with Rascher. In any case, all of that is Benninger's department. He's the expert. Can you manage, Benninger?"

"If I can just make a quick call to my home?"

"Go right ahead," Hurtil told him.

Benninger said, "Let me use the outer office. Then I can slip down, meet Hayes and bring him to . . ."

"Let's not waste any time with that character," David said. "Pick up his case on your way downstairs. Flash us when he arrives. Herr Hurtil can bring me downstairs and introduce us in the lobby. O.K.?"

Benninger agreed and left to make his call.

Hurtil said, "I shall tell Herr Rascher this evening that we are retaining you to protect his and our interests. I might as well call Mr. McGowan and Mlle. Abbott while we are waiting."

"No time like now," said David. "The sooner they know, the sooner I can talk to them."

Hurtil looked for a note on his desk and dialed a number. When the operator answered he asked for McGowan. David could hear the buzz as the operator dialed the room and then the click as McGowan answered. The too-jovial voice of the Texan came through. As the bank president explained the situation, David listened and could hear McGowan's voice become thick, alcoholic.

Despite the garrulousness of McGowan, Hurtil got across his information fast. We have retained Mr. David Christopher. He is the best man in Europe in this kind of emergency. He will be interviewing you. He is staying at the Regina Hotel in midtown Zurich if you wish to contact him. Otherwise he will see you at the Plaza.

McGowan was still explaining to Hurtil that he was just about to go out and have some chow, when Hurtil escaped and dialed a second number. David could hear the slightly husky seductive voice and didn't blame Hurtil for softening his voice in response as he repeated for Denise Abbott's benefit the story on David Christopher that he had given to McGowan. David was trying to imagine Denise in the flesh when he realized that Hurtil was talking to him.

"Oh, sorry. What was that?"

"It is Mlle. Abbott," Hurtil repeated. "She wishes to know if you wish to speak to her over dinner tonight. As it happens she is free." Hurtil looked slightly wistful, as if he wished that he were also free to have dinner with the entrancing Mlle. Abbott.

"Well, of course," David answered. "Is ninethirty O.K.?"

Hurtil relayed the message. There were some negotiations, and then Hurtil put back the receiver.

"She is a girl who knows her own mind," he said. "She suggests you come to her suite in the Hotel Bellevue for a drink at nine P.M. She will make a reservation for nine-thirty at the Greifen."

"I've got a feeling I'm being organized," David said.

A small buzzer sounded.

"That will be Benninger in the lobby," Hurtil told David. He picked up an in-house phone. "Yes? . . . We're on our way." Hurtil replaced the receiver on its cradle. "He's just arrived. Benninger is admitting him now and he has sent up the lift to meet us."

Hurtil retrieved the ransom demands from David and locked them in a wall safe concealed behind a section of his library. He collected his hat and topcoat and motioned to David to precede him to the elevator. When they got out of the elevator in the lobby, they could see Benninger talking to Hayes near one of the marble pillars.

Hurtil and Christopher walked through the lobby, pretending not to notice Benninger and Hayes. Their footsteps echoed eerily in the quiet building.

"Oh, Herr Hurtil," Benninger called.

Hurtil turned and approached Benninger. David followed but his position behind Hurtil obscured him from Hayes's view.

"Herr Hurtil, I'd like you to meet one of our very

60

good clients, Mr. Robert Hayes of Chicago." Benninger was studiously polite.

"We are desperately sorry to hear about your problem, Mr. Hayes," the president greeted him.

"Oh, yeah?" answered Hayes belligerently. "Then what the hell are you doing about it?" Politeness was lost on Hayes.

"This," said Hurtil. Like a master magician he stepped back triumphantly and gestured toward David Christopher.

"Hi, Bobby!" David said, stepping forward to meet Hayes.

The little man blanched. "What's he doing here?" he spluttered.

"You know each other?" Hurtil asked innocently.

"We don't mix socially," was David's fast reply.

"I want an answer," Hayes screamed.

Benninger stayed calm, smooth. "We have retained Mr. Christopher to protect our clients, Mr. Hayes."

"*Protect* us? You must be crazy. He's Justice Department." By now the little man was livid with fear and rage.

"Not anymore, Bobby. Not for two years now."

Hayes did not appear to hear David. "What is this? Swiss banks don't give out. Not to nobody. You—you . . ."

"You're right, Mr. Hayes," Hurtil told him soothingly. "Your affairs are sacred with us. But until the extortioners are uncovered, your life is in extreme jeopardy. Hurtilbank has hired Mr. Christopher to find the blackmailers. He is your ally. You may reach him any time . . ."

Nothing seemed to penetrate Hayes's monomania. He took a step toward David, and somehow the little man was not funny. Not pathetic. He was deadly. A grenade and the pin was drawn.

"Listen, Christopher. I'm giving you fair warning. I'm leaving this bank right now and I'm calling Big Lug person-to-person. If you're not out of town by morning they're gonna find you in the nearest meathouse. Along with the other dead sheep."

Hayes spun around and at a half-run made for the side door of the bank. Benninger had trouble keeping up with Hayes and in his nervousness fumbled with the lock. Hayes snarled, "Open that fucking door." Benninger undid the bolt lock and Hayes almost knocked him over in his anxiety to get out.

Neither David nor Hurtil spoke as Benninger relocked the door and returned to the two men standing by the tall marble pillar.

"I had no idea . . ." Hurtil began.

"Forget it," David said.

"That threat—I think—it sounded as if he were serious." Hurtil could hardly believe it.

"Oh, he was serious all right," David replied grimly. "But then so were a lot of his pals ten years ago. And they're dead or in jail and I'm working for Hurtilbank." David turned to Benninger. "You promised me a tour," he reminded the vice-president.

"Oh, yes. Immediately, Herr Christopher—er, David." Benninger was still recovering from Hayes.

"Good night, Herr Hurtil." David shook hands with Hurtil. "Don't forget to let Mr. Rascher know I'm at the Regina, if he needs me. Otherwise I'll see him in the morning."

"I'll let myself out, Benninger," Hurtil said.

"Don't keep Mr. Christopher too long. He has an appointment at nine."

"Which I wouldn't want to miss." David smiled.

Benninger made a small bow in David's direction. "This way, Mr. Christopher."

David followed him across the lobby and up the stairs, which Guard Brunnen had taken with such remarkable foresight earlier in the day. Benninger paused at the door.

"This is the computer room," he explained.

Benninger opened the door and seemed nonplussed to find the room blazing with fluorescent light. Then he realized that across the room Madame Florelle was still working at her desk. She looked up as the two men entered her domain.

"Mr. Christopher, this is Madame Florelle. She is in charge of the bank's computerized accounting system." David bowed to Florelle, who stood at ramrod attention.

"Perhaps I should explain, Mr. Christopher." Benninger seemed perturbed, as if he wished Florelle had gone home at her usual time instead of following the feminine intuition that told her some action was afoot. Benninger went on, "Madame Florelle knows about our problem."

"How long have you been with the bank, madame?" David asked her.

"Twenty-nine years, sir."

"She is my cousin and a shareholder," Benninger added quickly.

"If you can't trust Madame Florelle," David said, "who can you trust?"

"Precisely," Benninger answered. He appeared relieved, although not completely.

"Are the numbered bank accounts on the computer?" David asked.

63

"No, sir," Florelle answered. "We have discussed it, and under our system it would be safe but . . ."

"How do you mean, 'under our system'?" David wanted to know.

"Madame Florelle means that only President Hurtil, she and I can identify the person or group or corporation behind a secret-account number," Benninger offered.

"And you see, Mr. Christopher," Florelle took up the explanation, "only the figures would go on the computer cards."

"Thank you, Florelle. This way, Mr. Christopher."

Benninger led the way for David from the computer room to the ledger room and with a quick inclination of the head to Florelle, David followed him. He wondered why Florelle seemed to embarrass Benninger and tucked the thought away for future mastication.

In the ledger room Benninger went immediately to one of the Hong Kong desks, took out one of the massive ledgers.

"This is a secret-account ledger," Benninger said.

David leafed through it.

"As you can see," Benninger told him, "there is nothing there of a personal nature. Just figures."

"You must have some record of the deposit," David protested.

"How do you mean?" Benninger seemed mystified.

"Deposits have to be made in cash or by bank transfer or some such. Who knows that?"

"Oh, well, take any number and look for yourself."

Christopher took No. 320599 and looked for himself. Most of the records indicated cash deposits. A couple indicated a bank draft on a New York bank. There were half a dozen transfers from European banks.

"Who is Number 320599?" Benninger asked with a tinge of mockery in his voice.

"Guess you're right," David admitted.

"Our clerks are usually long-term employees," Benninger said. "And you would have to work in a bank to know what I'm saying. Figures are figures. Totally impersonal."

"Don't you ever get a bad apple?" David asked.

"Not in my father's time. Not in mine," Benninger declared. "Outside this room it is as though they have seen nothing, heard nothing."

David walked across the room to the row of flat desks. "What's the delivery system?" he asked.

Benninger showed him a stack of blank statements. "The clerks at these desks write out the numbered account statements by hand."

"From the ledgers?" David asked.

"No, from card index files in numbered series."

"Where are they?"

"In locked files under the supervision of Madame Florelle."

"Should be safe with her," David said.

"Safe?" Benninger said. "She makes a fuss if *I* ask for those keys."

"And then?"

"The completed statements are delivered by hand by trusted couriers."

"Every one?" David was incredulous.

"Not every one. They go by couriers to the different countries and are mailed there in plain envelopes—from different cities."

"Who are the couriers?"

"Men in high positions who do this as a sideline.

We've already checked on the present situation. No courier has handled more than one of the victims. No courier to these five knows any other courier."

Checkmated on this line of inquiry David asked, "Where do you keep the master list?"

"Which master list?"

"The one linking the numbers of secret account-holders with their actual names?"

Benninger looked pleased with himself. "Follow me," he ordered. Benninger took David from the ledger room to an automatic elevator where he pushed the Basement button.

"Upstairs," he told David, "we like to cultivate an antiquarian ambience. Down here you will see something different."

"I get the feeling you prefer this," David said.

"I supervised the entire reconstruction," Benninger told him proudly.

The elevator opened to a blinding fluorescent glare in a white-walled corridor leading to floor-to-ceiling steel gates. Benninger went to a house phone and signaled the lobby. A guard's voice answered.

"Yes?"

"Benninger."

"Yes, sir."

"I'm in the vaults."

There was a pause.

"I have you, sir."

David looked up to see a ceiling closed-circuit television camera focusing its suspicious eye on him and Benninger.

"Kill the alarm, Matzingen, I'm going inside."

"Yes, sir."

Benninger waited to give the guard time to deactivate the alarm. "There is a control board in the guard room which monitors doors, lifts, vaults and the entire alarm system for the building," he explained. "And another control board at our nearest police station." The vice-president used one of a bunch of keys to open the gates of the vaults and ushered David inside. Beyond the empty desk of the day guard, David found himself in a corridor between cages protected by massive steel bars. The first cage on each side held the safe-deposit boxes. The cages following contained trolleys of four-hundred-ounce gold bars or protected massive steel safes containing the bank's own money reserves and investment papers. Benninger led the way to the far end of the too glaringly lit corridor and opened the last left-hand cage. He motioned David inside the cage. David entered and found himself facing a safe set in to the reinforced concrete wall of the cage. This safe was small, its door gleaming under the fluorescent light. It looked like a tough door to crack. It had both a combination dial and a time clock protecting what looked like a good four to six inches of tungsten steel. From the look on Benninger's face, David guessed he was in the secret-account room.

"The master list is kept in that safe," Benninger said.

"Who has access to it?" David asked.

"I alone."

"Say you were killed in an accident? What happens?"

"The surviving directors would obtain the combination from the Federal Treasury vault in Berne."

David eyed the safe. "How much does that list add up to? Five hundred, six hundred million dollars?"

"Whatever it adds up to, Mr. Christopher, represents a bigger proportion of Hurtilbank assets than it should in this emergency."

Now Benninger was nervous again, his stomach turning over at the thought of that 39.87 percent of Hurtilbank assets which the secret accounts held. While he closed the gate of the secret-account room and walked rapidly ahead of David to the exit gates, Benninger was wrapped up in his own thoughts. How often he had remonstrated with Hurtil, insisting that they should broaden their base still more. It had to be done. It simply had to be done. Unless he could find some way to bring a big—what did he mean *big?*—a huge influx of funds into Hurtilbank and reduce that 39.87 percent, Hurtilbank was doomed. This emergency demonstrated that he had been right all along. Already it might be too late.

Benninger realized with a start that he had closed the gates to the vaults, buzzed the guard to reactivate the alarm, and taken David to the elevator in the lobby without saying a word. Now they were striding across the lobby of the bank to the tunnel exit. "Oh, I'm sorry, Mr. Christopher. Please excuse me. I was thinking of something."

"There is a lot to think about," David said. "And it's getting late. Thank you for your time and the tour. It was just what I needed." David shook hands with Benninger. "By the way," he asked, on his way through the door, "do you happen to know where Bobby Hayes stays in Zurich?"

"The St. Gallen. Always the St. Gallen."

"Till tomorrow then," David concluded with a wave.

As the door closed behind him and he walked down the tunnel toward the lobby of the office building, David thought about Benninger. That sudden silence. Was it because Benninger realized that nobody except Herr Franz Benninger had access to the information that made this blackmail attempt possible?

Because that was the way it stacked up. On the other hand, Benninger had said as much himself up in Hurtil's office. He had admitted, almost boasted, that only he had access to the vital facts—and if he were setting up victims for ransom, these would be the five he'd pick. Four of them anyway. Maybe not McGowan. Another thing. That was a kind of weird answer Benninger gave when he asked how much money was in the secret accounts. "Whatever it adds up to represents a bigger proportion of Hurtilbank assets than it should in this emergency." Seemed as if there was something bugging him. Questions. Questions. Only questions. How about some answers for a change?

David came out of 12A on to the Bahnhofstrasse at night. Nice. Very nice. With the lights filtering through the young leaves on the big limes. The buildings taking on the soft glow of night. Only a sprinkling of cars now. A nip in the air. Should have brought his topcoat. David looked at his watch. Eight o'clock. He would just have time to make those phone calls before his date with the Abbott girl.

He turned north on the Bahnhofstrasse and headed for the Parade Platz. It was only a short walk and the night air would do him good.

VI

IV

David adjusted the belt on his pale-blue London
Fog spring coat, took a final look around his room,
and was satisfied. He left, made his way to the elevator, and pressed the button for the garage.

The ball was in play. In the States Jack Foley at
Justice was sure he could have an up-to-date on
Hayes and McGowan by morning. Maybe tonight.
It was still midafternoon in the States, so no problem, David, lad. And how are the blondes in Switzerland? Not as good as the redheads in the States,
Jack, believe me. Jack's wife was a redhead, so it
was the right answer. And, Jack, if you happen to
get that stuff for me this evening, stick it on the
telex to my Geneva office, O.K.? Then I can get it
from my secretary first thing in the A.M., our time.
Jack said it was O.K.

In Paris Freddy Cohen said he thought he could
handle both Rascher and Villegas. If not he'd let
him know. Freddy was a wine exporter to the
States. So all the letterheads said. And the sign on

his office and his registration papers with French Immigration. And his passport. It was an innocuous and respectable front for a CIA agent and let Freddy run the necessary phones, telexes, staff and so on. Plus trips all around the Continent buying up wine. Leave it to me, Chris, Freddy had told him. We'll have those guys on a slide before dawn. Get your microscope ready. Where do you want it? David suggested the Geneva office telex again. Incoming calls could be a problem if anybody got to the hotel operator.

Which left just the blonde, Denise Abbott. David thought he would wait on that one. If the well-known Christopher charm was still working he should know more before dinner was over, and that would help him figure whether she was a case for Interpol or his friend, Dan Stillman of the U.S. Embassy in London, or whoever. Depended on where she lived, really. And what nationality she was.

David stepped out of the elevator into the hotel garage thinking that to be as far as he was by 8:45 P.M. on a job which he had first heard about at midday when he was 175 miles away in Geneva was damn good progress. Even if he said so himself.

This glow of self-satisfaction was doubtless the reason why David did not see the man wearing the tartan raincoat with a turned-up collar and a hat pulled down low on his forehead. That and a lively German rock number bursting out of the speakers feeding the garage. Somebody up there liked loud music.

The man in the tartan raincoat had his hands in his pockets; his right hand was curled lovingly around the butt of a .32 caliber pistol. He had evidently been waiting for David because, as soon as David began the long walk toward the office of the garage, the man in the tartan raincoat kept pace with him, two rows of cars away.

What with the rock music, the roar of car engines on the in-and-out concourse and involvement in his own thoughts, David was still unaware of the man in the tartan raincoat, even when the man moved a row of cars closer and took the gun from his pocket.

The man lifted the gun, straight-armed, like somebody very familiar with his weapon, got David in his sights and was squeezing the trigger when David stepped aside to make way for a long-haired, white-overalled attendant roaring along the aisle in a fawn Fiat. The gunman said "Shit," and ran after David for another chance. Time was running out. David was nearing the concourse and the car engines rising and falling and the attendants in white overalls.

Christopher changed direction just soon enough after the Fiat passed to catch a flicker of the man in the tartan raincoat. Puzzled, he turned to present himself as a full-fronted target. The man took barely a second to re-aim and fire. It was the second David needed to throw himself to the concrete floor.

The wind from the bullet was hot on his scalp and David heard a tinkle of glass as the bullet ploughed into the windshield of a parked car behind him. Already he was running forward in a low crouch, to put a car between him and the killer.

David heard a scuffle and lifted his head. Another bullet grazed his ear as he dived toward the next car. The man followed and there was a grim guessing game. Which way would which man move? David took a chance and started down one side of the green Mercedes 250 that was the only thing between him and death. Eyes wary, he saw the gun coming around the back of the Mercedes to meet him. In desperation he stood up and threw himself across the car. The murderous shot whined past him and spattered against a concrete pillar.

Now it was bad. The man was between him and the safety of the concourse. A scuttling crab, David backed away fast to the protection of a pillar. He looked around wildly. He must have a weapon or the next bullet would be it.

Behind the pillar David straightened up. Facing him was a car whose radio aerial stuck up some eighteen inches. David could hear the careful footsteps of the killer. In one savage move he jerked at the aerial, extending it to its full length while at the same time snapping it off the car. Then he stepped from behind the pillar and swung the aerial like a whip at his surprised assailant. The first cut took the man on the side of the face, drawing blood and making his fast shot go wild. A second cut slammed hard against his gun hand, momentarily paralyzing his wrist. Then David dived—a flying tackle aimed to knock the man off his feet and grab hold of the wrist controlling the gun.

As the two men went down, grappling, gouging, pushing, biting, kicking, growling, the music was cut off and in the distance David dimly heard the running feet of attendants finally aroused by the shots. David was busy mashing the gun hand of his assailant against the concrete floor of the garage when rough hands pulled at him. Despite his protests, an arm was around his neck, choking him, dragging him off the struggling body beneath him. Two strong men lifted him to his feet, demanding to know, in Schwyzerdutsch, why he was fighting with the other man. A pillar away, two other men were trying to extract the same information from the man in the tartan raincoat when he shoved an elbow into the belly of one man, chopped the second man hard in the throat and was away and running.

There were tears of frustration and rage in David's eyes as he saw his would-be murderer disappear.

"You goddam fucking fools," David roared. "You've just let him escape."

Completely confused, the garage attendants finally let David loose, but by this time the man in the tartan raincoat was through the concourse and gone. It was too late to follow him. Surrounded by four attendants violently arguing in a mixture of German and Swiss, David strode to the office, breathing heavily.

"What happened, sir?" the man in the office asked him.

"These damned idiots just let a killer get away. That's what happened," David said.

"Are you sure, sir?" the man in the office was suspicious of this unlikely story.

"Am I sure?" David was at breaking point, ready to smash in somebody's, anybody's face. "He fired four or five shots at me." David turned to the jabbering attendants. "Where is the gun?" One of the men came forward, disheveled, red-faced, and handed over the gun to David. Still the investigator, David put his hand in his pocket, took out a tissue and wrapped it around the gun. "If you know anything about guns," he said, "you'll find four or five empty shells in that." He laid the gun down carefully for the man to inspect, pulled a parking check from inside his jacket, and threw it on the counter beside the gun. "Now get me my car. I'm late already."

The night manager called to one of the attendants and gave him the ticket. When the man had gone he said to David, "I think you had better wait, sir. We have notified the police."

Tires screamed on concrete behind a wailing siren and a powder-blue Zephyr police car squealed into the garage followed by the green Peugeot which had trailed Hayes from the airport. Two policemen in uniform got out of the police car while the stocky man with the short moustache emerged from the Peugeot. His driver, a fleshy type, uncoiled himself from the driver's wheel of the Peugeot to reveal that he was over six feet tall and built like a heavyweight boxer.

The man with the moustache flipped a wallet in the general direction of David, the night manager, and the three gawking attendants.

"Captain Hans Frey, Swiss Federal Police. What's going on here?"

The night manager came out of his office talking at the same time as the three attendants, just as the fourth attendant arrived with David's Lamborghini. The fourth attendant left the Lamborghini's engine running and got out to join the babble of explanations. David said nothing.

Frey took in the scene, snapped one command. "Quiet!" The voices died suddenly. Frey nodded to the uniformed policemen. "Get their story." The policemen took the night manager and the four attendants aside, and the voices took up again at a slightly reduced volume.

Frey was a man with lots of time. He took a short walk around David, looking him over. Frey's partner, the big gorilla, stood against the Peugeot with his arms folded.

"This your car?" Frey asked unexpectedly, jerking his head toward the Lamborghini.

"That's right," David answered. He was conscious that the picture of sartorial elegance which had left his room a few minutes earlier had been ruffled in the interim. He wished he could have had two minutes to put himself back together. It put a man at a disadvantage, especially with someone as self-possessed as Frey.

"Like to switch off the engine?" Frey asked.

"Thanks," David said. He walked over to the car, leaned in the open door, and turned the key. He told himself to watch it. This Frey was a rapier ready to flick off buttons or go in neatly between the second and third ribs.

David thought it was time to try to regain the upper hand. He took out his wallet. "My name is David Christopher." He showed Frey his identification. "I'm a private investigator registered to operate in Switzerland. My office is in Geneva."

Frey said "Uh-huh" noncommittally while he looked over David's registration card. He handed it back.

"What are you doing in Zurich?" he asked casually.

David cursed silently. Anybody else but Frey, he would have played it dumb. Who me? In Zurich? Why it's just a private visit to see my girlfriend, Denise Abbott. As a matter of fact, Officer, Captain, I'm on my way to meet her and I'm late. Could we get this over and done with? Yes, anybody else but Frey. But with Frey you'd be asking for it. He'd never buy it. And then you'd have the son of a bitch under your feet for the rest of the investigation. Probably have him anyway. Well, here goes my forty-eight-hour undercover start.

"I'm doing an investigation for Hurtilbank," David said. Eye-to-eye. It was the only way to play it with Frey.

"May I ask what is the subject of this investigation?"

"You may not."

The two men locked eyes till Frey said, "No, I didn't think so. Well, no matter. I shall know soon enough." Frey took out a notebook. "Are you registered at the hotel?"

"That's right. Room 709."

"What happened here tonight?"

"A guy went for me. With a pistol. They have it." Christopher gestured toward the attendants. "The clowns have been mauling it for five minutes so you'll be lucky to lift a print."

Frey nodded to the gorilla, who strolled over to the policemen, took a handkerchief from his pocket, and with it rescued Exhibit A.

"Did you know the man?" Frey asked.

"Didn't have a chance," David said. "These—the four stooges." He was still seething. "I grabbed him in the dark over there. They came and grabbed me—and he got away. He was wearing a tartan raincoat, if that's any help. And a hat that didn't fall off—which is odd when you come to think of it. We were rolling on the ground."

Fred looked at David. "Who would want to kill you?" he asked.

"That's the hell of it," David told him. "Took me completely off guard. I'm licensed to carry a gun. Didn't bother to bring it."

78

David flipped open his topcoat and jacket to show Frey that he was clean. Then he buttoned his jacket and secured his belt again. He ran a hand through his hair. "I'm meeting this girl for dinner, Captain, and I'm already a half hour late. Do you think I could phone her hotel and then get going?"

Frey snapped shut his notebook and put his ball-point inside his jacket. "Certainly, Mr. Christopher."

David turned away gratefully.

"We'll be meeting again, I should think," Frey's voice followed him. "I'm in charge of the Bank Detail, Zurich."

David swung back to meet Frey's amused brown eyes. Knowledgeable. As if he had already guessed most of what David had heard tonight in the secrecy of Hurtilbank. Oh, hell. Just his luck. A case that must be kept from the police and who does he have to contend with? The Swiss Hercule Poirot. In person.

Son of a bitch.

The Bellevue Hotel was in the Bellevueplatz just a stone's throw from where the Zurichsee empties into the Limmat River. Fortunately for David, on wheels at night it was only a few minutes from his place and it was not yet 9:30 when he left his car with the attendant and went into the hotel.

In the second half of the nineteenth century, the Bellevue Hotel was the in-season gathering place of dukes, duchesses and fortune hunters. A hundred years later West German businessmen, African diplomats, American movie producers and elderly blue-haired Frenchwomen walked the faded carpets beneath the enormous crystal chandeliers.

A uniformed elevator operator took David to the sixth floor and pointed him in the direction of Suite 612. He knocked on the door and from somewhere inside a voice called, "It's open. Come in."

David went inside. His eyes crinkled with amusement at the scene that greeted them. Tall ceiling dropping a pear-shaped gleaming crystal chandelier. Aubusson rug. A vast deep burgundy velvet sofa. At the end of the sofa a polished antique table. On the antique table a porcelain vase—it looked valuable—filled with yellow tulips. The other furnishings matched these pieces. French windows framed by breeze-rippled, fine textured curtains led to a terrace. From somewhere he could hear the lilting strains of a waltz. It sounded as if it was being played by a quartet behind the palms in the grand ballroom of the Bellevue itself.

The radio suddenly switched to blaring hard rock. David turned with a start. She stood at the door of the bedroom, her finger on the wall panel controlling the Muzak. She was unashamedly posing for him, giving him time to take in the long honey hair, the shoulder-baring Pucci blouse, the clinging white sharkskin pants. Twenty-four. Thrillingly lovely. Languid. Superior. The princess and the pauper. It was a breathtaking entrance. It was meant to be.

She broke the pose, smiled and spoke. "Do you speak German?"

He shook his head.

"Words don't matter anyway." she consoled him. "I never listen to them."

She floated past him, close enough to envelop him in a delicate fragrance of Madame Rochas perfume, and went over to a traymobile set with bottles of liquor, glasses and a silver bucket of ice.

"Do you?" she asked.

David was wrapped up in the performance and the question took him by surprise. "Do I—er, what?"

"Listen to the words?"

"Ah . . . no. Not really."

"I suppose it's *de trop* or something to admit that," she said meditatively. "In these days of significant lyrics and the return of the philosopher-minstrel telling us the meaning of life in country-and-westerns. But frankly I don't give a damn. Now what will you drink?"

"Scotch, please."

"On the rocks, of course. You American, you."

"Of course."

She went to work efficiently on the drink while David watched her figure moving under the blouse and the skintight pants.

"Much better," he observed in considered judgment.

"Much better than what?" She half-turned and her breasts pressed against the blouse.

"Than those covers. *Elle* and *Vogue* and *Paris-Match* and *Oggi* and—even *Réalités*."

She brought over the scotch and handed it to him. As she did she looked up into his eyes and turned on full power.

"You have been doing your homework, haven't you, David Christopher?"

Their hands touched as he took the glass. Unable to resist the impulse, he leaned over and kissed her cheek.

"You may be the most beautiful girl I have ever been in danger of falling instantly in love with," he said. "And thank you for the drink."

"I like you," she said, and a smile glowed on her

face. She returned to the traymobile and poured herself a small martini from a thermos-decanter.

"I'm so sorry," she apologized. "Please sit down."

David obliged, sitting in a velvet-covered arm-chair and sinking into it a foot deeper than he had expected to. "Whoops!" he exclaimed.

She laughed, each note clear and musical like a well-played xylophone. "They're from the Ark," she said. "Designed by Noah himself." She curled up on the sofa, and her lithe body reminded him of a resting leopard. He wondered how accurate this image was.

"I know I'm very late," he said, "so you tell me when we should go. Will the Greifen hold our table, do you think?"

"They'd better," she said threateningly. "Or I'll scratch their eyes out." Then she grinned. "No, it wasn't that at all. I suggested nine-thirty because they have this wonderful group. You can only hear it till about ten-thirty. Then they all start singing at the top of their voices. The beer gets to them."

"Here's to . . ."

"Our secret bank accounts which are no longer secret," she said. And drank.

David was a little taken aback by the toast but decided to follow suit.

"And what is our big handsome private investigator going to do to protect us?" Denise inquired.

There was a prickle of irritation at the back of David's scalp but he fought the feeling. "I figure the others," he said, "but why you?"

"Why not me? Am I so fragile?"

"You're Beautiful People," he answered, ignoring what seemed to be a feline effort to anger him. "Money. Breeding. In demand as a model all over Europe. What have you got to hide?"

She swirled her drink, looked at him. If she were a leopard, David thought to himself, that would be her tail swishing.

"Everybody has something to hide," she said finally.

"Oh?"

"For example, Mr. David Christopher. What does he have to hide? Why did he leave the United States to work in Europe? Or is he so lily-white pure?"

"I had this delusion," David said equably, "that we were trying to solve *your* problem."

There was a sullen silence, and mentally David could hear the tail swishing, back and forth. For some reason he could not fathom he felt a tingle of apprehension. Suddenly she laughed.

"Just testing, David, dear." She finished her drink. "Shall we go?"

He stood up and gave her his hand. She came up easily.

"I'll just get my coat," she told him, "while you finish your drink."

The mood had changed again. This girl was like a bird, carefree in the spring. In a moment she returned, holding an exquisite white Dior coat and a gold rabbit Port-of-Call evening bag.

"Here," she told David. "Hold these a jiffy." She handed him the bag and coat while she fastened drop pearl earrings and a pearl throater with a diamond clasp. David stepped forward to help with the throater, but she was incredibly quick when she chose and had slipped the tongue of the clasp into its groove before he could reach her. She put both hands on her hips, swayed provocatively, and asked him in a deep husky voice, "How do I look, Big Boy?"

"Any more of that," David answered, "and this dinner is going to be indefinitely delayed."

"Promises, promises," she pouted. "That's all I ever get from you men." She stepped forward for him to put on her coat, then took her bag and pir-ouetted to give him the full effect. "Believe it or not," she said, "I think I'm ready. Don't forget your coat."

David picked up his coat from a chair and followed her to the door. He felt like an animal tamer. And his leopard was loose on the town.

"Maybe we lost him," Murdoch suggested.

"We lost him, we lost him," Johnson answered. Johnson was a philosopher and given to such pro-found analyses.

The two men were standing on the far side of the Parade Platz opposite the Regina Hotel. This way they could keep an eye on the hotel's main en-trance, which fronted the Parade Platz, and on the small side entrance on the Talacker Strasse, next to the Regina's garage. For the length of time they had been standing there the two men were remark-ably patient. But then patience and persistence were virtues necessary to men in their line of work.

Murdoch was a lean dark intense man of medium height. Johnson was perhaps five foot eleven, beefy-powerful. He had been a prizefighter until the Boxing Commission yielded to the mount-ing evidence that the outcome of Johnson's fights depended on instructions from "outside interests" and canceled his license. The "outside interests" were Luigi Valente Associates; Johnson was now one of their stable of hit men.

Murdoch and Johnson had been trailing Bobby Hayes all the way from Chicago. They had re-

ceived the word too late to catch the Swissair flight
to Geneva and Zurich direct from Chicago and had
barely managed to scramble aboard a British Air-
ways flight out of Chi to London. This had meant
spending a couple of hours cursing at Heathrow
while they waited to connect with a Lufthansa
flight that did not reach Zurich until midafternoon.
They had hired an Opel Kadett from Hertz, a little
compact job. Their orders were to be inconspicu-
ous. At least it had automatic shift. There were
some anxious moments while they nosed around
looking for Bobby. His car was not at the bank and
not at the hotel either. They didn't dare inquire in
case they ran into Bobby in public; he would smell
the kill right away. So they sweated it out. Murdoch with the car at the hotel. Johnson hanging
around in sight of the bank.

Then the break came. The Mercedes picked up
Hayes and took him from the hotel to the bank,
where he picked up his briefcase. Instead of going
back to his hotel or out to eat as they had expected, Bobby had left the bank in a hurry and gone
to the post office, where he picked up some tokens
and made some phone calls. When he came out
again the Merk took him to the Parade Platz. What
Murdoch and Johnson could not understand was
the green Peugeot. The two guys in it had cop
written all over them. What the hell were they
trailing Bobby for? It was like a goddam proces-
sion. The Opel trailing the Peugeot trailing the
Mercedes.

"We're havin' the funeral before the guy's dead,"
Johnson guffawed to Murdoch. Johnson was like
that. Always good for a laugh. It was why Murdoch liked to go on a job with Johnson. He made it
more fun. Otherwise it was the same old thing.

Follow the guy. Case the guy. Set him up. Burn him. Get the hell out. Lie low till the heat was off. Wait for the next one. A tough way to make a buck.

When Hayes got out of his Mercedes in the Parade Platz he had reversed his topcoat and was making like a Scot with the tartan. He left the briefcase in the Merk and told the driver to take off. Then he went inside the hotel. Thanks to the shitheads in the Peugeot, they could have lost him; the Peugeot just pulled up outside the hotel and sat there waiting. The driver got out and walked to the corner to cover Talacker Strasse.

The only thing Johnson and Murdoch could do was to make like they were just passing through, but they had a few anxious moments while they were looking for a place off the Tal-Strasse to ditch the Opel.

Fortunately when they meandered back, a couple of innocent sightseers, the Peugeot was still there and the big pig at the corner was still there, so they figured Hayes was still inside.

Then they had their first piece of luck. The shots came and the shouts. The big pig started toward the garage and then decided to check with his boss in the Peugeot. While he was checking, Hayes came running out, peeling off the tartan raincoat. He ducked straight back into the hotel through the side entrance next to the garage, and by the time the Peugeot and the backup police car squealed into the street Hayes was out of sight. Serve the pigs right, but what the hell was going on? Did somebody try to burn Bobby or vice versa?

They waited some more. The cool cat in the Lamborghini was the first to leave. The police car was next. Finally the schmucks in the Peugeot.

They slowed down a bit in the Parade Platz, and for a terrible instant Murdoch and Johnson thought the Peugeot was going to stop again. Then it headed off. Bobby would have got the hell away from the garage in the opposite direction. That's how the pigs would figure it. So they'd pick him up at his hotel or the airport. What difference did it make?

Normally speaking, no difference at all. But Murdoch and Johnson were not speaking normally. They gave the Peugeot just enough time to clear the square before they were in action. Murdoch took the side entrance and Johnson the front. It was a safe bet that Hayes would not take the garage route again, even without his tartan raincoat.

They met in the lobby and decided on the direct approach to the concierge. Fingering a twenty-five-franc note Johnson apologized to the concierge for disturbing him and explained that he and his friend had a problem. They were supposed to meet this American friend of theirs in front of the hotel but he had failed to show. He wasn't in the lobby. Was there some other place in the hotel he might be waiting? An American. Little guy. About so high. Wearing a hat with a big brim.

The eyes of the concierge lit up. Was their friend wearing a tartan topcoat? Maybe, Johnson and Murdoch said carefully. Because if so there was a gentleman such as they described inquiring for a Mr. Christopher about one hour earlier.

"Which Mr. Christopher is that?" Johnson asked.

"Mr. Christopher in 709," the concierge confided. "He is also an American. Your friend spoke to Mr. Christopher on the house telephone and then that is the last I see of him."

Johnson thanked the concierge for his help and

passed over the twenty-five francs. The concierge was grateful and eager to be friendly. "Of course, you know of Mr. Christopher's terrible incident?" he asked.

"What was that?" Murdoch said.

"He was fire on in the garage—somebody with a gun. He was nearly kill."

"No kidding?" Murdoch and Johnson breathed.

Murdoch and Johnson moved away for a quick conference. Bobby must have gone bananas. What was he doing trying to blast Christopher? Who the hell was Christopher anyway? Probably the cool cat in the Lamborghini. So where was Bobby now? Murdoch looked at Johnson and Johnson looked at Murdoch.

"Are you thinking what I'm thinking?" Murdoch asked.

"You wouldn't be back in the numbers game by any chance and laying bets on 709?"

Murdoch smiled the slow smile of a hunter who has waited all night and in the first light of dawn sees the biggest pair of antlers any buck ever wore.

It had seemed like a great idea at the time. Kind of obvious really. Where is the last place anybody would expect to find him just after he had tried to plug Christopher full of holes? In Christopher's room, right? All he had to do was sit there and wait for Christopher to come back. Then blip him.

Now Bobby Hayes was wondering. Frankly, he had expected Christopher to return to his room from the garage. To clean up and pick up his gun. Bobby had found the gun—a .32 like his own—thirty seconds after he closed the door of Christopher's room behind him. With the gun he had Christopher cold. But the prospect of a long wait

was getting to Bobby. Christopher could be anywhere. Probably spilling his guts to the police right
now. Bobby didn't like it. He'd heard about those
Swiss police. Stick a guy in jail and forget about
you for twenty years. Don't even bother to bring
you to court unless they feel like it.

Bobby decided to split. He could work out something else in the morning. Meantime he had to get
out. Fast. Bobby put his topcoat over his right arm
and kept the .32 in his hand. You never knew.
Could be just his luck to meet Christopher in the
street or something, and if his gun was in his
pocket the bastard might get away again.

Bobby was closing the door of 709 behind him
when the elevator doors opened and Murdoch and
Johnson stepped out. A man in danger of death can
be a very fast thinker, and Hayes was in danger of
death. While Murdoch and Johnson were still reacting to the fact that they were face-to-face with
their quarry, Bobby fired once, then again. Murdoch was winged in the shoulder, and he and
Johnson jumped back into the elevator.

Hayes raced for the exit stairs. In the elevator
Murdoch said, "I'm O.K. Go on. Run him down the
stairs and I'll get him in the street."

"We was supposed to make it look like an accident," Johnson protested.

"Shit, Johnson, run," Murdoch said desperately.

Johnson ran to the exit stairs. Below him he
could hear Hayes's feet pounding. He raced after
him thinking this was a terrible way to run an
airline. Thoughts like that came to Johnson at unlikely moments. The little cunt was giving them a
hard time. He, Johnson, would personally kick
Bobby's balls into chicken liver when he caught up
with him.

Inside the descending elevator Murdoch took off
his topcoat, shoved a handkerchief under his shirt
against the wound to stanch the blood, then threw
the topcoat over his shoulder to hide the damage.
Shoulder burning, he reached the lobby to find
that Hayes was ahead of him and half running
through the lobby toward the main Parade Platz
exit.

Murdoch signaled to Johnson as the big man
came pounding from the stairs. Together they went
after Hayes, trying to attract as little attention as
possible. From the steps of the Regina they could
see Hayes running at full speed for the Bahnhofstrasse. Murdoch said he would pick up the Opel.
If he took the Quai Bridge to the Limmat Quai he
might beat Hayes back to the St. Gallen and cut
off his escape. A worried Johnson watched him go,
but he seemed strong enough, so the big man took
after Hayes with the lope of an athlete whose track
work was not too many years past. He saw Hayes
cross over the Bahnhofstrasse, accompanied by
screaming car horns. By the time Johnson got
across, Hayes had almost reached the Munsterhof
Platz and was still running well.

Johnson thought of what would happen to him
and Murdoch in Chicago if he came back with the
news that Hayes had shot Murdoch and got away
from him. His adrenal glands began working
harder.

Tourists enjoying a quiet evening stroll around
the Fraumünster looked up in astonishment as first
Hayes and then Johnson thudded through the
square and on across the Münster Bridge to the far
side of the Limmat. Somehow it didn't look like a
game.

They were wrong. It was a game that was definitely up for Hayes unless he could get to the alleys around the Grossmünster. The massive eleventh-century cathedral dominating central Zurich was a shrewd choice on the part of Hayes. Its stone façade and three-story towers were surrounded by a rabbit warren of dark alleys where Hayes had a chance either to escape from Johnson or shoot it out on equal terms.

The St. Gallen was close to the Grossmünster, and Hayes had walked the cobblestone alleys a few times. He had a fair idea of its sudden, unexpected steps and the exits to more orthodox side streets.

In a way it was a fitting scene for a battle, even a minor skirmish in a petty war such as this one. On top of the south tower of the Grossmünster sat a colossal Charlemagne, sword across his knees. He must have been bored with centuries of Swiss peace. And in the pulpit of the Grossmünster, a parish priest called Zwingli started a religious confrontation with Rome that established the Reformation firmly in Switzerland and led to Zwingli's death in bloody battle at Kappel.

Hayes and Johnson had never heard of Charlemagne or Zwingli, but killing they knew about. Hayes started it from the shadow of the stone canyon with a quick shot in the general direction of Johnson. Johnson pressed close against the wall and sent just one shot back to keep Hayes on the defensive. By the time Johnson was around the curve of the wall, Hayes had disappeared into the darkness.

Johnson moved as quickly as he could in the direction of Hayes's running feet and caught up with Hayes on a steep rise toward the back of the cathedral. Here the streetlights gave some illumination and Johnson could see the outline of Hayes. He fired again and there was a shrill ping as the shot glanced off the stone foundation of the cathedral. Hayes heaved his way to the top of a set of steps angling away from Johnson and crouched on the rampart in the shadow of a thick outer wall. It was a good position for Hayes. Behind him was an exit to a street. In either direction the street could take him back to the Limmat Quai and the St. Gallen and safety. Alternatively, the alley vanished into darkness as it continued on its way around the base of the Grossmünster. It too would take him back to the Limmat Quai.

What Hayes had to do was stop Johnson. Kill him or at least wound him. A plan was forming in Hayes's mind. Feverishly he popped empty shellcases from his .32 and refilled the chambers. He would hold Johnson at bay until he was ready. Then he would let the big soldier think he was hit. Hayes exchanged more shots with Johnson then raised his hat till its shape was clear above the edge of the parapet. Johnson emptied his .38 at the hat. One shot caught the crown and sent it flying into the street. At the same time Hayes let out a ghastly bubbling scream of agony and dropped heavily to the rampart. Then he pulled himself up and waited for Johnson. He could hear the heavy-breathing, ear-cocked doubt of the gunman. There was a scrape of feet and Johnson began to move forward. Hayes gave him another dying moan to encourage his progress. The cautious footsteps became more confident. Hayes put his hand in his pocket and pulled out a switchblade. He moaned again while he sprang the blade and then, with the knife in his left hand and the .32 in his right, he waited, exultant.

Too late, Hayes realized that the stalker was being stalked. He heard the rush of feet and tried to turn, but a terrible blow from Murdoch's gun caught him on the side of the head. "You lousy little bastard!" Murdoch hissed.

Johnson called out, "Is that you, Murdy?"

"Yeah, it's me. Come and help me finish him off."

While Hayes lay crumpled on the stone rampart Johnson indulged his vengeance fantasy. He did his absolute best to pulverize Hayes's testicles into hamburger. His sadism fed on itself, and he and Murdoch took turns jumping up and down on Hayes's rib cage with their heavy shoes. They mashed up his internal organs in the process, and Hayes vomited blood from his mouth and excrement from his rectum. To make sure that he was dead they slammed his skull against the cobblestones until the last wheezing moans gave way to sighs and finally to nothing.

"Better take his wallet and stuff," Murdoch warned, panting for breath. "Make it look like a robbery."

"What about the body?" Johnson asked.

Murdoch thought about that. "Maybe we should dump it in the lake. Then we'll be back in Chi before the pigs find it."

Then Johnson had one of his ideas. "We can do better than that," he said.

"How?"

"You get the wheels. Bring it to the end of the alley and open the trunk. When it's all clear give us a whistle and I'll dump him in. Now we killed the mother I want to do him one last favor."

V

Small-time hoodlum Bobby Hayes ceased to exist in this dimension at 10:23 P.M. Zurich time. It was difficult to find a human being whose thoughts were on Bobby at the moment of his demise. In a Chicago suburb Bobby's wife was telling a friend that her feet were killing her and that she would have to find a new chiropodist. In the boardroom of Luigi Valente Associates, Big Lug was telling the board that they would have to come up with a gimmick if they wanted to get the Arab sheikh gamblers away from those MGM bastards in Vegas. He gave his board members forty-eight hours to come up with a gimmick.

Twenty thousand feet above Baltimore Carlos Villegas was sitting impatiently in an Aeronaves jet while the plane droned its way through a holding pattern waiting for clearance into Kennedy Airport, where Carlos would transfer to a Swissair flight to Zurich. Carlos Villegas was not thinking about Bobby Hayes. Carlos was wondering if the Hurtilbank problem would be resolved in time for him to buy the submachine guns he needed from Israel.

President Johann Hurtil of Hurtilbank was not thinking of Bobby Hayes either. Hurtil was sitting in the library of his mansion on the Bellerive Quai sipping an aged Napoleon brandy of which he was especially fond, comfortable in a burgundy-red house jacket. Ostensibly, Hurtil was watching television with his wife, Hildegarde. He could hear the clicking of Hildegarde's knitting needles as she worked away at some new scarf or sweater or sock for one of the grandchildren. Privately, Hurtil was convinced that Hildegarde would still be industriously knitting for the grandchildren while the doctor was diagnosing that her heart attack was fatal. Hurtil was not really watching television. He was thinking of David Christopher and asking himself if he had done the right thing in bringing him in to help solve the Hurtilbank crisis. Actually he seemed a bright enough young man and the people at Crédit Suisse had been satisfied. Tomorrow there would be Villegas to console and then there was a meeting of the Swiss Central Banking Authority. When would things ever return to normal?

David Christopher might have been thinking about Bobby Hayes if he had not been so absorbed in the strobe-succession of Denises who were his dinner companion. She was snarling leopard and forest faun, little girl and sex goddess, girl-next-door and flaunting whore, exquisitely soignée model and madcap hoyden in such lightning

switches that she was gone before David could fo-
cus properly on the woman who had been there.

The Greifen turned out to be a smoky night spot
in a cellar in the shadow of the enormous
Hauptbahnhof, the railroad-cum-bus-cum-parking-
cum-meeting-eating-shopping center and *rendez-
vous-ordinaire* for the half million people of Zurich.
There was a feeling about the cellar that suggested
it might once have served as the kitchen of a convent in the days when convents were massive stone
fortresses resting on one-ton granite blocks. Somehow the bearded young men with their braless
girlfriends in jeans, the mikes and amplifiers and
loudspeakers and spotlights on the booming
beaded group—they billed themselves as the Sitting
Sioux—and especially the tourists, wrongly dressed,
smiling fatuously, trying to be with it—all seemed
like invaders of a sanctuary who would shortly
be cast into eternal darkness for their sacrilege.
There could be no question however that it was
Denise's kind of milieu. She flourished in it like an
exotic night flower. Apparently well-known to the
beards-and-jeans crowd, she first chatted in fluent
German with one table about a new night spot in
Munich and a fabulous group in Soho. Then, while
David fretted and shuffled even more impatiently
she found some French friends. To David's un-
tuned ear her French sounded at least as indigenous as that of her friends while they discussed
this marvelous singles spot in Paris and Denise
stated confidently that the "in" place this summer
was definitely going to be the Anatalya strip on the
Mediterranean coast of Turkey.

Their own table was against a pillar under an
arch that looked as if it were supporting the entire
Hauptbahnhof on its single span. Denise assured

David that the house wines were Swiss and terrific.
On the rushing torrent of her enthusiasm they
started with a pewter flagon of icy Fendant. The
Fendant went with a *soupe du jour* that Denise
seemed to command by clapping her hands lightly
in the middle of the increasing babel of music and
voices. It was steaming hot and resembled a light
pea soup flavored with pork and finely sliced vegetables.

David and Denise had not yet exchanged a word
of personal conversation and in the cacophonous
enthusiasm of the guitars, banjos, drums, organ, triangle and accordion of the band, backing a
screeching male singer, it did not seem too likely
that he would repair the omission in the Greifen.

"You'll adore the next course," Denise shouted,
cupping her hands to her mouth.

"What is it?" David asked her.

"It's the geschnetzeltes Kalbfleisch. You know,
the minced veal with creamed sauce. Zurich's famous for it."

"No kidding," David answered.

"Really," she told him seriously, "with a side dish
of Rosti. Hope you don't mind."

"Rosti?" he queried.

"You Genevoises," she mocked. "You don't know
what real food is."

"Tell me."

"It's one of our German Swiss dishes," Denise
lectured him. "They boil whole potatoes. Then they
dice them and fry them and finally they bake
them. They are absolutely divine."

"How do you keep your figure on Rosti?" David
asked.

"It's all the exercise I get," she dropped her voice
to a conspiratorial whisper, "late at night." She was

openly taunting him. David wondered how long he could resist the impulse to fight back.

The waiter brought two plates of geschnetzeltes Kalbfleisch on a tray. Using a napkin, he placed one in front of Denise and gave the other to David.

"Watch out," warned the waiter, "the plates are hot. Some red wine?"

"What is it?" David asked.

The waiter was nonplussed. "I'm not sure," he confessed. "Probably Dole. It's local." He leaned over and spoke confidentially—or as confidentially as one could speak at the equivalent noise level of a subway rounding a curve under Manhattan. "There's some Beaupolais out there if you want it. Seeing as you're with Mlle. Abbott."

Denise looked up and smiled a slow sweet smile at David. An American who elects to live in Europe tends to delusions of grandeur when it comes to dining out, with himself as the gourmet impressing his date with his profound experience of the wine list. The Greifen had been a perfect choice. She knew that David could cheerfully have reached out, put both hands around her throat and squeezed hard.

"Well?" the waiter asked. He was unconscious of the battle of the sexes being waged silently in his presence.

"The Dole will be fine," David said, "with or without Mlle. Abbott." His nod dismissed the waiter to Hades.

"Naughty, naughty," Denise chided him. "Your fangs are showing."

"Just the points," David answered grimly. "I'm working up to the full fang."

They ate in silence while the waiter disappeared and then reappeared with another pewter flagon of wine and two more glasses. He poured the wine and vanished again.

To David's surprise the acid rock of the Sitting Sioux suddenly gave way to a softer interlude. The group, proving more versatile than he would have guessed, cut back to a piano, a guitar and a double bass and the voices of the crowd at the Greifen unconsciously lowered their pitch. David decided to attempt a more personal exchange with Denise.

"Where's home base for you?" he asked her.

She shrugged her shoulders. "All over."

"Have you ever been to the States?" he pursued.

"Not really."

He sensed her resentment across the table and could not understand why she would feel it. "I have to take my hat off—figuratively speaking—to your gift for languages," he tried again. "Not being a linguist myself. What's your first language?"

"If you're trying to put me in a slot," she flared, "forget it. I don't like slots and I don't like people who try to put people in slots."

David put down his fork carefully and engaged Denise's eyes against her will. "To say nothing of your manners," he said, "you suffer from a poor memory. You suggested this dinner meeting, as I recall, so that we could meet and talk over matters that might have some bearing on your present predicament. I've been hired by Hurtilbank to protect its interests. Its paramount interests are its clients . . ."

"The bank doesn't give a damn about us." She almost spat out the words, and he wondered where the venom came from and for what reason. "It only cares about itself."

"How the hell can the bank care about itself," he demanded, "if somebody is attacking it through clients who refuse to let the bank protect itself by protecting them? This is the damnedest thing I've ever experienced. You're as sensitive as an exposed nerve. What's with you? Anybody would think I was on the side of the blackmailers. Can't you get it through your dumb and beautiful head? I'm on your side."

Denise put down her knife and fork. "Do you have a tissue?" she asked him.

David looked up. Tears were glistening on her lashes and one stray tear escaped from the corner of her eye and trailed its way down her cheek.

"Of course," he answered. He put his hand in his jacket pocket, took out a couple of tissues, and handed them across the table.

"I apologize," David said, "I didn't mean to sound off like that. Guess we got off on the wrong foot somehow."

Denise dabbed her eyes. Then she stood up, came around the table, took David's face with both her hands, and kissed him on the mouth. "You're really very sweet," she told him, "underneath all that *muy macho* bravado. And I've been beastly to you. Forgive me?"

"I'll definitely take it under serious consideration," he told her. David stood up while she went back to her seat. "While we're appraising my etchings."

Denise laughed. "Etchings do nothing for me," she said. "I turn on in the Louvre."

"There's a plane at midnight, so hurry up and finish your whatchamacallit."

Denise stuck out her tongue. "And that's the truth," they said in unison.

Dwight McGowan was another man in Zurich

who was not thinking about Bobby Hayes at 10:23 P.M. Actually McGowan was not thinking about anything very much. He was too drunk. The Plaza Hotel, where he was staying, was in one of the choice areas of Zurich: a towering, tree-lined square two blocks back from the Uto Quai promenade along the eastern bank of the Zurichsee. The hotel itself had a variety of restaurants where McGowan might have eaten—a café-restaurant called the Piccadilly, the Plaza Grill, the swinging Palm Garden, the Intimo Bar, and the Pfederstall and the Vodka, two restaurants specializing in German food.

For reasons best known to himself in his inebriated state, McGowan decided not to eat in the hotel. He ordered the taxi driver to take him to some place where he could have some real Swiss chow. Skilled in the likes and dislikes of visitors to Zurich, the taxi driver decided on the Zeughauskeller in the Parade Platz, a decision which put McGowan within a few feet of the Regina Hotel and the ominous preliminaries to the death of Bobby Hayes. Not having any reason to be aware of this, McGowan stumbled into the Zeughauskeller and found himself in a béer hall of which all other beer halls can only be pallid imitations. Once an army arsenal, this beer hall still has a special appeal to Swiss soldiers. Apart from their compulsory military training, public parades and guard duties and service at the Vatican, Swiss soldiers have a lot of time on their hands. Those in the Zurich area find the Zeughauskeller an ideal setting for long night sessions of eating, drinking and yodeling. The high vaulted ceiling, the massive wooden crossbeams and the great supporting pillars partially concealed under a fuzz of birds perched on grape-laden vines—alas, artificial—seem to absorb the most raucous laughter, shouts and singing and encourage still greater efforts.

Sitting down cautiously at a table under a wall crowded with broadswords, pikes, halberds and coats-of-arms, McGowan, with considerable help from a jovial waiter, ordered an "Entrecote 'Café de Paris' mit schmelzender Kranterbutter and Pommes Frites," plus a liter stein of Feldschlossen beer. The plate of food was larger than McGowan could finish, despite an appetite that went with his bulk, and the beer turned out to be the perfect chaser for his bourbon. McGowan bought a giant pretzel from a waiter who sold them off a walking stick. The salted biscuit maintained his thirst at a level where the beer was needed to alleviate it.

At some time during the night a Swiss band started up, complete with alpenhorns, trumpets, clarinets, trombones, B-flat horns, and drums. The players were dressed as Gruyère herdsmen. Each of them wore a velvet black skullcap and an Empire canvas jacket with puffed sleeves called a bredzon. There was edelweiss embroidery on the bredzon lapels and silver-thread thorn-points on the body. The Texan was no musician but he liked to hear people sing, and yodeling took on new meaning when it was done by a chorus of martial voices in a stube like the Zeughauskeller. One of the soldiers, almost as drunk as McGowan and just as friendly, learned that McGowan was an American. To McGowan's astonished delight, the bandleader made an announcement in German. There were halloos and clapping. Soldiers, businessmen, tourists, students, husbands, wives—the whole beer hall turned in McGowan's direction. A weaving forest of giant bechers, rugelis and steingutkrugs of beer pointed at him and then everybody was roaring at full throat behind the blasting instruments of the band, "When the Saints Come Marching In." Tears streamed down McGowan's face. It was as though he had penetrated the essence of life in Switzerland and found it to be some mysterious combination of camaraderie and alcohol. Everything was going to be all right. But then he had known everything was going to be all right ever since the customs officer had let him keep his bourbon.

Helmut Rascher, the man from Bonn, was definitely not thinking about Bobby Hayes at 10:23 P.M. Helmut also had other things on his mind. Like Dwight McGowan, Helmut was a man who lived with a fear that was constantly threatening to overwhelm him. Helmut's fear was those Africans. One day they would get him. Helmut knew that. Because thousands and millions of them were never far away. Plotting a horrible death for him. Every minute of the day.

He met Hurtil on schedule at his home. Rascher insisted that it had to be Hurtil's home. A public meeting was asking for trouble. The African spies would learn about it and then it would be all over with Helmut. Rascher drove himself to Hurtil's villa. He didn't trust chauffeurs. Half of them were Africans. The other half were in the pay of the Africans. Hurtil's home sent shivers up and down Rascher's spine. It was on the lakefront. There was a big stone fence around it with iron spikes on top. Heavy iron gates. Weird-looking trees. In the dusk they could conceal an army of Africans. The house itself was tall. Dark-gray stone. Mullioned windows with amber and purple glass. Rascher was glad when the butler led him to the security of the interior. Hurtil was waiting for him in the big old library and Rascher accepted a small sherry to settle his quivering nerves. But the combination of the secret bank-account disclosure threat and Helmut's fear of the vengeance of the Africans did not make for light conversation. He told Hurtil to pay the ransom and be damned. Rascher did not think the bank had any case for procrastination. As if the bank would miss a few stinking million francs. What were a few francs to Hurtilbank? After all, the Africans wanted his heart. Alive and beating in their pink palms while they stabbed it.

But Rascher was forced to sit there while Hurtil told him about David Christopher. Who needed David Christopher? What he needed was the bank to pay the ransom so Helmut Rascher could escape from Zurich before the Africans caught up with him. "Christopher is a good man. He's done some great things, Rascher. I have a feeling he will solve this case, find those scoundrels and bring them to justice." It was enough to make a man shit in his pants while he sat there. Christopher would still be bringing criminals to justice when he, Rascher, was dangling by his toes over a caldron of boiling rat fat, waiting for the Africans to drop him in.

Rascher got away from Hurtil as quickly as he could and drove off in a near-frenzy. His refuge was a little-known hotel. It was small and old-fashioned, used mostly by the local Swiss. At the foot of the hill below the University. The hotel appealed to Rascher. It was on the north side of the city in the direction of the airport. Only half a dozen people ever slept there. No Africans. And it had an unusual advantage: Inside the hotel was a funicular station sending cars up the steep slope to the University. It was an escape route that Helmut Rascher appreciated deeply.

The little hotel had one other quality that appealed to Rascher. It was within a few meters of the best brothel in Zurich. Helmut was afraid of alcohol. A little too much to drink and he might let down his guard. The Africans would not miss a chance like that. But sex. That was different. You could forget your troubles. And afterward you could sleep in peace.

Rascher drove to the hotel, parked his car in the street, washed up in his room, and ate in a main-floor dining room that was just a large space with long plank tables which people shared. It was fine with Rascher. He enjoyed the food and was indifferent to the company. Tonight they had fresh Kalbsbratwurst, direct from farm calf to hotel table, with still-warm bread and moist creamy butter, washed down with a raw Valais wine served in a large pitcher. Then out came the great earthenware cooking pot bubbling with its fragrant Gruyère fondue. The owner of the hotel was also the chef and prided himself on serving the best fondue in Zurich. Only Valais white wine. Only the most fulsome garlic. Only his own spices, the most aromatic. Only his special house Neuchâtel kirsch. Everybody cheered when it arrived and the chef personally set it on a brazier which nobody was allowed to regulate except himself. Only when the brazier was exactly right and the fondue was bubbling to perfection, by which time the twelve open mouths at the long table were unashamedly salivating in anticipation, would the chef let out a bellowing *Ja* which expressed his own satisfaction and gave the diners permission to begin. In unison twelve toast-pointed forks plunged into the fondue and the feast began. Tonight Rascher had lost his toast and had to pay for a bottle of wine. This rare gracious act for him had released some of his tension like steam escaping from a pressure cooker.

He had arrived at the brothel with a bottle of wine for Gretel. Gretel was a heavy German-Swiss girl with bursting breasts and a lust for sex that not even prostitution had been able to diminish. For one hundred francs, Rascher was able to stay with Gretel as long as he wanted. And tonight he wanted.

First they had a drink with Madame Brabant and a couple of the girls who were off duty. For Helmut it was part of the ritual. The room was too small, but Madame liked a fire and the heat made the girls glow. The smell of a female was a powerful stimulant to Helmut, and he breathed deeply of the heavy musky odor of the room while he poured the cool wine. He liked the nearness of the girls and their warmth. Their loose gowns over their black briefs. Their generous hair falling over near-nude shoulders. And their full-mouthed kisses as they greeted him or thanked him for the wine or enjoyed some word of flattery.

When he was aroused to the point of agony, Helmut was overcome by an urge to establish his sexual qualifications. He had Gretel unzip his trousers and proudly display the distended penis for the girls' inspection. There were oohs and ahs of approval, and much envious begging of Gretel to lend them Helmut for just this one night. After he had been properly admired, Helmut told Gretel to zip up his trousers, left the wine with Madame Brabant and her girls and then took Gretel to bed.

Rascher had been married once, but the experience had disgusted his wife and angered him. Now

Helmut's former wife was married to a farmer and lived in a tiny village called Fürstenzell outside of Passau. Helmut did not believe that the farmer was enjoying much of a sex life. When he contrasted the narrow-minded puritanism of his wife with the easy cooperation of prostitutes like Gretel, Helmut was all for the prostitutes.

They were hardly inside Gretel's room when her warm mouth enveloped his penis in a caress so scintillating that he was not sure he could hold back his orgasm. He fought free and lifted her up. Her body was pressing against his as he dropped her gown to the floor and reached for the hook at the back of her bra. She paused only long enough to help him take off his shirt and his undershirt. As soon as he was naked she dropped onto the bed and stretched out her legs so that he could drive himself crazy deciding which orifice to fill.

Her mouth was open and begging again for his tool. As Helmut straddled her he felt her mouth suck his penis down into her throat until her lips were—almost incredibly—at its base. But now his own experienced tongue was savoring the exciting acidic juice of her vagina and flicking at her clitoris with rough demanding urgency. He felt her writhe in pleasure and gush a first flow of orgasmic juice into his mouth.

He rolled off her to come up for air and felt her climbing on top of him, feeding his still-distended organ greedily into her vagina, lowering herself until the end of his penis was pressing against the mouth of her uterus. She moved experimentally to test his rigidity and found him hard and confident. Her weaving back and forth became faster as her aroused clitoris sought more and still more pleasuring.

Helmut's mouth nuzzled her breasts and drew in each nipple in turn as if he expected the bulging mammaries to yield him a feast of mother's milk. As their movements became faster with increasing passion, Gretel started a series of orgasms, moaning with pleasure like a keening puppy. Instead of coming with her, Helmut swung her body around and under him and brutally plunged his penis deeper and deeper with such force that she cried out for him to stop. Instead he laughed, sneeringly with male power, and continued torturing her until agony went over the brink into ecstasy and she exploded with a shuddering delight that affected her whole body. He stayed in her, on his knees, braying his victory like an hysterical donkey.

When Gretel had quieted down she heaved him off her with a surge of her powerful hips. Then she turned over and rose to her hands and knees, presenting her spread buttocks to Rascher. The sight of the curving creamy flesh surrounding the inviting dark well aroused the old savagery in him. His moist drooping member rose to the challenge as fresh blood pumped into it and, growling with fury, he searched for her anus. He did not care that her tight sphincter muscle resisted him, but pushed viciously until it gave him entry and he could plunge his penis all the way in.

This was the moment of oblivion. By day Rascher was a ruthless businessman filled with fears that his two-timing would catch up with him. At night he turned into a snorting, rearing, uncaring beast. He clawed and scratched at Gretel's milk-white body, leaving red burns and bloody trails as he struggled for the fierce frenzy of the ultimate climax. As he achieved it he was howling like some fearsome monster from the misty marshes of primeval earth.

He definitely was not thinking of Bobby Hayes, even though the time was exactly 10:23 P.M.

Nor was Hurtilbank vice-president Franz Benninger thinking about Bobby Hayes. Benninger was also a man with other things on his mind. The things on Benninger's mind at 10:23 P.M. did not include his wife and children. Contrary to his conservative public image the things on Benninger's mind rarely included his wife and children. This was partly due to his preferred life-style and partly due to Friedel. Friedel was an old-fashioned wife who let herself turn dowdy and go to fat while she waited hand and foot on her husband and her three children. She could not have foreseen that while she was faithfully fulfilling her wifely duty as she understood it, wives with a different viewpoint would be enjoying satisfying liaisons with her husband.

Benninger was discreet in his indiscretions. He kept an apartment on the Badener-Strasse for assignations with his mistress-of-the-moment. He deliberately had affairs only with wives who, as far as he could judge, were satisfied with their marriages but wished to expand their love lives. He did not believe in serious affairs. Business and pleasure were separate compartments in his life.

Or they had been until tonight. When Benninger closed the door of the bank behind David Christopher at 7:45 P.M. he went back to his office to collect his topcoat and briefcase. He assumed that he was going home to his wife and children—for a change. He would certainly have done so if he had not been suffering still from that terrible moment of despondency that hit him when he was in the vaults with Christopher. The thought of the too-easy vulnerability of Hurtilbank to the black-mailers still irritated him. He had to protect the bank from Hurtil's damagingly facile assumption that the money in secret numbered accounts was safe money. Today had proved that he was right and Hurtil was dead wrong. One slip by Hurtil or Christopher or Florelle or himself, one whisper to the police, one unguarded word from any one of the five investors being threatened and this thing would blow sky-high. Poof. The end of Hurtilbank.

There was only one solution. A huge influx of secure money to reduce the secret-account invest-ment in Hurtilbank down to a manageable pro-portion of their gross reserves. But where . . . ? how . . . ? Benninger had his topcoat on. His briefcase was packed and ready. He was looking around his office for any signs of untidiness. His hand was reaching for the light switch when there flashed into his mind the face of Rita Jensen. His heart be-gan to race. He sat down, breathing heavily. Rita Jensen, by God. Rita Jensen. He saw her. The ath-letic body. Lithe and long-hipped and small-breasted just the way he liked a body to be. The jet-black hair. The amused hazel eyes. Suddenly his longing for her was an ache in his groin.

He had seen her first at one of those dull recep-tions. OPEC or OECD. What did it matter? At the time their meeting seemed accidental—the drifting together of two pieces of flotsam on the aimless tides of the reception. He was mouthing polite nonsense to an American banker from Paris who seemed more anxious to demonstrate his heavy-handed proficiency in French than to say anything intelligent. She was warding off an insistent Italian who said that his Ferrari was waiting to take her to dinner, preferably room service in his hotel, wherever she wished. At the same moment each of them turned to escape and their drinks clashed and sprayed slightly.

"Sorry," he said instinctively in her general direction, without really looking at her. He started for another corner of the room.

"No damage," she answered. There was something about the voice, something cool and offhand which caused him to turn back for a focused look.

She was wearing a simple black knee-length Cardin cocktail dress with a single strand of pearls around her throat. She wore no makeup except lipstick. She was appraising him with cynical eyes, assaying his worth objectively, unemotionally.

"Are you francs, marks, sterling or petrodollars?" he asked her.

"I'm gold," she answered. "Which are you?" He spread his hands. "All five I expect. I'm with Hurtilbank here in Zurich."

"Oh," she said, as if the news were inconsequential. Afterward he realized that she already knew, that she had been stalking him all night and in seconds would begin to spin the web for her mildly curious little fly.

"There is a certain schizophrenia about oil," she said, "don't you think?"

"In what sense?" he asked her. He was interested that a woman had an opinion on oil but was not very interested in the opinion.

"Our Arab brothers are sitting on their sea of ooze," she said. "The quintessence of all that antediluvian fauna and flora squelched by all the earthquakes and lava and folds and whatnot."

"Colorful image."

"I'm sure I must have read it somewhere," she told him. "That ooze is our twentieth-century Circe. In this role it is decoying the world's financial reserves in the form of petrodollars."

"Go on," he encouraged.

"Now the Circean ooze reveals its schizophrenia. It turns into Cyclops. It is a monster terrifying the world with those same petrodollars as it goes about like a roaring lion seeking where it may invest. Don't you agree?"

They spent the rest of the reception together discussing recycling, and Benninger was intrigued to discover that she was at least as familiar with the complexities of the reinvestment of petrodollars as he was himself. At the end he regretted that the reception seemed to be over so quickly and that Hurtil was at his elbow suggesting that the car was ready.

Fortunately he had memorized her name and her address—when she told him that she had just come to live in Zurich and that she had found an apartment in a new building off the Alfred-Escher-Strasse on the western shore of the lake. Because of his golden rule about not mixing business with pleasure he had no real intention of calling her. But nature took its course, and after a few days it became less and less important that she was involved in some kind of international finance—gold she had said although who knew if she was serious?—and more and more important that she was somebody he found attractive. The image of her lean flowing body kept recurring to him.

Finally he called her and suggested dinner. She seemed to take a while to consider the suggestion before she said, "Franz, there is a price on my head."

"What do you mean?" he asked. There was another long pause and for some reason her answer became important to him. "Well?"

"I mean," she said, "that . . . it is stupid to discuss such a thing over the telephone."

"Where, then?" he wanted to know.

"You may come to my apartment or I shall go to yours—you have one, Franz, I suppose?"

"I have one."

"Good. Or we can meet in any hotel or café or bar that you wish. The choice is yours—but I must warn you that this time we will talk business. No games."

"In that case," Benninger told her, "we will be businesslike. Let us meet tomorrow afternoon at four P.M. in the Kreuzgang. After that we shall see."

Benninger had not risen to preeminence in Hurtilbank to go to Rita's apartment like a lamb to be slaughtered by its possible microphones and hidden cameras. Neither was he going to introduce her to his own secret place which she could bug with equal ease after their first meeting. Common sense dictated that he write finis to the acquaintance there and then, but it was not easy to follow the dictates of common sense when the girl was as intelligent, as direct and as attractive as Rita. Benninger told himself he could at least listen to her proposition.

They met in the Romanesque cloisters of the Kreuzgang at exactly 4:00 P.M. It was only courtesy on Benninger's part to suggest she take five minutes to have a quick look at the Fraumünster itself. Rita agreed that this was an excellent idea. She had been meaning to drop in and see the Fraumünster ever since she arrived in Zurich but just had not gotten around to it. While they admired the ogive-vaulted nave Benninger told Rita that this interesting example of medieval architecture actually dated back to a convent for women founded in 853 by the grandson of Charlemagne dubbed Louis the Germanic. The twin arcaded galleries were an obvious fifteenth-century addition, but they had a certain style even so.

In the gloom underneath the overhanging galleries, Benninger quietly asked to see Rita's handbag. She handed it to him without a word. He examined it carefully. There was no tape recorder. Without waiting to be asked, Rita took off her sable jacket and handed it to Benninger. Then she removed her Hermès scarf and shook free her short-cropped jet-black hair.

"I'll take off my dress too if you like," she said, "but you're wasting your time, Franz. What I am offering is a business proposal. If I had wanted to blackmail you, I would have let you take me to dinner—and gladly gone with you to your love nest. You telephoned me, Franz, remember?"

Feeling as foolish as she meant him to feel, Benninger helped Rita on with her jacket and waited while she retied her scarf. She took her handbag from him.

"Actually, Franz, I am not upset. I would have been disappointed in you if you had not been careful. Now may we have a drink and talk business?"

It was March, still chilly in Zurich with the winds whistling down from the surrounding mountains. Benninger took Rita to an inn in the old town. They sat in a dark-paneled booth and watched the flames leaping in the great open fireplace while the waiter served them espresso coffee and a bottle of Rhine wine. They assessed each other

wordlessly. Rita wondered what was going on behind the careful impassive face of Benninger. She
was afraid that she had a hard sell in front of her.
This was a man in control of his emotions. He liked
her, but hardly enough for what she wanted. Rita
was less pretty and more appealing than Benninger
had fantasized her. He realized that her broad intelligent forehead made her face heart-shaped.
From within the heart her eyes, long-lashed, calm,
at ease, met his unafraid.

When the waiter had gone, Rita took a packet of
filter-tipped cigarettes from her handbag and asked
Benninger if he would object to her smoking. He
shook his head and took out a box of matches from
his pocket to light her cigarette. Accepting the
light, she said, "Franz, may I ask two favors of
you?"

"If they are reasonable and within my power."

"They are reasonable and within your power."

"What are they?"

She carefully tapped her cigarette in an earthenware ashtray, then took a sip of wine. "First, hear
me out. Hear the whole story before you say yea or
nay."

"That's reasonable enough," he agreed. "What is
the second?"

"If you cannot help me, promise to treat what I
tell you in confidence." She put up her hand to indicate that she was not finished. "You are afraid
that I may hurt you. Actually it is the other way
about. May I have some more wine, please?"

"I'm sorry." Benninger took the bottle and
poured wine into Rita's glass, then replenished his
own. Rita was nervous and she was not the kind of
girl to be nervous. Benninger's curiosity grew. He
waited, conscious of the taste of the wine, the smell

of the coffee, and the way Rita's lips moved when she drew on her cigarette. He wanted to feel those lips on his and had difficulty putting away the thought.

"I represent the government of Ethiopia," Rita began.

"You what?" Benninger was taken completely by surprise.

"That ruffles your cool, doesn't it, Herr Benninger?"

"What is it you want?" Benninger inquired—but he already knew what she wanted and knew that she knew he knew.

"You know what I want," she told him, "but let me put it in perspective." Having opened the subject, Rita was now in control of herself. "Our government is not very popular in the Western world, I'm afraid. We have made mistakes. We have done stupid things. It happens. Some people have died. Perhaps unnecessarily. We are still new in all of this business of government. We are learners."

She crushed out her cigarette, and then seemed to feel the need of coffee to remove the taste it left in her mouth.

"One thing that people have not understood—the people who feel emotional about the old Emperor and his family. He and his ancestors have had centuries to do something for the people of Ethiopia and what have they done? Yes, we have killed a few dozen. Because of the decades of neglect of the mass of the people, hundreds of thousands died. They died because simple things were left undone. Engineers were not hired to plan water conservation and irrigation. Agriculturalists were not brought in to teach our people modern farming. We have had almost no help from the international agencies. In the days of Solomon our civilization was the wonder of the world. That a woman as important as our queen would condescend to visit Solomon became one of the legends of history. And what are we today? A primitive backward poverty-stricken race starving in a world that knows better. You see why we have not very much respect for the old Emperor. All that he is or was we made him, and what did he give us in return?"

It was a rhetorical question and Benninger knew that he was not expected to answer.

"Somewhere in Zurich Haile Selassie has invested about one billion dollars in gold. At this moment it is sitting, feeding on itself, multiplying in value. For whose benefit? Right now for the bank's benefit. Whichever bank has it sitting in a cage. We need that gold for our people. Morally that gold belongs to the people of Ethiopia. It can be invested in their future. It represents the water, the grain, the farm machinery, the expert advice, the collateral against World Bank loans, the local participation in United Nations Special Agency programs, the incentive for the big foundations to come to our assistance . . ."

"You've chosen the socialist path," Benninger protested.

"Deliberately," she replied, "and after profound study of the alternatives. We think the socialist path means the greatest good for the greatest number. It may be the slowest path, but at least you begin with the right theory—that the whole nation owns the total capital resources of Ethiopia. Soon enough the strong will begin to destroy the weak and seize their possessions—as the Rothschilds and the Rockefellers and the Carnegies and the Krupps

have done before them. But at least let us begin at
the beginning."

"Why come to me with all this?" Benninger
asked her.

Rita laughed. It was a hard metallic laugh with
no music in it and no humor. "Oh, Franz, rant and
rave or tell me you won't deal or do anything—but
for Christ's sake don't treat me as a fool. I've done
my homework, Franz. There are only three banks
where that money could be. Personally I am convinced that that gold is in the vaults of Hurtilbank
because the other two banks don't match up with
the rest of our information."

"And if it is?"

"If it is, Franz, your president, Johann Hurtil,
knows about it. Probably your chief accountant,
Madame Florelle, also knows about it ... but you,
Franz, you control it. You have the key. You know
the number. Only you can say open sesame. I told
you that I've done my homework, Franz."

Benninger looked for his topcoat. "I've enjoyed
our chat," he said. "Shall we go?"

Rita was calm. It was the reaction she had expected. "Just one more minute of your time,
Franz."

Benninger looked at his watch. "I'm afraid I'm
running late as it is," he apologized.

"Relax, Franz. From what I know of your
friends, she won't mind your calling at the last
minute."

Benninger blushed and stood up. "Good afternoon, Mlle. Jensen."

"Don't be an idiot, Franz. Listen to me for sixty
seconds. Until we get across to that gold, Franz, I
remain here in Zurich. Same telephone number.
Same address. We do not want simply to withdraw

the gold. We will make your bank our agents—to negotiate with our funds on a normal commission basis. You will buy and sell investments for us—stocks, bonds, shares, securities, companies, you will negotiate loans, pay for our purchases of imports on the international market, deal for us with the West and with the East. With the East too, Franz. Think of that. What have you got to lose?"

"Only my reputation, the reputation of Hurtilbank, and the respect of Switzerland before the world—to name a few things. What do you take me for?"

"I had hoped a man," she replied quickly. "A humane and decent man."

Her words were lost. Benninger threw a note at the cashier and left without looking back. Rita saw him go and lit another cigarette. Then she refilled her wineglass. She felt tired, drained, but not as depressed as she had expected. His reaction had been too sharp, too violent. Her proposition had touched a chord. She did not think she had seen the last of Franz Benninger.

For the next few days Benninger was impossible at home, irritable at work, preoccupied, seething with resentment. Rita had taken advantage of him. She had used a typical woman's subterfuge. Attracted him sexually and tried to bribe him with her body. Despicable. Simply despicable. As if he, Franz Benninger, a leading Zurich banker, would contravene the code on which Switzerland had built its economy: the inviolable sanctity of the depositor. That was the problem with women. No morals. No sense of ethics. And absolutely no sense of law whatsoever.

Benninger shuddered to think of the consequences of doing what she had asked of him. Tacit

revelation of a numbered account. Illegal appropri-
ation of the funds of a depositor without the authorization of the depositor or his representative—in fact
violently against the publicly known will of the depositor. Rita could say what she liked about the
funds belonging by moral right to the people
of Ethiopia. That was a transparent pretense.
High-sounding poppycock. What would stand up
in a court of law? That was the only issue germane
to the case. One thing that certainly would not
stand up in a court of law was misappropriation.
And he, Benninger, would be the one person the
law could prosecute. Not Rita. Not the people of
Ethiopia. Just Franz Benninger. In jail for the rest
of his life. The laughingstock of Switzerland. The
byword of the banking world. Trapped by a
woman. Another Samson. Another Solomon. Another Mark Antony.

Benninger first distracted himself with a woman
who was everything that Rita was not. She was
red-haired, teetering on the edge of overweight because of a passionate fondness for Swiss chocolate
during those arid times when she had to go as long
as two or three days without sex. In the past Benninger had always parted with her weighed down
by a sense of failure—the sneaking suspicion that
he had merely whetted her appetite. In his raging
resentment of Rita he discovered new sexual
prowess and evoked from his redhead an orgasmic
flood of passion which sent her from him delirious,
light-headed, satiated.

The victory restored Benninger's ego and he
closed the door on Rita Jensen forever.

Forever lasted exactly five weeks and two days.
Until tonight. Until Benninger, deep in his slough
of despond, was about to leave the bank after his

session with David Christopher. In a blinding flash
of illumination Benninger saw what he had missed
completely: The Haile Selassie gold was the key.
Transfer that from a secret account into general
funds and in one bold stroke he would cut the deposits in secret accounts from a terrifying 39.87
percent of Hurtilbank reserves to a comparatively
harmless 7.3 percent. Then let the blackmailers do
their damnedest.

Excited, Benninger strode up and down his office
weighing out the issues in his mind like moves in a
chess game. As far as he could judge, his position
was impregnable. Certainly Haile Selassie's heirs
were in no position to claim the money. If the
former Emperor had executed a power of attorney
in favor of anybody else, would Hurtilbank honor
it? It would become an international *cause célèbre*.
The government of Ethiopia would take it to court.
The case would drag on for years. Until long after
Benninger was dead and gone.

Moreover, Benninger had one enormous advantage. The Haile Selassie funds were in gold.
Down below in the Hurtilbank vaults there were
ten carrels of gold. Standard four-hundred-troy-
ounce gold bars, 99.5 percent fine, each worth
some eighty thousand dollars. Benninger issued
chits daily as Hurtilbank bought and sold gold for
its clients and the gold shuttled back and forth
from bank to bank up and down the Bahnhofstrasse. There was nothing quite so anonymous as a
bar of gold. That fifteen thousand of them in the
carrels of Hurtilbank were theoretically attached to
a dying Abyssinian through a number in Benninger's head was of no consequence. As many bars
and more changed banks in Zurich every day.

Benninger's hands may have been trembling

slightly as he dialed the telephone number of Rita Jensen, but his head felt crystal clear. Actually he felt calmer than he had felt in months. Even years. The blackmailers had in a way done Hurtilbank a favor. They had forced Franz Benninger to take a step long overdue. For the good of Hurtilbank. Benninger heard the musical beep tone as Rita's phone began to dial out, a click as she picked up the receiver, and then the husky voice he remembered so well. Franz was not a religious man. Nor was he given to poetry. He had no conscious mental preparation for his own voice as it said, "Rita. This is Franz Benninger. See, winter is past, the rains are over and gone. The flowers appear on the earth. The season of glad songs has come, the cooing of the turtledove is heard in our land." Perhaps the Queen of Sheba had inspired the words from Solomon and they were apropos now.

"I think that is the sweetest thing anybody has ever done for me, Franz," Rita told him. He suspected she was crying. "Does it ... I hope it ... oh, Franz, help me. Have you had dinner yet?"

"Now that you mention it," Benninger replied, "no."

"Good," she told him happily. "I'm a marvelous cook. Why don't you join me?"

That is why Franz Benninger was not thinking about Bobby Hayes at 10:23 P.M. They had spun dreams together for the future of Haile Selassie's gold over a tender Wiener Schnitzel. Now they were making love together. To seal the agreement.

David and Denise had reached the don't-care stage where it seemed pointless to end the night. They left the Greifen at 11:30 P.M. As soon as they were settled in the comfort of the Lamborghini,

Denise decided that she wanted to see the Zurich-see by moonlight. David drove her to the Mythen-Quai, where she got out of the car and waited for David to take her arm. They strolled through the gardens to the beach. Despite the chill, she suddenly slipped off her shoes and ran to the edge of the water. She tested it with her toe, squealed at the cold and waited for David to come crunching to her.

"You'll freeze," he warned her.

"I don't care," she said. "I love it. I just love it. Where else could you get gardens and a beach and a mini-ocean and an old town and a modern city and the Juras smiling down on it all, hoary and wise and ancient. Mountains are really God, you know. I worked it out once."

Unexpectedly she turned up to him, pulled down his face to her and kissed him hard and long and deep, as if she wanted the kiss not to end. She hardly broke the kiss to say, "Thanks. I needed that. Let's go."

Denise retrieved her shoes and they walked back to the car, arms around each other for warmth. In the car she told him, "Take me to see your hotel. O.K.?" Not knowing or caring what she wanted, David drove slowly back along the Mythen-Quai to the General-Guisan-Quai and into the Tal-Strasse. When they reached the Parade Platz he circled around to the front of the hotel. Abruptly she said to him, "Let's put the car in the garage. Maybe I'll come and see your etchings after all. Or maybe we'll just walk back to the Bellevue."

David was tempted to ignore her, to slip the car into Drive and take her back to her hotel. This was one hell of a jumpy female. A cat on a hot tin roof. The trouble was he didn't know why. It was not sex. The way her body moved, she could handle him and a dozen more like him before breakfast. But she was jittery about something. That was for sure. Maybe it was the blackmail thing. That could be it. He decided to go along with her. Ride with the whims a little longer.

The Lamborghini purred into the Talacker Strasse and David guided it smoothly to a halt at the garage office. The night manager rushed out to give him personal attention.

"Good evening, Mr. Christopher."

The manager opened the door for David and gestured to a driver to open the door for Denise.

"Evening," David said curtly.

"I trust you had a good evening, sir, after that unfortunate . . ."

"Did they find the man?" David cut him off.

"I'm afraid not, sir. He disappeared completely."

Denise's curiosity was aroused. "What's he talking about, David? What happened?"

"Nothing. Nothing at all," David assured her. "Come on, let's move it, huh?" He took Denise's arm to hurry her from the garage, but the manager was unshakable.

"Oh, just a minute, Mr. Christopher, I almost forgot. The gentleman from Hertz delivered your car."

David swung around to face him. "You're out of your skull. What car? What gentleman from Hertz?"

"The Cortina, sir. It's right over here." The manager fluttered into his office and returned with a set of keys, flustered but eager to restore the good name of the garage by extra service, wanted or not. "The gentleman from Hertz asked me to be sure to let you know that the package you asked him to pick up for you was in the trunk."

"Package? This is crazy ..." David tried again to get away from the persistent manager.

"Calm down, David," Denise said. "There's probably some simple explanation."

"I'm sure there is, sir," the manager said soothingly. "Here are the keys, sir, with your name right on them."

From the keys dangled a white tag with the name DAVID CHRISTOPHER scrawled in crude biro-printed letters.

"O.K., O.K.," David growled. "Open up the trunk. We'll go along with the joke."

The manager bustled ahead of them importantly and pointed to a red car, nose in to the wall. "This is it, sir. We'll see what the package is." He inserted the trunk key, twisted and the lid swung up easily. *"Mein Gott!"* the night manager gasped.

Denise began to scream uncontrollably, her screams reverberating through the concrete basement in waves of horror. David took hold of her and tried to hold down her hysteria. It was not easy when his own stomach was churning with nausea at the shock.

Their reaction was understandable. Inside the trunk of the Cortina was a corpse. The eyes stared up from a mutilated face and a smashed and bloody skull spilled out from under a familiar wide-brimmed felt hat. The broken contorted body was clad in a tartan raincoat. Johnson and Murdoch had done Bobby Hayes one last favor. Now let David Christopher try to explain him.

VI

For two hours David Christopher tried to explain
Bobby Hayes to a squad of slow-thinking night-
duty detectives who took down everything he said
in longhand and at 2:30 A.M. were still convinced
that he had more to tell them than he was willing
to admit. In the end it was Denise who put a
period to the interrogation by quietly dropping to
the floor of the police station office in a waxen-
faced faint. When she came to, the police agreed
to call it a night and chauffeured her back to the
Bellevue and David to the Regina, where he
dropped off into a restless sleep at 3:30 A.M.

At 8:20 the following morning David was awak-
ened by a polite, apologetic but insistent Captain
Hans Frey, who claimed that it was imperative
that he speak to David immediately. David barely
had time to fumble his way into a mauve silk
dressing gown and feel his groping feet into a pair
of Gucci slippers before Frey was at the door,

knocking for admittance. Hair tousled, unshaven, bad-tempered, David let him in.

Frey was, if possible, neater, cooler and more in control of the situation than he had been the night before. He was dressed in a dark-gray pinstripe suit, a white shirt, a tie striped in silver and black, black shoes and silver-gray socks. A gray felt hat with a green-blue peacock feather completed his ensemble. Frey was just what David needed to complete his depression. With Frey was his sumo-like assistant. Frey introduced him as Sergeant Alfred Schwand. David thought sourly that if Frey was not satisfied with his answers he would probably wiggle his moustache at Schwand and leave the room while Schwand softened him up for further interrogation.

"It seems, Mr. Christopher," Frey said in his precise voice, "that you have a genius for trouble."

"Another explanation could be that the Zurich police do a lousy job of protecting the citizenry."

Schwand shuffled and looked at Frey. David thought he looked like King Kong eagerly anticipating a command to crunch a few of his ribs, just to teach him respect. Ignoring both the appeal from Schwand and the insult from David, Frey took out a notebook.

"Mr. Christopher," he began, "could I have a few . . . ?"

"Look, Frey," David protested, "I was up half the night with a bunch of your goons. Before you start on me I'd like a cup of coffee. O.K.?"

"Certainly, O.K.," Frey replied.

Before David could move, Frey crossed to the telephone, dialed room service and grunted orders in German. The voice at the other end asked something and Frey turned to David. "What kind of juice, Mr. Christopher?"

"I don't believe this," David said to the ceiling. "Grapefruit. Fresh-squeezed. Warm bread rolls. Butter. Marmalade jam. Oh, yes, and fresh cream with my coffee. Not hot milk. Translate that into Schwyzerdutsch."

"Certainly," Frey answered. Imperturbable, he gave the order in Swiss German.

A half hour later David had repeated his account of the evening with Denise Abbott and their return to the garage of the Regina for the grisly discovery in the Cortina. His coffee, juice and rolls, exactly as ordered, had restored some of his confidence. "Look, Frey," David broke in, "you know all this stuff backwards. Let me ask you a question for a change? That Cortina? It was stolen, wasn't it. It was no Hertz car."

Frey paused before he said, "Why do you say that, Mr. Christopher?"

"Modus operandi of Big Lug's boys, Frey. Whoever blipped Bobby . . ."

"Bobby? Big Lug? You knew Mr. Hayes then?"

David let out a neigh of mockery. "Come on, Frey. Quit the routine. You know all about that guy. I'll bet you've been on his tail ever since he landed yesterday morning. You're Bank Detail, remember? What are you doing here, questioning me on a murder rap?"

"Murder? You were there?" Frey snicked with the rapier.

"No, I wasn't there, goddam it. What's with you, Frey? You know I'm covered minute-for-minute last night. What's your problem? Want me to solve your murder for you?"

This time David got through. Frey closed his

notebook with an audible snap. His gray-green eyes were glacial as he looked at David. The seconds ticked off in a silence charged with antipathy. "You mentioned that you were registered to investigate in Switzerland, Mr. Christopher," Frey said at last.

"You saw my card."

"It would be a pity, Mr. Christopher, if you lost your registration, would it not?"

"You bastard, Frey. You wouldn't."

"Oh, yes I would, Mr. Christopher. So, watch it, eh? As you Americans say . . . watch it." Frey stood up. "I asked you last night what you were doing in Zurich."

"And I told you," David answered.

"May I also remind you," Frey went on, "that in Switzerland as in the United States, it is a crime to withhold information on a murder case?"

"What I know is certainly not information on Bobby Hayes's death," David said sharply.

"Let us discuss that," Frey told him. "You are working for Hurtilbank?"

"I am."

Frey was like a skilled surgeon peeling off layers of flesh with a scalpel. "And Hayes is a client of Hurtilbank?"

"You know he was."

"Was Hayes part of your investigation?"

"Well—yes, but . . ."

"Did you meet Hayes yesterday?"

"I did. In the bank. At seven-fifteen P.M. Unless I miss my guess you saw Hayes enter and leave the bank. By the way, where did Hayes go after he left the bank?"

"The PTT. He made some phone calls. Why do you ask?"

"Just wondering how he knew where to find me."

"Why didn't you tell me last night that it was Hayes who tried to kill you? You knew it was Hayes, did you not?"

David needed time to frame his answer to that one. He decided to pour himself another cup of coffee.

"I'm waiting, Mr. Christopher."

David stirred sugar into his coffee. "Two reasons, Frey. One was that Hayes reversed his raincoat. He was wearing brown when I saw him. Sure I suspected it was Hayes. But I was not certain."

Frey thought over the answer before he asked, "And the other?"

"He was part of my investigation—which is confidential."

"Mr. Christopher, really. We are both intelligent men. How can you go on with this pretense that your investigation has nothing to do with this murder?"

David drained his coffee and put down his cup. "It may sound stupid to you, Frey, but I'm leveling with you. My investigation is an internal Hurtilbank matter. Hayes tried to kill me because I used to be with the U.S. Justice Department. I put away some of his mob. He thought I was after him for U.S. Justice. That's God's truth."

"Why was Hayes killed?"

"Frey, I'll do you a favor. Just go away and leave me alone with my little investigation for Hurtilbank and I'll solve your murder for you. Deal?"

Frey was wary, noncommittal. "It is possible. What is your solution?"

David stretched and yawned. "Frey, you've got to do better than possible. Come on, now."

"Very well, then. Who killed Hayes?"

David smiled. "I'm glad you asked that question.

131

Hayes was killed on orders from his boss, Luigi Valente of Chicago."

"How do you know?"

"I don't know. I smell it. If you want proof, you'll have to get your legmen to do some checking. More than likely you will find that two of Luigi's soldiers flew into Zurich yesterday. They picked up a rental at the airport. They watched Hayes until they got the chance to burn him last night. They checked their car back in at the airport. They took a midnight flight out of Zurich to any place there was a plane. Paris or London, I'd bet. Right now they're in Paris or London boarding a flight for Chicago."

"Why?" Frey asked.

David shrugged his shoulders. "Maybe Hayes got itchy fingers and Big Lug found out about it? Who knows?"

Reluctantly Frey closed his notebook and nodded to Schwand. The big detective opened the door for Frey. "Perhaps we shall meet again, Mr. Christopher."

"I hope not," David answered.

"Meanwhile, thank you for your cooperation." Frey inclined slightly, touched his hat and walked through the door ahead of Schwand. The silent sergeant twitched a muscle of his face at David and followed his superior out.

David grimaced, chained the door, looked at the time. "Shit," he groaned. He went to the telephone, dialed for an outside line, heard the ringing of the through tone and called his office in Geneva. He heard his secretary answer. "Corinne?"

"She must have kept you up late. I've been sitting here for an hour."

"I know. I know. Enough of the wisecracks.

132

What have you got for me?"

"O.K. Keep your shirt on. We have two signals from Jack F. in D.C. and two from Freddy in la belle whatsis. You following?"

"I'm five years old and retarded but I'm following."

"I get it. You tried all night and never made it."

"Corinne, you're fired."

"Too late. I just quit."

"For Christ's sake, Corinne. Will you give me those messages? They're urgent and I've got seconds to save Switzerland from bankruptcy. Now come on."

Corinne switched roles and for two minutes fed information to David while he listened without interrupting.

"That's great, Corinne, just great," Christopher told her.

"I always knew you would come to love me," she sighed huskily into the phone.

"Shut up and listen. Get back to Jack in D.C. as soon as it's dawn over the Potomac and tell him one of Big Lug's legmen, Bobby Hayes, was killed here in Zurich last night. Almost certainly two of Valente's soldiers. Almost certainly they'll be flying into Chicago today from Paris or London. Maybe—just maybe he can pick them off. Hold them on something until we check prints with Zurich. O.K.?"

"Got that," she said. "What else?"

"Call Freddy in Paris, Dan Stillman in London and somebody in Interpol . . ."

"Like Otto Goldhagen?"

"Perfect."

"Tell them I'm looking for a rundown on a blonde called Denise Abbott."

133

"Ah!"

"What do you mean, 'Ah!'"

"She's the one you didn't make it with and you want to know if she's lesbo?"

"Shit, Corinne!"

"Naughty, naughty. In front of a lady."

"Listen, she's part of the deal here. I want to know everything about her. Everything."

"She the model?"

"Right."

"Gotcha. Anything else?"

"No, I don't ... yes, damn it. My .32's been stolen."

"Somebody setting you up, maybe? You be careful, boss ..."

"No, I mean, yes. Listen, get my .38 across to me, today, O.K.? Delivered to the hotel. Preferably this morning."

"Done. Boss, did that bank crowd give you a down payment?"

"No, why?"

"It's just that IBM is threatening to seize my typewriter."

"You're a tonic, Corinne. Just what I need to set me up for the day." He cradled the phone on her laughter and looked longingly toward the shower. He stood, stretched, shook his head, and reached out for the phone again. He called Hurtil on his private number. The president came through on a wave of anxiety.

"Christopher?"

"That's right, sir."

"Thank God you've called. We're nearly out of our minds over here. About Mr. Robert Hayes, I mean. What happened? I understand ..."

David cut in and soothed down the panicky

president with the suggestion that a telephone was not a good medium for a discussion on Hayes. He would be at the bank shortly to share with Hurtil all the information he had. In the meantime could the president hold Señor Villegas for him when Villegas arrived from the airport? Hurtil said he had planned to do just that. And, David pursued, would the president be kind enough to have his secretary set up appointments for him with McGowan and Rascher—preferably before lunch? Hurtil assured David that he would be delighted to attend to those matters and anything else David might need.

David managed to terminate the conversation while this aura of reciprocal goodwill prevailed. At last his shower. He was heading for the bathroom, when his phone buzzed demandingly. Puzzled, David returned to answer it.

"Christopher," he said gruffly into the phone.

The voice that came through was Spanish, speaking English in somewhat injured tones. "This is the desk, sir. Your message light, we make it light, sir. You not answer it."

"Sorry," David replied, wishing the desk to hell and back. "Guess I must have missed it. What can I do for you?"

"There is a M. Armand Frey, sir, who call his brother, Captain Hans Frey, from Paris. It is *muy urgente, sir.*"

"So?"

"Captain Frey, he is with you, no?"

"Sorry. Can't help you. He was here but he left about ten minutes ago. O.K.?"

"Not O.K. There is one more thing."

"Well, give it to me fast, will you? I'm in a hurry and I'm already running late."

"Yes, sir. My apology, sir. But my friend, Genaro, he wish me to tell you about the two men . . ."

David's impatient disinterest disappeared. Now he was really listening. "Which two men? Where? When?"

"Last night, sir. About nine-thirty. They ask for Mr. Hayes. You know? The one who is kill?"

"What sort of men?"

"American, sir. One is big and very strong, like a fighter, a boxer, you know?"

"I know. And the other?"

"Mean, sir. Very mean. Genaro say he no like the look of them. To him they look like the gangster. He think they maybe kill Mr. Hayes."

"Genaro could be right. What . . . was there anything else?"

"Yes, sir. This is bad, sir . . . and Genaro, he is very sorry, sir, but he was not thinking nothing you see and he tol' them your room number, sir, because Mr. Hayes, he also was looking for you, sir. He call you on the house telephone, no?"

"No, he did not call me on the house telephone."

The voice from the desk sounded excited. "Ah, hah, you see. Mr. Hayes only pretend. That is what we think also."

"What's your name?" David asked.

"Julio, señor."

"Good for you, Julio. Was there anything else?"

"Well . . . maybe, Mr. Christopher. Maybe."

"Maybe what?"

"Genaro, he think the two men go look for Mr. Hayes in your room maybe. Just maybe. Afterward they come out very fast. They run through the lobby."

"Julio," David assured his informant, "you should

be a detective. And Genaro, too. Tell him from
me."

"*Muchas gracias, señor.*"

This time David made it to the bathroom undis-
turbed. He thought to himself it was funny how
your best information came like that. Out of
nowhere. When you least expected it. That explained the missing gun. The two guys, no, not the
two guys. Hayes himself. That's how it would have
been. Hayes lost his gun down in the garage. He
must have run straight back into the hotel and into
my room. Found the .32. Might have been waiting
for me here until he was disturbed by the two soldiers. Something like that. He'd figured it pretty
well all the same. It was easy, knowing the routine.
Why was Hayes so desperate to kill him? David
wondered. He douched his face with soap and hot
water and began to lather up, talking to himself in
the mirror. It was years since the Justice investigation. Maybe Hayes thought any kind of investigation would blow the whistle on him with Big Lug.
That could be it. But of course somebody had already blown the whistle, which was a damn funny
thing when you came to think of it. Had the blackmailer goofed? Or had he deliberately passed the
secret bank statement to Luigi Valente even before
the payoff? Very tricky, but it might make sense.
Kill off Hayes and scare hell out of Hurtilbank and
the other victims in the process. David began to
shave.

The cascading hot water rinsing the shampoo
from his hair and the soap from his body, the
foaming toothpaste in his mouth, the fresh menthol
lather on his face: The whole morning routine had
not felt so good to David Christopher in a long
time. While he went through the ritual he thought

about Denise Abbott. She was a nervous filly if ever he met one. High-strung like a racehorse. Elusive as a snowflake. He had spent five hours with her nonstop last night and what the hell did he know about her? Basically no more than when he walked in the door of her suite at the Bellevue. She spoke English with an English accent, but what did that prove? She also spoke French with a French accent and German with a German accent. She could have been English educated in Switzerland or maybe French educated in England or Belgian educated all over. Who the hell knew?

A couple of things were certain. She was beautiful, for one. She was talented, for two. She seemed to have money, for three. She'd been around, for four, and would have been quite willing to dally a moment with one David C. But—and here was the big but—something was making her plenty nervous. She was frightened. She was more than frightened. She was terrified. Somebody or something had her by the short hairs. The blackmailers. Well, yes, the blackmailers of course. That was the easy answer. But like he said the night before, she was Beautiful People. What did she have to hide? What did the blackmailers have on her that was going to come out if she didn't pay up? That was the trouble with a girl. You never really knew. It could be that she was part of a plot to blow up London with a hydrogen bomb. Or equally and more likely, it could be that she was really a redhead who dyed her hair blond.

McGowan, Villegas and Rascher. No problem. What Suzanne had given him this morning confirmed what he already suspected: They were vulnerable because they were skating on the edge of the law or they were flouting the law or they were crooks. It did not really matter. He had them in their slots. The mystery man was Benninger.

While David dressed he put his mind to the mystery. There were moral possibilities and psychological possibilities and possibilities that fitted the facts. If you took the moral possibilities it seemed unlikely that Benninger was responsible. He obviously enjoyed the complete confidence of old Hurtil. Benninger seemed ill at ease with Florelle, but on the other hand he had her confidence. Benninger would hardly be likely to run amok at his age. Or would he? The roaring forties. You had to throw in then the psychological possibilities. Benninger was a very smart guy. He weighed things out. You could see he was the one human being who had that whole bank in his hand. Its executive vice-president. A kind of operations comptroller. Why would a man in that position, if he wanted to embezzle bank funds, choose a way that was as bizarre as blackmail? If any one of the victims got a hint that Benninger was putting the squeeze on, his life was not worth a cracker.

The problem was that Benninger did have something on his mind. No doubt about that. And it was not very likely that a man in charge of a bank threatened with blackmail would have other things on his mind besides the blackmail. Moreover, there were the facts. And only Benninger fitted the facts. Only he knew those accounts. So you were back to the mystery. Benninger could not have done it. Benninger was the only one who could have done it. Take your pick.

David took a final look at himself in the mirrored door of his closet. He had chosen a Bill Blass cream silk turtleneck shirt. His rust-red Pierre Cardin jacket was double-breasted. He had on pale fawn Dax slacks and gold-buckled alligator shoes. Just once he thought to himself he would like to meet that goddam Captain Hans Frey when he was freshly changed instead of the way he always seemed to be when the ubiquitous captain came on the scene.

David spent a quick half hour getting a client's-eye view of Hurtilbank before announcing himself to Benninger and Hurtil. He took the main entrance, had a word with Guard Brunnen and won his confidence by congratulating him on the unerring instinct he had shown in taking yesterday's letter straight to Madame Florelle. It showed a fine sense of judgment, David told Brunnen, and he could personally assure Guard Brunnen that while Madame Florelle might say nothing, she was really deeply grateful.

Guard Brunnen was so relieved by the news—he had hardly slept the night before—that he confided to David that Switzerland was going to the dogs. It was those young hippies, of course, who were the cause of all the trouble. No respect. Dropping envelopes on the floor. What next? David agreed and recommended that Guard Brunnen watch out in case the same thing happened again. If it did, David told Brunnen in a confidential whisper, the president of the bank would like Guard Brunnen to take the envelope direct to him. Brunnen was aghast.

"You mean upstairs to his office?"

"Shush," David said sternly. "To him personally, understand?"

Eyes wide, Brunnen nodded. Then, as David left him, he mopped his brow. This was dreadful. The responsibility made his ulcer quiver like a violin string.

David watched the operations in the lobby, visited the vaults, spoke to the guard there long enough to watch staff coming and going and see how the bank worked. Then, to the glee of the typists, the interest of the computer-operators and the barely concealed consternation of the Gorgon herself, he visited Madame Florelle and satisfied himself on the logistics of the operation she controlled. Last night the bank had been a museum. Today it was a living organism, digesting money in its myriad forms.

After familiarizing himself with the ledger room, this time under the gimlet eye of Madame Florelle, David went on to Hurtil's office. Florelle would tell Benninger he was snooping around. That was what he wanted. If anybody in the bank was involved—such as Benninger—just his snooping around should be enough to precipitate the next step in the extortion scheme. Until the blackmailers moved, Christopher felt he was marking time at best. True, he was getting the feel of the bank. He was meeting the victims, and that, he hoped, would eventually pay off. Somewhere or other there had to be a lead back to the criminals themselves.

Anna, Hurtil's secretary, was waiting for David. "Good morning, Mr. Christopher," she said to him, getting up from her desk. "Herr Hurtil is expecting you. He said I should take you to him immediately. Señor Villegas is with him."

"Er, one moment, Anna?"

"Yes, Mr. Christopher?"

David took out a card from his wallet and handed it to her. "This is my office address in Geneva. I wonder if you could forward the down payment on my fee to my secretary."

"Why certainly, Mr. Christopher." Anna smiled at him. "Did she remind you?"

"How did you know?" David asked. "Don't tell me. She called you. The—"

"Now, now, Mr. Christopher," Anna soothed him. "We secretaries stick together, you know. As a matter of fact, we telexed the payment straight through to your bank account in Geneva. Your IBM is safe." She led David to the door of Hurtil's office.

"All that stuff about the IBM," David protested. "She makes it up, you know. If you ever want a job in Geneva . . ."

The door of Hurtil's office was already open and Anna was saying, "Herr Hurtil. Mr. Christopher has arrived."

David whispered to Anna, "It's our secret, huh?" Then he was shaking hands with Hurtil and being introduced to Señor Carlos Villegas.

Villegas was a man of medium height, square, strong, handsome. David thought he might be ruthless. Whatever Villegas was, David knew that he was a force to be reckoned with.

"We are all of us grateful for what you are doing to protect us, Mr. Christopher," Villegas said.

"You know the others then," David asked him.

"Only by hearsay, I'm afraid," Villegas said. "Herr Hurtil has been kind enough to brief me. Also on the tragic events of last night. I understand one of us . . ."

"Yes, Christopher," Hurtil broke in, "I've been anxious to ask you. Exactly what happened?"

While the faces of Hurtil and Villegas showed increasing concern, David told them briefly of the murder of Bobby Hayes and how he and Denise had been accidentally involved.

"But why?" Hurtil wanted to know. "Why in a car left for you?"

David looked at his hands. "A warning, I guess. Careful or you'll be next. That kind of thing."

"This is dreadful," Hurtil said. "Simply dreadful. Can we go on like this? Will we be forced to go to the police in spite of the dangers?"

"Just let's cool it a while," David said. "The police have information on the killers. There is a fair chance they will be caught. Now, if I could ask Señor Villegas a few questions?"

"Anything at all," Villegas answered.

"You're the nephew of the President of Santacosta, if I recall"

"The former President. It makes a difference."

David appreciated the point. "It does indeed," he admitted. "Especially to the ownership of the former President's Swiss bank account."

Villegas was not ruffled. "My uncle was a thoughtful and careful man," he said. "There can be no dispute about my right to the funds here in Hurtilbank."

"Unless you try to spend them in Santacosta," was David's dry comment.

"It is a hard world, Mr. Christopher. I have a better chance of enjoying it if that secret-account number remains a secret from the present military dictatorship of Santacosta."

"I think it might be more accurate to say that you have a better chance of enjoying life if the purpose of the funds in that account remains a secret from the military dictatorship you hope to overthrow."

Carlos Villegas went rigid. His eyes narrowed.

His hands clenched. When he spoke his voice was low and intense. "I have killed men for knowing less than you know, Mr. Christopher."

"I know that too," David said.

"What do you want of me?" Villegas asked.

"Just the truth. All of it."

The Latin American slammed his right fist into his left hand. "*Dios*. What can I tell you? My base is Rio. From there I am in touch with a band of counter-revolutionaries, brave, honorable men, faithful to my uncle and now to me. I had a good life. Now I spend it raising funds to buy weapons so that one day I can oust those bloody assassins who are castrating my people. This is no crime. Except in the eyes of the criminals I hope to kill. If this becomes known—hundreds, perhaps thousands of Santacostans will die. That is why these black-mailers, whoever they are, have me by the balls—if you will excuse me, Herr Hurtil. One whisper of this affair and the hopes of Santacostan freedom perish forever. That is why the bank must pay. I make no accusations. I place no blame. This I must say: If Hurtilbank does not pay what these—these cruel extortionists demand, it will have many murders on its conscience."

Hurtil, embarrassed, wanted to finish the discussion. "It seems to me, Mr. Christopher, that we do not need any further information from Señor Villegas ..."

"If I may ask a couple of quick questions, Herr Hurtil?" David looked at Hurtil and received his grudging assent. Hurtil had no stomach for interrogation. "How were you blackmailed?" David asked Villegas.

"By mail ..."

"Here it is, David," Hurtil said. He handed David

a photocopy of Villegas's secret account statement. Scripted with the familiar red felt pen were the words:

> SEÑOR CARLOS VILLEGAS
> UNLESS YOU PAY US
> ONE MILLION SWISS FRANCS
> TO BE SILENT
> YOUR SECRET BANK STATEMENT
> WILL BE REVEALED
> TO THE RULERS OF SANTACOSTA

David looked over the statement carefully. "Do I see an envelope there?" he asked.

"Sorry," Hurtil apologized.

David stood up and reached for the envelope. His brow furrowed. "That's—er, uh, all?" David asked lamely, a man changing his thought in midsentence.

"That's all," Villegas confirmed. "As soon as I received this threat I telephoned Herr Hurtil and told him I would be arriving this morning."

"Well, thank you, Señor Villegas. I don't think we need to hold you any longer. You must be tired."

Villegas stood up.

"There is one more thing," David said. "Where can I contact you in Zurich?"

Hurtil also stood. "I have invited Señor Villegas to be my guest," Hurtil told David. He turned to Villegas. "You will forgive me, Carlos, if I do not accompany you. My chauffeur will deliver you safely to Hildegarde, who will make you comfortable. If you should need the car during the day . . ."

Villegas put up his hand. "I am about to make

willing surrender to fatigue. The thought of your beautiful quiet villa is already making me sleepy." Villegas picked up his briefcase and topcoat and bowed formally to David. "Mr. Christopher." Then he went with Hurtil to the door of the office.

When Villegas had gone, Hurtil returned to his desk, looked over his pipe rack. "Did I imagine it?" he asked David. "Or did something disturb you?"

David showed Hurtil the envelope used to blackmail Villegas. "Did you notice that this was postmarked Zurich?"

"Can't say that I did," Hurtil told him. "Is that important?"

David returned to his easy chair. "Maybe," he answered. While Hurtil took threads of tobacco and dropped them into his pipe, David sat frowning and thoughtful. "How was Bobby Hayes contacted?" he asked finally.

"He spoke to Benninger," Hurtil said. "Just a moment." Hurtil dialed an intercom number and waited for Benninger to answer. "Benninger ... Hurtil. I'm here with David Christopher. He was asking—did Hayes happen to say how the blackmailers contacted him? ... I see ... No, no ... it is not vital. Just a thought."

Hurtil put down the telephone. "He specifically asked Hayes that question and Hayes refused to answer. Said it didn't matter."

David sat thinking, tapping the envelope on his knee.

"What exactly is your—er, suspicion?" Hurtil asked.

"Not a suspicion. It might be helpful if we could prove that all the blackmail threats originated from one point—say, here in Zurich. What about Mlle. Abbott?"

Hurtil paused. He had his pipe in his mouth and was applying the flame from the silver Ronson to the tobacco. "She gave me her statement. You have seen that. No envelope. Definitely no envelope."

"Did she mention where she was when she received the threat?"

Hurtil sucked on his pipe and blew out a cloud of aromatic smoke. "Paris, I believe. I'm almost certain that she mentioned Paris. If you like I'll check." Hurtil reached for the intercom to give orders to his secretary.

David stoped him hastily. "No, no. Never mind. It may come up later. And time is getting on. Were you able to arrange appointments for me with McGowan and Rascher?"

From his desk Hurtil picked up a memo with a typed message. "McGowan is waiting for you at the Seeblick. It is a restaurant on the lake across the Burkliplatz. You can't miss it."

David got up from his chair and took the memo from Hurtil—a reminder from Anna of his meeting with McGowan. He smiled. Perhaps all good secretaries treated their bosses like retarded five-year-olds. "And Rascher?" he asked.

Hurtil grimaced. "Friend Rascher is a problem," he explained. "Because of his mortal terror of his real or imagined enemies . . ."

"Don't blame him," David said. "Or them."

Hurtil looked up at David. "You have information on Rascher?" he asked.

"Some," David answered. "Where do I nail this guy?"

"He suggests you go to the Rietbergmuseum after you talk to McGowan. Perhaps a taxi would be best. It's on the Seestrasse . . ."

"I know it," David said. "Where will he be?"

"He suggests you do not go inside but walk from the front of the villa toward the lake. He will contact you if he thinks it is safe." Hurtil was apologetic. "It was the best thing I could arrange," he said.

"Think nothing of it," David told him. "A screwball is a screwball, except that this one has reason to be." David handed Villegas's statement and the envelope it was sent in back to Hurtil. "It will be best if you lock all the evidence in your personal safe," he suggested.

"Of course," Hurtil agreed. He got up, swung back the library section, twisted the combination dial expertly, and opened the door of the safe. "Do we have a chance?" he asked.

It was the nearest to naked emotion Hurtil had ever come with David, and David's heart went out to him. "We have to work so quickly," he confessed, "that right now I would not make any bets."

Hurtil looked suddenly old as he locked the safe and swung back the library section. "That's not so good, is it?"

"It works both ways," David consoled him.

"How do you mean?"

"The blackmailers are also under pressure. They must now give you instructions about delivery. Delivery means a point of contact. A chance for us."

"You really think so?" Hurtil's sagging shoulders gained strength.

"Definitely. Meanwhile, we have a lot of irons in the fire. We're getting facts. Somewhere among those facts is the one we need. The break. The lead. It is only a matter of recognizing it." David smiled. "Auf Wiedersehn, Herr Hurtil."

"Auf Wiedersehn, David—and good luck."

Another sparkling spring day seemed to have attracted a substantial proportion of the inhabitants of Zurich to the Bahnhofstrasse and the lake for the day. The Bahnhofstrasse's roadway was choked with cars and buses while shoppers jammed its sidewalks. Although it was still only midmorning, the Burkliplatz gardens were thronged with girls who seemed to be on lunch break. At eleven o'clock? Or else, David thought, they had invented urgent messages which took them out-of-doors. David did not blame them.

He looked around. A green Peugeot slid away from the curb on the far side of the street, and David thought he recognized Frey and Schwand. It would not be a great shock to the system if he was right. David had no illusions about Frey. The detective knew that something was cooking at Hurtilbank and he would not give up until he found out what it was. He would just play it a little closer to the chest from now on. That was all.

David turned and walked briskly to the end of the Bahnhofstrasse. He waited for the pedestrian light to change to *aller* and stepped out to cross to the lakeshore. As he did, an Opel Kadett, with two men in the front seat, squealed around the corner from the Bahnhofstrasse heading straight for David. David's peripheral vision told him that the velocity of the car had to take it wide toward the center of the dual roadway, so he back-rolled on his shoulder in the direction of the sidewalk he had just left. The Kadett grazed his left jacket sleeve, making a jagged tear in it. Instead of stopping, it accelerated along the General-Guisan-Quai until it was lost in the traffic.

Two men and a woman rushed to help David to his feet. As they asked anxiously if he was all right, he brushed the dust from his jacket and slacks, tried to assess the damage to his sleeve, and assured the Samaritans it had been an accident. While they were arguing about what happened and shaking their fists in the direction of the hit-run driver, David withdrew and hurried across the Burkliplatz for his appointment with McGowan. The incident had shaken him up badly—not so much the fall as his own miscalculation. Once again the pattern was too familiar. Two men. A motor accident. David smelled Big Lug. But how? And so fast? He remembered what Frey had told him. Hayes went to the PTT and made some phone calls after he left the bank. He'd threatened to do it, of course. Must have contacted Big Lug without knowing that his own time was up. When Hayes's killers called in to Chicago to report mission completed they must have received new orders. They didn't leave on the midnight plane after all. They were still in Zurich. With a second assignment. Get David Christopher.

The busy, plump middle-aged matron who was the part-owner and the manager of the Seeblick Café-Restaurant was known to her customers as Jolly Gretchen. Her staff, who worked long hours under Gretchen's slave-driving tongue, called her Gruesome Gretchen—and worse. All agreed that she provided service. If there was a hint of warmth in the morning air, even a likelihood of sun, Gretchen was setting up colorful striped umbrellas and outdoor tables before the first white sail was on the lake. It was, after all, a favorite spot for both the people of Zurich and the tourists. It was close to the Bellevue Platz streetcar and bus terminus. It connected with the lake quais, the Bahnhofstrasse and the nearby parking for passenger cars. It was beside the marinas and the terminuses for the ferries which carried sightseers around the Zurichsee. If there was a hungry or a thirsty human animal in the area, it was not Gretchen's fault if the hunger stayed unsatisfied or the thirst remained unslaked. She gave good value. For the price of a drink a tourist had a view of the lake and the wooded slopes of the Zurichberg and the Adlisberg and the Uetliberg and a cross-section of Zurich to boot.

By the time David Christopher had made his way along the quai to the Seeblick, there was already a sprinkling of customers at the outdoor tables. Mothers and nurses with children eating ice cream or sucking Pschitt through straws, couples drinking coffee and beer or enjoying an early salad lunch. McGowan's fawn Stetson hat was visible on the edge of the patio. He sat at a table alone, sipping bourbon from a paper cup and looking thoughtfully at the ferries and launches on the lake.

David signaled a waiter, ordered a beer and indicated that he would be with McGowan before he went over to the Texan and introduced himself.

"Mr. McGowan? I'm David Christopher."

The husky westerner struggled to his feet and shook hands with David. "Sure glad to meet you, Davey boy. Dwight's the name. Dwight McGowan. Sit down. What will it be?" McGowan looked around for a waiter.

"That's O.K., Mr. McGowan," David said. "I've got a beer coming."

The waiter arrived with a Heineken, removed the cap and poured half of the bottle's contents into a tall glass. Over McGowan's protests, David paid the waiter. "Next time," he told McGowan. "Cheers!" David took a long mouthful of beer and let the cool liquid lubricate his throat.

"You've seen my ... what those skunks are tryin' to do to me?" McGowan asked. His broad face showed anxiety under the big hat.

"You can't afford it," David told him.

"Damn right I can't," McGowan agreed. "I got a few bucks stashed away. Sure I have. Who hasn't? Ninety G's maybe. These days all that can do is help me buy my bourbon."

McGowan laughed an embarrassed laugh and took a swig of liquor from his paper cup. Immediately he rubbed his stomach as if there were some instant reaction of his ulcer to the bourbon. "I got this ulcer," he explained to David. "Very thirsty. Feeds on bourbon." His laugh brayed out over the lake, masking the worry in his eyes.

David let McGowan play out his act until the Texan's laugh subsided into an uneasy silence. Then he spoke quietly. "According to my information, the United States Internal Revenue Service would be more than willing to take that ninety G's on account."

McGowan brayed again. "If you mean those tax claims you can relax, Davey boy. Dwight McGowan ain't about to cheat ol' Uncle Sam. No sir. I got me a deal simmerin', Mr. Christopher, that'll set me flyin'. You can count on ol' Dwight McGowan to settle every penny of every ol' tax claim Uncle Sam likes to put up." McGowan was suddenly very serious. "It's plain old American horse-sense, Davey. Believe me. Let me give you a piece of advice from an old horse thief. A man gets himself charged with evasion of taxes, concealment of assets, what the hell, why he's dead with the big money. Yes, sir, he's dead. Those financiers. Bunch of stuffed shirts, but you do it their way or else."

McGowan drank again. Then again he went through the ritual of rubbing his stomach. "I shouldn't touch the bourbon, Davey, but I bred me this thirsty ulcer." McGowan's worried eyes looked at David, trying to assess his reaction.

"How well did you know Bobby Hayes?" David asked. His face was grim. He was getting annoyed with the man's fawning, phony sincerity.

McGowan frowned. "Never met the gentleman, I'm afraid. Now I never will, I guess. I heard what happened to him. Do you think it was the black-mailers? A kind of example, to show us they mean business?"

"Maybe," David replied shortly. The interview was making him uncomfortable. "What about a man called Carlos Villegas?"

McGowan shook his head.

"Helmut Rascher?"

Again the Texan shook his head mournfully.

"The woman then? Denise Abbott?"

"Mr. Hurtil mentioned they were bein' black-mailed too," McGowan replied. "But I never met 'em. Sorry. Can't help you there, Davey. Guess that's your problem, eh?"

McGowan took another mouthful of bourbon and refilled his paper cup while David poured the rest of the beer into his glass.

"Who handled your bank statements?" David asked McGowan.

"Me."

"What about your wife?"

"Little lady and I have been divorced for nine years. Anyway, only a damn fool lets his wife know about a Swiss bank account. I'm not a fool.

153

Might be havin' me a bad run for the last year or two, but then a good many Americans are in the same boat as me so I don't feel so bad."

"What about secretaries, business managers, tax advisers? Have you any clue about how somebody might have got to your numbered-account statement?"

McGowan's fingers felt the bottle of bourbon, seeking physical support from the Southern Comfort label. "Sittin' here with my bourbon, Davey, I probably look like an ol' goat to you. Mebbe I am an ol' goat. But one thing you have to believe: I guard that bank statement with my life, Davey. Nobody—and I mean nobody—except me ever lays eyes on it." He looked up at Christopher. "Listen, Davey, you're workin' for the bank . . ."

"I'm working for you and the bank," David reminded him.

"Sure, Davey, sure. But we aren't payin' your fee. The bank is. You gotta look after Hurtilbank's interests. That's O.K. That's what you're gettin' paid for. But when you ask all your questions and get all your answers, one thing's gonna be certain: Whatever went wrong, went wrong here in Zurich. Maybe Hayes made a mistake. Or maybe I made a mistake or maybe Mamzelle from Armentiers made a mistake. But all five of us, Davey boy. We all made mistakes at the same time? Who you kidding, Davey? There's only one way to find out about five people who bank at the same bank, Davey. At the bank, right? Now why don't you go back to ol' Mr. Hurtil and tell him to be a good boy and pay that ransom and get those bastards off my back. They're going to ruin me, Davey. I ain't got time for setbacks like this."

"How was your ransom demand delivered?" David asked McGowan.

McGowan fished into his pocket and handed David a plain brown envelope. It was addressed to McGowan at a Los Angeles business address. It was scripted with the familiar red felt pen. The envelope had a Swiss stamp and was postmarked Zurich. David looked at the envelope. For some reason he could not put his finger on, the envelope made him feel disappointed, depressed, as if he was expecting something else.

"May I keep this?" he asked McGowan.

"Why not?" McGowan answered.

"Thanks," David said. "I'll get back to you."

He left McGowan sipping bourbon from his paper cup, in exactly the same position as when David found him. A lonely man. Trying to be cheerful and not succeeding, despite the warming sunshine and the happy shouts of children and happy people reacting to the friendly blue water of the Zurichsee.

In his office at Hurtilbank Franz Benninger used his personal direct outside line to call Rita Jensen.

"Good morning, my dear," he said softly into the phone when Rita answered. He listened to her reply and then told her, "I'm glad you feel like that. It was for me also something unique—a meeting of mind and body, shall we say? Something all too rare, I'm afraid. Now to business . . . apropos of our plans . . . naturally I understand that you must refer back decisions to your government. That is why I am calling. This is what I propose. Over the next one to two months, depending on the market, I shall begin to move the gold into Swiss francs or German marks or Eurodollars. You agree? . . . That's right. About one hundred million dollars to begin with ... gold is a sensitive market and we do not wish to disturb it ... I understand ... that's right ... half will go into the Ethiopian Government's reserve fund with Hurtilbank for the purchase of commodities ... right ... Exactly ... now for the other half I am drawing up a list of recommendations for investment: a cross-section of things—U.S. Government treasury bonds, perhaps one or two of the multinationals—then there is a Canadian company I think we could acquire a controlling interest in without exciting too much unhealthy interest among the gentlemen of the press ... Good. Yes. I will have a plan typed up recommending a diversified investment portfolio for the first fifty million dollars. Before I dispose of the first bar of gold I want a statement in writing from the Supreme Progressive Council of Ethiopia giving me power of attorney to convert its assets in Account Number so-and-so over to its new corporation account. I'll get a sample statement typed up and include the forms you will need to have signed by the Supreme Progressive Council opening a Hurtilbank corporation account. Will this be satisfactory? ... Fine. Now when can you pick up these papers? They should leave for Addis Ababa tonight, if possible."

Benninger and Rita agreed to meet at 3:00 P.M. in the neutral lobby of the office building disguising the exit of the discreet Hurtilbank tunnel. Rita would have a courier waiting to pick up the papers from her and fly them to Rome. In Rome the Ethiopian Ambassador would meet the courier, seal the papers in a diplomatic pouch and put them personally on the Ethiopian Airlines flight for Addis Ababa. They would be in Addis Ababa by morning.

"Rietbergmuseum *bitte*?" David Christopher instructed the taxi driver in what he felt smugly was a passable German accent.

"Certainly, sir," the driver answered cheerfully in English. "And what part of the United States do you come from?"

"I live in Geneva," David answered sourly.

"Ah, yes, sir," the driver agreed. "So many Americans live in Geneva. The United Nations. The churches. The voluntary agencies. The big international companies. Not so many in Zurich, I think, although all the banks are here. Is this your first visit to Zurich?"

"Not really," David grunted. He hoped that his unwilling tone of voice would penetrate the mind of the taxi driver and paralyze his speech center. The driver was immune to such hints. His social life and his business were one entity. He slowed down for a red light at the entrance to the General-Witte-Strasse.

"There, you see?" the driver proclaimed victoriously. "That just goes to prove my point."

"What point?" David felt forced to ask.

"That people keep coming back to Zurich. Famous people. You know what I mean? James Joyce—you know, the writer. Liked the wine here, he said. I'll bet you'd never think of Zurich as a place for great wine, but that's what he said. And Goethe you know—the great German. For him it was scenery. The mountains. The trees. The lake. All that sort of thing. He's right, you know. When you live here you get used to it, but when you look around on a day like today I expect Zurich is O.K. I mean it's not every country has this kind of scenery. And then there was Lenin. That kind of caught you off guard. Eh? Eh? Yes indeed. Lenin.

The Russian. Did all his study here in Zurich at
our Central Library. You wouldn't think the Russian revolution started in the Central Library in
Zurich, would you now? And there was Wagner.
The German who wrote the music. Had a
girlfriend here. Mad for her, he was. That's funny.
That's really funny."

David sighed, "What's funny."

"This girlfriend of Wagner was Madame Wesendonck. Good-looking, they say. A real beauty."

"I don't get it," David said.

"You don't get it? I thought even a tourist would
get that one. You see, Madame Wesendonck was
rich. She had her own villa. Beautiful place. Beautiful trees. Gardens. Near the lake. Do you get it?"

"No," David growled. He wished the loquacious
driver would be struck dumb long enough to let
him enjoy the magnificent grounds of the museum.
Not grounds, really. A lovely park of majestic
woods with its own view of the Zurichsee.

"This is it," the driver said, as if he had created
the whole scene this morning after breakfast for
David's private delectation.

"What is it?"

"The Rietbergmuseum used to be Madame
Wesendonck's villa. Now it belongs to the city and
they keep Baron von der Heydt's collections in it.
He was the great traveler, you know. Peru, India,
Khmer, Armenia, Japan, Tibet, China—he saw them
all before you and I were even a twinkle . . ."

"How much?"

"Twelve fifty."

David gave the friendly driver fifteen francs, got
out of the taxi, made as if to enter the villa, then
turned to admire the view of the lake from the
steps. He waited for a departing couple to get into

the cab and, when the driver had gone, began to walk toward the wooded park in the direction of the lake.

David found himself alone. His feet crunched on the golden-yellow gravel of the path. There was a sough of wind in the upper branches of the elms and the oaks. He could hear birds and a muffled drone of traffic on the Seestrasse. A ferry hooted from the lake. He started when a voice hissed, "Christopher!" David turned to see Rascher beckoning him from the pathway to a clump of rhododendrons.

As David walked over to meet Rascher he put together in his mind the things he knew about Rascher. They didn't add up. Rascher was on the short side, round and plump of face and body. David's first reaction was amusement, but Rascher was no funny man. Scheming, cunning, ruthless, deadly, vindictive, yes, but not funny.

"I'm David Christopher," David said. "You must be . . ."

"Helmut Rascher," the man said. "We can sit on this bench."

They walked over to a cast-iron-framed bench with a wooden seat. David sat down. Rascher gave a final careful look around the woods before he entrusted himself to the seat.

"I need to ask you a few questions," David began.

"It's all a bunch of shit," Rascher said.

"Why?"

"What the fuck can you find out in a few hours that's going to be any good to any of us? Tell me that."

Nice man, David thought to himself. Very attractive type. I may not wait for the Africans. I may murder him myself. With an effort David stayed calm. "I can only do my best," he began.

"Your best is not good enough if they catch up with me while I'm sitting around on my ass ..."

"O.K. Let's talk about 'they.'"

"Who?"

"'They.' The Africans."

Rascher pulled back to the end of the bench. "How do you know about them?" he demanded. There was real fear in his face. No doubt about that. Good, David thought to himself. Now we've got the little bastard on the run.

"You're an arms dealer, right?"

"I don't see that's any fucking business of yours."

"You'll see, friend. You'll see. Your clients are the new African governments. Preferably poor. Preferably desperate."

"I made honest business deals," Racsher bleated.

"Honest, hell. As I hear the story you milked their treasuries of every cent they had ..."

"The prices were fair, damn you, fair."

"Like hell they were fair. As I get it, they were double what anybody else would even dare to ask."

"Lies, all lies," Rascher ranted.

David began to tick off points on his fingers. "I must say that I've met a few slimy characters in my day, but you make the Mafia seem like the Salvation Army. First, you gouge your clients for prices that are sheer robbery. Second, you purchase inferior weapons—obsolete or OS or no ammo available. Third, you tip off neutral countries and have the shipments seized at their borders, en route to your clients ..."

"I won't listen to this. I don't have to listen to this," Rascher was screaming.

"Oh, yes you do, Rascher. Fourth, you negotiate

160

new under-the-table deals with the neutral governments and sell the arms cheap to them—like for
only twice what you paid for them . . ."

"Hurtil is a friend of mine. He will never allow
one of his clients—"

"And then you tell your original clients that you
used their funds to buy the arms which, alas, have
now been seized by other governments so there is
nothing you can do about it except—a matter you
neglect to mention to your clients—put all that
lovely money into your numbered account with
Hurtilbank. How am I doing, Rascher? Close to the
story?"

This time Rascher said nothing. He took out a
large handkerchief and tried to clear some of the
sweat from his face and eyes. David let him suffer
in silence. Then he asked, "How were you black-
mailed?"

In a small, almost unrecognizable voice, Rascher
answered, "First, by telephone."

"By telephone?" David asked in astonishment.

"Yes."

"Where were you?"

"In Bonn. I have a villa there. Guards. Dogs. It
is the only place I am safe."

"Was the telephone call local or long-distance?"

"I couldn't say. Long-distance, I believe."

"Did you recognize the voice?"

"Yes—no—I don't know."

"Who did it sound like?"

"It sounded like Franz Benninger."

"Who?"

"Benninger. The vice-president of Hurtilbank.
You don't know him?"

"Yes, I know him." David spoke slowly, carefully. "What happened then?"

"I received this in the mail." Rascher put his hand in his pocket and took out a plain brown envelope. Nothing about the envelope surprised David. It was addressed to Rascher in script with the blackmailer's red felt pen. The stamp was Swiss, the postmark Zurich. Inside the envelope was a copy of Rascher's numbered-account monthly statement for March, with an additional message:

> HERR HELMUT RASCHER
> UNLESS YOU PAY US
> ONE MILLION SWISS FRANCS
> TO BE SILENT
> YOUR SECRET BANK STATEMENT
> WILL BE REVEALED
> TO YOUR AFRICAN CLIENTS

Rascher grabbed David by the sleeve. Saliva dripped from the edge of his mouth. He began to babble. "Those Africans. They're savages. Straight from the jungle. If they learn about this money they will torture me. You don't know what they're like . . ."

"You could give it back to them," David suggested.

"Are you serious?" Rascher asked him, still clutching his arm. "I've offered to get it back. All of it. If they'd only give me time . . ."

"And what did they say to that?"

Rascher drew his hand across his throat and rolled his eyes. He looked as if he were about to have an epileptic seizure. David shook him. Suddenly Rascher jumped to his feet. "They're coming," he said. "That's my only protection. I can always hear them coming." He ran off into the

woods, circling away from David in the direction
of the Rietbergmuseum exit.

David stood up and walked slowly back toward
the main villa. While he had always considered
that Benninger must be listed as suspicious, in his
mind Benninger was like the butler. An obvious
suspect he was using as the hypothetical villain until the real villain showed up. It shocked him to be
faced with the probability that his hypothetical
villain was the real blackmailer. He found it difficult to cope with the thought.

While he waited for a taxi at the entrance to the
museum David decided that he would have to do
something about Benninger. He looked at his
watch. It was one o'clock. Perhaps it would be better to eat first. No, first he would call Corinne in
Geneva. Might as well have her call off Jack Foley
in Washington, seeing as it looked as if Luigi's
boys were still in Zurich. Might make more sense
to see if Jack could trail them from Chicago to Europe. At least he would know who his enemies
were. Might even pay to pass the information on to
friend Captain Frey. Kill two birds with one stone.
Deliver him Bobby Hayes's murderers and get
them off his own back at the same time. Come to
that, Frey was probably ahead of him. If the two
soldiers left any prints around on the stolen car,
Frey could be getting a make on them through Interpol. So five minutes with Frey were definitely on
the menu. A check-in with Hurtil too. The blackmailers' instructions might have come through by
now. Christ, there were never enough hours in the
day.

While he was thinking, the taxi came. David decided to go back to his hotel. There he could
change his torn jacket, wash up, phone, eat. In ad-

dition he would be close to the Lamborghini in case he was in need of transportation. David was not sure just how many verbose taxi drivers he could take.

It was the advertisement in the morning paper that did it. As far as Guard Brunnen could make out, the machine was something even a man on his limited budget could afford. You could put together your own mixture, anything you liked. It could be pork one day and veal the next and a saveloy mix or a salami another day. It was up to you, really. You could add spices, if you liked, or cheese or lard or vegetables. That was the great thing about it. You could be your own butcher. You dumped all this stuff into the machine and ground it up to suit your own taste. Then you pressed a lever and the ground-up mix fed into the casing. That was another thing about the machine. It could take any size of casing and make a Wurst any length you wanted. The mix would feed in. Galump. Ga-lump ...

"Excuse me," the voice interrupted his reverie.

Guard Brunnen could not believe it. Every time he started to think about Wurst it happened. He was almost afraid to open his eyes. When he did, sure enough she was there again. The same little old woman with the same black scarf and the same black shawl and the same drab handbag and the same beady black eyes.

"There's another one," she said.

"Another what?" Brunnen asked. It was only to gain time that he asked. He already knew what it was going to be. For answer she pointed downward, and his unwilling eyes followed her pointing finger to the floor.

Guard Brunnen gulped and his stomach sent a surge of stinging scalding acid up his esophagus and into his throat. He swallowed his own juice, forcing it back into his abdomen, and picked up the envelope. It was as if time had reversed itself to yesterday morning and he was starting that better-forgotten day again. The same white vellum envelope. The same glo-red script. The same address to "Herr Johann Hurtil, President" and the same notification that it was "URGENT." While the little old woman watched him with her unwavering lidless gaze, the guard waited for his brain to reorder itself and tell him what to do.

Then Brunnen held the letter away from his body, like the first one, and began to stride majestically—or as majestically as a frightened guard can stride—toward the computer room and Madame Florelle. Then he remembered. The nice American had said he should take the letter direct to the president. Guard Brunnen paused, took a deep breath, and made his way to the elevator.

"Take me to the president," he ordered the operator.

It was ten to three when David Christopher got up from the table in the Parade Platz, shook hands with Captain Hans Frey and headed for the Bahnhofstrasse and Hurtilbank. It had been a satisfying interview. Well, satisfying enough. One could not really tell with the careful captain. He had admitted that he was initiating some inquiries through Interpol on the prints found in the Cortina, but he was not sanguine. The killers might have used gloves and the prints could simply be those of the local owner and his family.

David told him about the incident on the Quai

bridge and the Opel Kadett that had tried to run him down. Frey said he would check the rental companies. David admitted that he was only guessing. It might have been just a couple of drunken citizens afraid to stop. Still, in the light of Bobby Hayes's threat the night before, a connection was at least possible. Frey asked David how his investigation for Hurtilbank was progressing. David told him only so-so. Just one foot at a time. Frey also suggested that it was time David told him what the investigation was about before he became an accessory to the concealment of information in a murder case. David earnestly told Frey that as soon as information on a murder case came his way, Frey would be the first one to know about it, which was the reason why he was having coffee with Frey right now and telling him about the men in the Opel. Frey did not seem convinced, but there was not too much he could do about that and so they shook hands and parted.

Walking down the Bahnhofstrasse David thought that his interview with Frey would at least keep Frey close on his own trail and, in the circumstances, that might not be such a bad thing. At least it would keep Big Lug's gunslingers at a distance—that is, if the two men in the Kadett were his soldiers and if they had orders to fry him. If. If. If.

David found himself in front of 12A and decided to take the tunnel-entrance into the bank for a change. Inside the lobby there was a newsstand, and he went over to pick up a *Herald Tribune*. Just as he turned away from the newsstand he noticed her. She was a damn good-looking girl. Brunette. Flowing shoulder-length black hair. Probably early thirties. Dressed in white. The dress was so simple that it had to be good and expensive. What with the matching little white boots, David guessed it was a Courrèges. Her handbag was also white, with a gold clasp. She was doing a good job of being extremely nonchalant, but David pegged her to be waiting for somebody. The somebody she was waiting for ought to be coming from Hurtilbank because her orientation was in the direction of the tunnel. On a hunch he decided to remain near the newsstand and read his *Herald Tribune*. The flow of customers was a good screen and he could watch unobserved.

When the neat, integrated figure of Benninger debouched from the tunnel and the girl moved forward to meet him David almost dropped his newspaper in surprise. Their meeting was elaborately casual as only the meeting of a couple who have been intimate and are trying to disguise it, can be. A black portfolio changed hands so unobtrusively that David would have been willing to bet that he was the only person in the lobby who noticed it. As their hands suddenly touched lightly, she made a move to indicate a kiss and then Benninger returned to the tunnel and the girl was walking casually toward the street.

David waited until Benninger was out of sight and followed the girl into the street. She was already heading for the nearest corner to cross to the far side. David watched while she went straight to a waiting taxi and stepped inside. The taxi was facing north, in the direction of the railroad station, and David took a risk that he could keep the taxi in sight at the slow pace of the thick midafternoon traffic on the Bahnhofstrasse. He crossed to the east side of the street and trailed the cab three blocks north. Opposite the Parade Platz it turned into the old town and took the Storcheng. In the narrow winding street, the taxi was still traveling little faster than David on foot. He followed the cab between the townhouses of the oldest section of Zurich. The houses, ornamented with elaborate corbelled loggias the Swiss called *Erker* and with rich wrought-iron symbols dating from the late Middle Ages, leaned over the alley as if curious to watch a man chasing a motor vehicle on foot.

At the Weinplatz the taxi stopped for a second beside the wine-grower fountain to let out the girl in white. Immediately it shot forward, crossed the Rathaus Bridge and disappeared across the river and on to the Limmat Quai. The girl was no longer carrying the portfolio. It did not take David's finest investigative talent to deduce that the girl had given the portfolio to the small dark man who had been waiting for her in the taxi. That was spilt milk. Meanwhile a bird in the hand . . .

Obviously the girl had achieved the goal of the moment and was now at a loose end. She strolled among the tables of the Weinplatz Café, found an empty one with a view of the old Flemish-roofed houses and the Rathaus across the Limmat, and sat down. There was only the surprise attack left to David, and he made it.

Walking briskly up to the table where the girl was making herself comfortable, David drew out a chair and sat down. "Sorry to be late, dear," he said in an easy conversational tone, "but I got caught up in the traffic back there. Anyway, here I am. What are we drinking?"

"I'm afraid you have made a mistake . . . I'm sure . . ."

"Mistake?" David was indignant. His indignation was greatly helped by the fact that the girl was intrigued as well as startled by his effrontery—just enough to see how he would play out the charade. "No mistake at all. It's David. Don't you recall? David Christopher."

"Oh, David Christopher. I . . ." Rita suddenly realized that she was not supposed to know any David Christopher and blushed at the additional realization that she had heard all about him when she was in bed with Franz Benninger the night before. David seized the initiative again.

"How did you say you spelled your name again?"

"J-E-N-S-E-N . . . but . . ."

"Not your last name, your first name."

"R-I-T-A."

"Of course. How stupid of me to forget. White O.K.?"

David signaled for the waiter.

"White. Two glasses. A carafe. O.K.?"

The waiter nodded and David turned to Rita with a warm smile. He used a tissue to mop his brow delicately.

"I'm so glad I found you," he said. "For a moment there I thought you were going out of my life forever."

Rita was in a quandary. She obviously knew who David was and had reacted too openly to pretend anything else. It was equally impossible for her to explain how she knew him without bringing in Franz Benninger, and that could bring her whole castle of dreams tumbling around her. Fortunately the waiter arrived with the carafe of wine and David decided to risk a little clowning while Rita composed herself.

"Thank you, Otto," he said to the waiter.

The waiter paused in his pouring. "But how did you know my name, sir?"

"A secret, Otto. I'm very big on secrets."

The waiter decided to join the game. "And what is my wife's name, sir?"

David beckoned him down and whispered, "Your wife's name is Gretchen but your girlfriend is Ingrid."

"*Mein Gott!*" the waiter gasped. He finished pouring the wine and left the table in a panic.

David raised his glass in a toast to Rita. *Gesundheit!*" he said.

She drank with him, some of the offhand amusement coming back to her face, but there was too much at stake for Rita to be her usual poised self.

"You're not Swiss," David said to her. "You could be Austrian ..."

"Don't press your luck. I was born German."

"Maybe," David admitted. "But I would wager my miserable fortune that you went to school in the States."

"And England. And France," she added.

"Which would argue a father in the diplomatic service."

"Don't practice ..." she began, and could have bitten off her tongue.

David poured her some more wine. Rita looked at him, was about to say something, changed her mind, picked up her bag. "Thank you for the wine," she said, "and the pleasant chat, but the time has come, as the walrus said." She made to rise.

David put out a gentle hand to stop her. "Don't go yet. I have something to say which I think you will want to hear." Rita hesitated. David smiled up at her. "Besides—you're getting your quotations mixed. What the walrus said was that the time has come to talk of many things. I'd like to talk of just one thing."

Rita smiled her sweetest heart-shaped-face cupid's-bow smile. "No deal." She was fully on her feet and had her bag. David rose with her.

"I'd like to talk about Franz Benninger," David said quietly. His eyes met Rita's and he was sorry to see sadness welling up to cloud her face.

"All right. A couple of minutes then."

She sat down again and Christopher waited for her to settle before he sat down himself. Both of them reached for the carafe of wine at once.

"Allow me," David insisted. He poured wine into both glasses. "Yesterday there were eight people who knew what I was investigating for Hurtilbank. I have a feeling that today there are nine."

Rita fluttered her hands in protest. "It's none of my business."

"Maybe." David noticed her feeling for her bag. "If you want to smoke, go ahead," he told her. "We're in the open air and the solution to pollution is dilution."

While she found her cigarettes and lighter David went on, "If you don't know what I am doing, there is no harm done. You will not understand— the—the—double-talk."

David noted that Rita was an efficient girl. Her lighter worked on the first spin of the contact wheel. He waited for the smoke to clear.

"I'm listening," she said. She was steadier now. "But you're not saying anything."

"At this point in my investigation the odds are strongly in favor of one Franz Benninger as the villain." Rita gasped. "That is why it disturbs me to see Franz passing papers covertly to you. If there is an explanation give it to me. If there isn't, you and Franz are likely to be sharing twin cells in the Zurich prison."

"Why, that's ridiculous," Rita blurted out.

"I hope it is, but all I know is what I see."

Rita drew on her cigarette, exhaled the smoke and took a mouthful of wine. "Normally I eschew American slang," Rita told David. "On principle. But this is a standoff."

"How do you mean?" he wanted to know.

"You think you have a security problem," Rita said. She laughed, and for that instant David had a glimpse of the woman underneath the girl he was interrogating. "Your problem pales into insignificance compared to mine. The trouble is: I cannot confide in you, any more than you can confide in me."

"It doesn't help, does it?" David commented.

She shook her head. "That's my dilemma. That's why it's a standoff. Scylla and Charybdis were never like this. I can only say that the papers Franz gave me are confidential papers relating to business I have with Hurtilbank. He is handling my business for me."

David realized that this was as far as he would get in this round. "May I ask where you can be contacted?"

"Why not? It's public knowledge. I have my own apartment on the Alfred-Escher-Strasse and I am in the telephone book."

"If you change your mind on this confidentiality bit," David said, "I'm at the Regina on the Parade Platz. Twenty-four-hour service." David looked at his watch and groaned. "I was due at the bank a half hour ago. See what happens when I meet a beautiful girl?"

"Run along, David. If you don't mind, I'll stay with Otto and finish the wine."

"Careful of Gretchen," David grinned. "I hear she's insanely jealous."

David bowed, stopped by Otto to pay for the wine, told him to be discreet with Ingrid, allowed himself five seconds to admire the statue of the wine-grower carrying his basket above the delicate fountain and went briskly on his way.

Rita watched him go. She thought that he was a good-looking man with a well-knit athletic body. She wished that he was much less observant. She regretted intensely that she had agreed to meet Franz in that lobby. Her intuition told her that it would lead to trouble. All her months of careful preparation. All her careful planning. Those harried weeks of waiting for Franz to break. Then the unbelievable coup. And now this feeling that she had destroyed it all by one silly carelessness in front of one watchful man. It was not fair. Really. It was just not fair.

David Christopher met President Johann Hurtil and Vice-President Franz Benninger and Chief Accountant Madame Elsa Florelle, in Hurtil's office at Hurtilbank. The subject of the emergency 4:00 P.M. meeting was the latest letter from the blackmailers. As the last one to join the meeting, David was the last one to read the page of carefully scripted instructions in the familiar red of the criminals' felt pen:

TOMORROW MORNING YOUR REPRESENTATIVE
AND ONE HOSTAGE, MLLE. DENISE ABBOTT,
ARE TO DRIVE ALONE TO THE VILLAGE

OF NEUFSUZERAIN REGISTERING AT THE
GASTHAUS AND AWAITING FURTHER INSTRUCTIONS.
NO POLICE. NO SURVEILLANCE.
OR THE LIFE OF THE HOSTAGE IS FORFEITED.
THE PAYMENT IS TO BE ONE UNMARKED CHAMOIS
    BAG
CONTAINING UNCUT DIAMONDS
TO THE VALUE OF TEN MILLION SWISS FRANCS.
AFTER PAYMENT IN FULL
OUR SILENCE IS GUARANTEED.

When David had finished reading—he read the
page twice, the second time aloud—he handed the
sheet of vellum back to Hurtil and returned to his
white leather armchair. Hurtil, Benninger and
Florelle looked at him expectantly. Christopher
said nothing.

"Well?" Hurtil asked him.

"About what I expected," David answered deliberately. "There are some aspects of the instructions I want to think over, but on the whole . . . no
surprises."

"Then the bank must pay?" Madame Florelle
asked with a touch of indignation in her voice.
David looked at her as if she were some new and
unwelcome element in the meeting. He had the
sense of having to start his explanations all over
again from Point One.

"Madame," David told her carefully. "We have
had a number of meetings on these blackmail
threats. We have agreed on one basic principle.
Paying the ransom is secondary. Buying secrecy is
primary."

Hurtil cleared his throat. "That's exactly right,
Florelle. You may have been unaware of our feeling on this point." Hurtil turned to David. "The

reason Madame Florelle is with us this afternoon is that we felt, that is, Benninger and I felt, we could not approve such a large sum without the agreement of our chief accountant."

"Fair enough," David answered. "Can you get the stones?"

"The stones are no problem," Benninger asserted. "We do some dealing in uncut stones and there is always a supply in our vaults."

David thought to himself that it was interesting that the blackmailers should ask for payment in a commodity which just happened to be plentiful in the vaults of Hurtilbank. He decided to plunge. He owed it to Hurtil and Florelle, and if Benninger were the blackmailer it would not hurt him to know it either.

"There is something I should explain," David said. "In the States we have unfortunately a lot of experience with blackmailers. Of course this situation is different. The blackmailers are not holding a human being as hostage, but they are in possession of information which is lethal. The principle on which law enforcement agencies in the States have always operated is this: First, pay the blackmail, release the hostage and then go after the criminals. I believe we should operate on the same principle here."

"I don't see . . ." Florelle began.

"What don't you see?" Christopher asked her.

"It's just not the same," Florelle insisted stubbornly.

"Why not, Florelle?" Hurtil asked.

"Because . . . you are a father. Your baby is kidnapped. You pay the ransom. The kidnappers give the baby back. Now you have your baby you can arrest the kidnappers. What do we get back when we pay? I think we get back nothing."

The three men digested this objection.

"What do you think of that, David?" Hurtil asked.

"Up to a point, Madame Florelle has a valid argument. I admitted our situation was different."

"Then what do we gain by paying the ransom?"

This from Benninger, with a look of genuine concern. David wished that either Benninger was not present or that his innocence was established. It was too confining to have to explain your game plan to the man who might be the captain of the other team.

"What do we gain?" David echoed the question. "First, we gain time. Even if these bastards intend to come back for a second bite, ten million francs is a lot of francs. It is going to take time for them to dispose of the stones, share out the proceeds, change their way of life, maybe move to a new country. While all that's going on, we are not just sitting paralyzed. Hurtilbank is doing a lot of soul-searching, to protect itself from further leaks. Every hour for me is a step closer to the identity of the blackmailers. I already have a prime suspect . . ."

The excitement in the room was intense.

"You have a suspect?" Hurtil, Benninger and Florelle asked in unison.

"A couple, in fact," David answered smugly.

"Who are they? You must tell us," Hurtil insisted.

"When my evidence will stand up in a court of law, that's when I tell you," David replied. He calmed down their protests. "Listen, every man is innocent until he is proved guilty. It would be defamatory for me to name persons who may be innocent."

Hurtil started to speak. "But . . ."

"Hold it," David interjected. "I'm not finished yet. Hear me out. This drop tomorrow. The payment, I mean. As long as I can protect Mlle. Abbott—and I mean to protect her—the drop could be our big chance. I'm going out to this place . . ." He clicked his fingers.

"Neufsuzerain?" Benninger asked.

"That's the one. I'm going out there prepared for any eventuality. All I need is one slipup on their part. Somebody has to be there. To make the pickup. You can't leave four million dollars' worth of diamonds sitting around a mountain for very long. When they make their pickup—that's a chance for me. I don't mean to miss it. That's what you're paying me for."

David stood up, and Hurtil, Florelle and Benninger followed suit. Hurtil smiled warmly at David.

"You have given us a glimmer of hope, David. I would not have thought that was possible."

"You know what they say about hope," David answered. "It springs eternal. What time can I pick up the diamonds in the morning? The earlier the better."

Hurtil looked at his subordinates. "Benninger? Florelle?"

"Whatever time Mr. Christopher suggests, we will be here. We can prepare the package tonight."

"Let's say seven A.M. then?" David suggested.

"Front door," Benninger told him.

"Aren't we all taking something for granted?" Madame Florelle asked.

"Like what?" David said.

"Like Mlle. Abbott. Has anybody inquired whether she is willing to go?"

The three men looked at each other ruefully.

Now that Florelle mentioned it, it had escaped their minds.

"Er, thank you, Florelle," Hurtil apologized, "I'll call Mlle. Abbott personally." He turned to David. "You're welcome to use my car and chauffeur if you like."

"Thanks, but I'd prefer the Lamborghini," David said. "If these characters want to play hard to get, they could say we broke the rules by bringing a chauffeur along."

"Should we advise Herr Rascher and Señor Villegas and Mr. McGowan?" Benninger wanted to know.

"Let me handle that one," David said. "Except maybe Villegas, I guess. He's staying with you, sir."

"It's no trouble," Hurtil began.

"Better this way," David assured him. "Gives me an excuse to talk to them again. McGowan's at the Plaza, right?"

"Correct."

"And Rascher?"

Hurtil looked dubious. "He is so insistent . . ."

"Look, Herr Hurtil, we are trying to save his miserable life. Surely he will be glad to get this piece of news."

"I suppose so." Hurtil was not really convinced. "He's at the Lindenhof on the Florhofgasse."

"Thanks," David said. He waved to Hurtil, Benninger and Florelle. Then lifted his thumb in a victory sign. "Here's to good luck tomorrow. Don't bother to see me out. You will have things to talk about."

In the outer office David stopped to have a word with plump, middle-aged Anna, Hurtil's receptionist-secretary.

"Good afternoon, Mr. Christopher. I trust . . .

that is ..." Her voice trailed off lamely. Anna was not supposed to have an inkling that anything was afoot.

"Anna, my dear," David said, "you can help me."

"Anything, Mr. Christopher. Anything at all."

"Good. Call that secretary of mine in Geneva and tell her I would appreciate it if just once, just for today only, she would work through till five o'clock. Maybe even five past five. I want to talk to her. When she stops swearing you can tell her I'll be calling in fifteen minutes from my hotel."

"Certainly, Mr. Christopher. A pleasure." With a gurgle in her throat that sounded suspiciously like a giggle, Anna reached for the telephone.

VII

Of the passengers who left the Swissair DC8 from
Abidjan at Zurich International Airport, none was
more conspicuous than Gaston le Grand. Gaston
was a tall man in his own right, certainly over six
feet, and his Afro hair and the black, silver-braided
pirate hat atop it gave him another six inches. Gaston wore leather boots up to his thighs over black
velvet trousers. His shirt was flaming red, open at
the neck. He wore a silver-embroidered waistcoat
which did not conceal a broad leather silver-
buckled belt. His carved wooden-beaded necklaces
were the envy of the girls on the plane. You could
wait at Zurich Airport for the whole summer and
not see such an exotic African as Gaston.

If Gaston's appearance was slightly bizarre by
the conservative standards of Zurich, his French
was impeccable. In a brief time he was through
Immigration, had picked up an army-green knapsack, rented himself a Volkswagen, and was on the
way into the city with his radio blaring out hard

rock from a French-speaking station. Gaston's body moved in time with the music and his left hand beat a tattoo on the steering wheel. It was difficult to believe, watching Gaston go by, that he was the living embodiment of all that was most terrible in the neuroses of Helmut Rascher.

Sometimes David Christopher wondered why his conversations with his secretary always seemed to end up with him apologizing. Other men terrorized their secretaries. His secretaries always managed to terrorize him.

"Corinne? This is Chris."

"Get lost, Big Brother. I have just put up a For Rent sign on your office."

"Corinne, you wouldn't."

"Oh, yes I would. I did."

"Corinne, it was just . . ."

"Don't come sniveling around me. I quit yesterday. Remember?"

"Corinne, my darling, my indispensable, vital, essential, necessary . . ."

"You have your Roget open. Page 326."

". . . ally in my lonely war against crime, what did you get on Denise Abbott?"

"Nothing."

"Nothing?"

"Nothing."

David thought that one over. "Corinne, I told you this was business. Now come on, give me what you've got."

"O.K., but no more cracks to that Anna. Secretaries have feelings too, you know. Stay till five for gosh sake!"

"I apologize. Now give me the Abbott stuff."

Corinne spoke rapidly while David took notes to help him digest the information.

"You're a honey," he said when she had finished. "Now what can you get me on Rita Jensen?"

There was a long suspicious pause from Corinne. "Who he?" she asked him slowly.

"German woman. About thirty-two. Daughter of a diplomat. Educated in the U.S., England and France. Living in Zurich. Try the CIA. Maybe Interpol. Nothing to go on. Just a feeling."

"So you gave up on the lesbo, huh?"

"Corinne, did anybody ever tell you that you have a dirty mind? A very dirty mind?"

"Not dirty. Just realistic. Let's face it. When did you ever go a night without sex? Except for the lesbo, that is?"

"Fortunately I am beyond such snide remarks, which are stimulated unfortunately by a frustrated sex life on the part of the snide remarker. Adios, my little one. My sympathies to your husband."

David hung up before Corinne could answer. He felt a long one coming on. He was tempted to call up Denise Abbott and invite her to dinner again. Now that he had her case history he stood a chance of making more headway than he had made the night before. On the other hand, with a moody female like Denise he could never be too sure about the way she was going to react if he pushed her, and he would have a few hours with her tomorrow when they made the ransom payoff at Neufsuzerain. David decided to let it ride for now. Tomorrow could be a heavy day and a decent sleep would not do him any harm. Especially after last night.

Gaston le Grand drove off the Rami-Strasse into

the inviting campus of the University of Zurich. He seemed to know exactly where he was heading because he drove quite confidently until he came to the parking lot in the vicinity of the University railroad station. He drove around the lot until he found the parking space he wanted. In the evening dusk it was well away from the main traffic arteries and not well lighted. Gaston turned off the ignition, slipped the keys into the pocket of his velvet trousers and stretched luxuriously. He looked at his watch. Then he took off his pirate hat and his Afro wig. Underneath the wig his hair was cropped short, close to the scalp.

He got out of the car and looked around carefully. When he found that he was alone, Gaston quickly removed his beads, his waistcoat, his shirt and his leather boots. He slipped on a black turtleneck and hush-puppies, also black. He was almost invisible. From the rear seat of the Volkswagen he took his knapsack and unstrapped it quickly. He took out a black .45 and a silencer, a switchblade and a lariat. The .45 and the silencer went into a shoulder holster which he also found in the knapsack. The switchblade was attached to a strap which fitted snugly around his right ankle underneath the leg of his velvet trousers. The lariat he attached to a silver hook on his leather belt. The knapsack yielded finally a black leather jacket which Gaston slipped on and buttoned up. He patted himself and found everything in place. He turned away, then remembered one more thing. He leaned into the VW, picked up his waistcoat and took out his wallet and some Swiss coins. The wallet slipped into his rear pocket while the coins dropped into the right-hand front pouch of his velvet pants. Gaston was ready.

"Hi, there, stranger. Long time no see."

David Christopher was passing through the lobby of the Plaza Hotel when the girl spoke to him from a leather armchair next to a solid square marble pillar. It was Denise Abbott, and she had a definite surprise advantage on David.

"Well, I'll be damned . . ." he said.

"Indubitably," she agreed.

"How . . . ? What? I mean, aren't you . . . ?"

"Give up, David," she said. "I am about to remove the veil from the Feminine Mystique. Our esteemed president, Herr Johann Hurtil, told me that you were out doing your detective duty by informing Mr. McGowan and Herr Rascher of their rights or some such. I took a chance on the Plaza. It must be all of a hundred meters from the Bellevue. And here I am."

She uncoiled in the armchair and stood up. Denise was wearing a long, roomy, multicolored Saint Laurent chemise. In the right lighting it was see-through to the flesh-colored bra and pantyhose underneath and in the wrong lighting it gave nothing but frustration to male birdwatchers who wanted to view it in the right lighting. Denise shifted onto the balls of her feet and pecked David on the cheek.

"I've just seen McGowan," David said, offering her his arm, "and I'm about to drop by Rascher. Like to come along? Maybe we could share a Wimpyburger or something later on?"

"I'd like that," Denise told him frankly. "Seeing as we have this grand secret assignation together tomorrow, I thought we could make some plans tonight. Actually I'm scared to death. Every time I hear a sound in my room I jump seven feet into the air. I'd really like to tag along if I may."

"We're all in this together," David said. "No reason why friend Rascher should object. *Allons, ma petite.* I happen to have my coach and four at the front door."

Gaston le Grand got out of the funicular train he had taken from the University to the Lindenhof Hotel. He mingled with the departing passengers as they walked to the Kantonschul-Strasse and followed two students into the Florhofgasse, which ran around to the rear of the hotel. He left the protection of the students at the delivery entrance of the hotel, picked his way carefully through the parked cars of the staff, negotiated the garbage cans at the door of the kitchen, carefully turned the handle of the door, and found what he expected to find: The door was not locked. From the right-hand pocket of his leather jacket, Gaston took out a flesh-colored stocking mask and slipped it over his head, adjusting it until the eyeholes were in position. From the left pocket he took a pair of white-skin gloves that he drew on until his fingers were snug. Then he took out the .45 from the shoulder holster, fitted the silencer to the muzzle, hefted the gun in his right hand until the feel was right, carefully turned the handle of the door with his left hand, and slipped inside.

Gaston could not have timed his arrival better. Jacob, the chef-owner of the Lindenhof, had arrived at the penultimate moment in the preparation of his fondue, when he demanded the undivided attention of Hans, his kitchen boy and apprentice chef, as he shouted for more kirsch or another spice. Gaston carefully closed the door behind him with his left hand while he kept his .45 ready in case of emergency. He oriented himself in the room, fitting the real-life scene into the plan he had studied while he was preparing the job. His information had been exact. To his left was the heavy-doored pantry, to his right the cool-room and the sinks for the pots and pans. The preparation benches lined the walls and the stove was centered in the kitchen under a heavy steel exhaust flue. Jacob and Hans were working at the stove with their backs to Gaston. Beyond them, on the opposite side of the room, was the swing-door leading to the passageway into the dining room. Gaston was satisfied. There would be no hitches as long as the little shit was inside. Eating his last meal. Shovel down that soup, man, Gaston told Rascher. Your stomach will never have time to digest it.

Gaston waited until Jacob tasted the fondue, lifted his left eyebrow in judgment, and found his creation good.

"*Ja?*" asked Hans.

"*Ja!*" exclaimed Jacob.

"*Nein,*" announced Gaston.

The two men swung around in disbelief and protest and looked into the long snout of Gaston's silencer. Still disbelieving, they looked up to the face above the silencer and saw the terrifying stocking mask and the black eyes through the narrow slits. Their hands slowly rose above their heads.

Gaston gestured toward the pantry with his gun, and the two men stumbled, in their haste to obey his order. At the door of the pantry Gaston halted Jacob, removed his large white chef's cap, and indicated that Jacob was to take off his white coat. Again Jacob obeyed with nervous, fumbling alacrity. Gaston took the coat, then ran the chef inside the pantry after Hans, slammed the door behind them, and slipped the heavy bolt. The stone walls of the pantry were covered with plaster which in turn was lined with wood—a fragrant spruce—and there was little chance that the two men could be heard even if they decided to yell and pound on the door. From their fear of his .45 Gaston estimated that it would be at least ten or fifteen minutes before they risked any noise at all. By that time, Gaston hoped, it would be too late.

Gaston put on the chef's tall cap, adjusting it to a jaunty angle. The coat was large enough to fit over his leather jacket. Gaston put the gun in his pocket, went over to the stove, picked up the heavy bowl of fondue, and walked toward the dining room. This was it, brother, and may the God of justice be on the side of Gaston le Grand.

There were six men, four women and Helmut Rascher at the long wooden picnic table in the dining room. Jacob, the chef, was celebrating something or other tonight. Helmut could not remember whether it was his mother-in-law's birthday or his cousins's nephew's marriage or simply Mayday. Whatever it was had produced a special flagon of red wine from Jacob's cellar and a couple of toasts at the start of the meal, along with a thick minestrone soup. The wine was a Mezzana from Ticino, a red wine with the punch of a light gin that had caught Helmut Rascher off guard. By the time Helmut had waded his way through the minestrone Jacob had been simmering for three days in preparation for the evening, an entrée of fish from the Zurichsee and toasted cheese, washed down with more of the Mezzana, he was as merry as he had dared to be for some years. He had almost forgotten the Africans.

When Jacob came through the door hefting the great bowl of fondue high in front of his face, Helmut joined the tympani section of the orchestra of approval, banging with his spoon and fork on the wooden table and shouting for Jacob to hurry. Jacob did not hurry. He moved slowly along the table until he was opposite Helmut. Then he sped up wafting the fragrant fondue past the noses of the shouting slavering diners until he was behind Helmut. To the horror of the six men and the four women who shared the table with Helmut, he upended the heavy bowl of fondue and brought it crashing down on Rascher's head. The hot cheese scalded Rascher's face, and he screamed in agony as he tried to lift the bowl from his head.

Gaston put his hand inside the white coat, took the lariat from his belt and slipped a noose over Helmut's head and around his neck. He drew the noose tight, then flicked the other end of the lariat over a heavy crossbeam above his head. He drew the rope taut, hauled hard, and Helmut's writhing body lifted out of place to dangle before the popping eyes of the paralyzed company. Gaston stepped onto the bench, then onto the table and half-hitched the rope twice under the beam so that it was firm. He jumped back down to the floor, leaned down, and took the switchblade from its anklepouch, flicked the blade open and plunged it twice into Helmut's back behind his heart. From the terrible shudder that shook Helmut's body, Gaston was sure that he had found his mark. But he was not taking any chances. This one was for ten million fellow-Africans whom Rascher had ripped off. Gaston slipped the switchblade into his left hand, took the .45 from his pocket, and jammed the nozzle into Rascher's anus, pointing it vertically so that the bullet was aimed at Rascher's head. Gaston pulled the trigger and the heavy .45 bullet tore its way up through Rascher just in front of his backbone. There was a tremendous convulsive heaving reaction to the bullet in Helmut's body, and his legs slammed against the heavy trestle table with such force that it overturned, throwing plates, knives and forks and spoons, glasses and wine and bread and butter and people into a screaming heap of messy terror on the floor.

Holding his gun and knife extended, Gaston backed away from the scene toward an exit door leading into a corridor connecting the Lindenhof with the funicular station. Gaston need not have worried. In the confusion of sobbing wives and shouting husbands trying to find each other and wanting to get away from this nightmare of brutality that had invaded their peaceful lives, hardly anybody saw Gaston go.

The distance between the Plaza Hotel and the Lindenhof was hardly enough to give David a chance to get the Lamborghini out of first gear. Still, time is not everything. It was long enough for David to become conscious that tonight Denise was another girl entirely. Not any of the women he had met fleetingly the night before. Sitting beside him in a full-length delphinium-blue light wool cape, the leopard was pliant and anxious to please, ready to agree to whatever he suggested. David was realistic enough to understand that Denise was frightened, that she wanted to be around somebody who could protect her, and that the most available somebody was himself. The knowledge of her motives did not alter the warmth of her presence. This kind of girl he could go for all the way. This kind of girl would not leave him on the mat outside her door. She would feel much safer with him beside her in bed. The thought appealed to David. In a way it combined business with pleasure. If they got to know each other well tonight they would be much better allies tomorrow.

David ran up the Rami-Strasse to the corner of the Zurichberg-Strasse, made a left into the Kantonschul-Strasse, and found a parking spot opposite the hotel.

"This should only take a minute," he said to Denise.

"If you think you're leaving me alone in this car, David Christopher," replied Denise indignantly, "you're crazy."

David smiled, got out of the car, went round to the passenger side, and opened the door for Denise. When she was out, she immediately clung to his arm while David slammed the door of the car.

As they crossed the street and walked up the steps into the lobby of the hotel they could hear the shouting and screaming. David hurried inside, dragging a reluctant Denise with him. There was a plump elderly woman at the reception desk.

"Quickly!" she appealed to David. "Something terrible is happening." She pointed toward the dining room. David turned to run, but Denise clung to his arm.

"Please, David," she begged. "You might be killed."

"That's my job," he said, throwing off her arm.

When he reached the dining room, people were picking themselves up from the floor. The body of Rascher hung from the crossbeam, but nobody was paying any attention to Rascher. David jumped onto a bench, but it was too low to allow him to

reach the half-hitches under the beam. He heard
Denise scream—a high-pitched keening scream that
turned every head toward her—and as he groped
on the floor for a knife he could hear her voice
above the rest:

"Oh, no! Oh, no! Please God!"

David finally came up with a breadknife and
looked around for something high enough to stand
on. Then he took a calmer look at the body and realized that Rascher was dead. David dropped the
knife and went across to Denise. She was still crying, so he slapped her face hard and said, "Denise!
Damn you, these people need help." He shook her
until her rigor subsided and her fear-glazed eyes
saw him. "Help these people while I call the police." She nodded dumbly and looked around to see
what she could do. Satisfied that she was over her
hysteria, David went back to the fat woman at the
desk.

"My husband," she begged, "how is he?"

David answered, "I don't know. Who is your
husband?"

"The cook," she said. "He is the chef. We own
the hotel."

"Call the police," David ordered, "and I'll go find
out. Ask for Captain Hans Frey to come also. Talk
to him personally. Tell him David Christopher
asked for him."

Gretel, the bulbous-breasted girl who had been
Helmut Rascher's preferred bed companion from
among Madame Brabant's stable of prostitutes,
stepped off the funicular at the Hotel Lindenhof
station and noticed the black man swing aboard at
the rear of the train just as it started to move up the
steep gradient toward the University. That's funny,

she thought to herself. Helmut was always muttering to himself about Africans. Funny to step off the train and see one. Just like that. Gretel had heard about black men and was always hoping that one of them would come to Madame Brabant's. According to the gossip among the girls, they were a terrific lay. They had tools like horses and could fuck you forever before they came. At least that's what this girl from Geneva said who claimed she had actually been with one. She said she was sore for days. But it was worth it because she'd come six times herself, and then when he came it was like when they burned the giant "Snowman" in Zurich at the end of winter and you never thought the firecrackers would stop. Gretel wished the black man who got on the train would only come to Madame Brabant's tonight. She could feel him in her already. It would be just terrific. Then Gretel remembered she was running late and Madame would give her hell again, so she forgot about the black man on the train.

By the time Gretel was back at the brothel, enduring her expected tongue-lashing from Madame Brabant, Gaston le Grand was in the Volkswagen speeding along the Winterthurer Strasse that connected with the autobahn to the airport. Gaston had resumed his disguise as a swinging African with the Afro hairdo, the hat, and the dark glasses. He was tempted to remain in Zurich and eat, but temptations of that kind did not trouble Gaston for long. He was a careful man as far as his profession allowed, and would take his pleasures in the safety of Brussels later in the evening. He had timed himself to catch the 8:50 P.M. Sabena flight and was right on schedule. Gaston liked a smooth operation. It was good for business.

Captain Hans Frey's short black moustache bristled with suspicion. His square strong body was more tightly contained than usual if that was possible. His gray-green eyes sent beams of glacial light through the shivering souls of the unfortunate guests whose only crime was that they had witnessed Zurich's most brutal murder in a decade.

The shrewd detective's real concern, superseding even the killing, was David Christopher. He knew that Christopher was afraid of him or at least uneasy in his presence. To him the American investigator did not seem particularly bright, and he invariably seemed to be caught with his pants down. He was a rival in a sense, but unworthy of the talents of Hans Frey, recognized as one of Switzerland's most successful policemen. On the other hand, how could you write off a man who seemed to have a nose for trouble? Who was always on the scene of the crime before you were? Who always knew what was happening and why, or at least thought he did? Up till now Frey had kept a close eye on David Christopher because he knew that something was wrong at Hurtilbank, something that Hurtilbank was keeping from the police but which, Frey suspected, was actually a police matter. Now Frey began to wonder if Christopher might not be involved somehow himself. How could a man consistently show up at the scene of the crime if he was not part of the crime?

To add to Frey's chagrin, Christopher seemed to have assembled all the facts of this particular case before the first policeman was on the scene. He had rescued the chef and his assistant from their pantry-prison. He had learned from them how the assassin had done the deed—entry through the delivery yard and the kitchen, using the chef's cap and coat as a disguise, escape almost certainly on the funicular. Only the identity of the assassin remained to be discovered. Frey was almost afraid that Christopher would come up with that as well, if he gave him half a chance.

Frey assigned the interrogations of the chef and his assistant and the guests to the radio patrolmen whose cars sat sprawled at awkward angles on the Kantonschul-Strasse, blinking blue warning lights to a curious crowd of sightseers. Two detectives from Homicide had also arrived, together with a police photographer, two ambulance men, a doctor, and several reporters who, like vultures, had scented the carcass. Frey, accompanied by his faithful Saint Bernard, Sergeant Schwand, reserved the interrogation of David Christopher and Denise Abbott for himself.

The detective had found a small parlor-cum-writing-room for the interrogation, away from the logorrhea in the lobby, the dining room and the kitchen. He sat Denise and David down in two uncomfortable nineteenth-century upright chairs with velvet-covered seats and looked at them across a center table of dark polished wood, capped with a dusty bowl of artificial violets. Schwand took up his customary stance by the door. David had the random thought that Schwand stood by the door in the hope that he and Denise might try to make a run for it and give him something more to do than be a dumb show behind Frey.

"Mr. Christopher," Frey began, "you seem to have suffered another misfortune ..."

"Not me, Frey," David cut in. "Rascher. He suffered the misfortune. He's the one who's dead. Remember?" Frey tried to outstare David. "I will

ask the questions, Herr Christopher. You will answer them."

"O.K., O.K.," David agreed. "Ask away. Just stop
editorializing and get on with it."

Frey was not conversant enough with the American vernacular to understand the meaning of "editorializing," but the gist of David's remark was obvious. Frey's breath shortened, but he controlled
himself. "What were you doing here tonight?" the
policeman asked.

David sighed impatiently. "We're going round in
circles, Frey . . ."

"You will please answer my question."

"I am carrying out an investigation for Hurtilbank and some Hurtilbank clients. One of the
clients is Mlle. Abbott. Another is—was—Herr
Rascher. I came to the hotel with Mlle. Abbott to
speak to Herr Rascher. We arrived just after the,
uh, killing, murder, what have you. That's it."

Frey's face, as far as he allowed any change of
expression to mar his studiously impassive de-
meanor, mimed the resigned patience of the mar-
tyr.

"Mr. Christopher . . ."

"Yes?"

"Mr. Christopher, this is now the second occasion your investigation for Hurtilbank has become involved with a murder. I have told you
that concealment of information in a murder case
makes you liable to prosecution for criminal conspiracy . . ."

David interrupted with an irritation that could
not be concealed. "For Christ's sake, Frey. I'm a
lawman, remember? You don't have to tell me the
laws of Switzerland . . ."

"Then tell me the subject of your investigation."

"My investigation has absolutely nothing to do with this murder or the one last night."

"Come on, Mr. Christopher. Do you take me for a fool? Perhaps to you all policemen are fools."

"I do not think you are a fool. On the contrary. You're only being stubborn. If you want to know why Rascher was killed and who killed him, I'll tell you."

Frey and Schwand exchanged the resigned looks of parents whose four-year-old son has just confided to them that Jiminy Cricket painted their Chinese bamboo wallpaper with ketchup. In a voice that Frey trusted was dripping with concentrated acidic irony, the detective ordered, "Very well, tell me why Rascher was killed and who killed him. I'd like to know. The entire police force of Zurich will be in your everlasting debt."

"Thank you, Captain," David answered sweetly. "I know that comes from the bottom of your heart."

"Tell me," Frey snapped.

"Rascher was an arms dealer," David told him. "Lived in Bonn. If you could possibly spare the time to check with Interpol you will find that he was a crooked arms dealer who swindled African revolutionary governments. It was only a matter of time before they caught up with him. This job was done by a pro. One of the best, I'd say. Not a nice man, but one of the best."

Frey tried to walk a few steps while he pondered this answer, but he came up against a cumbersome wall cabinet encrusted with sticky varnish that clung to the twill of his jacket sleeve. There was an audible hiss as he jerked his sleeve away from the varnish, hoping that David and Denise had not noticed. It was proving out just as

Frey had feared it would. This infernal meddling American was in danger of solving the murder right under his nose. He made it all sound so simple, so logical, so undeniable. There had to be a catch. Frey swung on Denise.

"And what do you think of all this, Mlle. Abbott?"

"She knows nothing about it," David answered for Denise, "She just—"

"Herr Christopher," Frey said sternly, "I am speaking to Mlle. Abbott. You will please not to interrupt. Mlle. Abbott?"

"I know nothing about it," Denise told him. "I just came along for the ride."

If Frey had been able to indulge his fantasies he would have ordered Schwand to pick up David with one mighty arm and Denise with the other and drop them both in the Zurichsee. Instead he turned to David.

"You will remain in Zurich," he instructed, "you will hold yourself at all times available for questioning." Then Frey turned so abruptly that he was too close to the door for Schwand to open it. He had to step back to allow the big man to get at the handle. Leaving the door open behind them, Frey and Schwand left the room.

David and Denise stood up. As David took a step toward the door he felt Denise clutch his arm. He turned just in time to grab her before she crumpled to the floor in a dead faint. He helped her back onto the upright chair and lowered her head between her knees until she recovered.

"A deep breath," he encouraged her. "Come on, now. A big breath."

He felt her heave under his hands and let her sit up straight. For a minute she sat in the chair breathing deeply while the color came back to her cheeks.

"I'm a big help," she said. Her smile was wan.

"Sure you are," David answered, lifting her to her feet. "You said nothing, which is the only way to deal with a guy like Frey."

Denise tested her strength, still holding tightly onto David's arm. "I feel such a damn fool," she confessed. "I was really looking forward to spending the night with you. You know, soft lights, music, dinner, champagne and then back to your place for the big seduction scene. Now all I'm good for is a couple of aspros and an early bed. Can you ever forgive me, David?"

"Never," he replied sternly. "At least not before morning. Then I'll think about it."

VIII

It was exactly 6:40 A.M. on Thursday morning when David swung his car from the Regina Hotel's garage onto the Talacker Strasse and turned left again into the Parade Platz on his way to the Bahnhofstrasse and Hurtilbank. There was no particular reason for David to pay close attention to the flower stall in the Parade Platz. He expected flower stalls in Switzerland to be open and doing business at that hour of the morning. For this reason he did not see the man in the cloth cap. The man was galvanized into action by David's unexpected appearance. He hurried into the stall, picked up a two-way radio and signaled. He had to signal three times before his speaker came to life and a voice asked in German, "What's so important?"

"Christopher."

"What about him?"

"He just went past in his car. He's turning into

201

the Bahnhofstrasse right now. Direction of Hurtilbank."

"Christ. Is anybody covering the bank?"

"No. Heidegger is in the Bellevue Platz. He's watching the girl."

"O.K. I'll contact Heidegger. You go after Christopher."

"On foot?"

"No, you blockhead. Use your wings. And hurry or Frey will have your ass for this. If he doesn't stop at the bank try to flag down a taxi."

The man in the cloth cap stuffed the two-way radio into the capacious pocket of his bedraggled topcoat and left the flower stall at a run. He was in such a hurry that he took no notice at all of the avocado-green Mercedes drifting down the Bahnhofstrasse and halting two blocks back from Hurtilbank under a greening lime tree where the two men in the car had a clear view of the golden Lamborghini parked in front of the bank. The two men inside the Mercedes were more observant. They saw the poorly dressed workman in the cloth cap go running past them on the sidewalk. They noticed him stop abruptly, turn into a shop window as if he had been overcome by an irresistible impulse to study the couture dresses on display there, take out something from his pocket, and bring it to his mouth.

"Shit," Johnson said to Murdoch. "This prick is guarded by a goddam army. We'll never get to him."

"They can't guard him all the time everyplace," Murdoch answered. "Besides, I don't think they're guardin' him. I think they're watchin' him, same as us."

"To knock him off?" Johnson asked incredulously.

Murdoch moved impatiently, then groaned as the movement hurt his shoulder. "To put him away, dummy," he growled.

"You O.K., Murd?" Johnson asked anxiously. "Yer shoulder givin' you trouble?"

"Some," Murdoch told him. "Lucky the bullet went right through so I didn't have to go to no quack. That would have given us away for sure. The alcohol is keepin' it clean. No pus or nothin' like that."

"You're sure, Murd?"

"Sure, I'm sure. I'd just like to get this son of a bitch Christopher in his grave, that's all, so we can get the hell out of this place. It's startin' to give me the creeps."

"Me too," Johnson confided. "Who knows? Maybe we'll get lucky this morning and shove Mr. Goddam Christopher and his fancy goddam wheels over the nearest cliff."

Murdoch was gloomy. "We should be so lucky."

As soon as the buzzer sounded inside Hurtilbank, the door opened and Benninger was standing there.

"Come in, Mr. Christopher," he greeted David.

Florelle was standing inside the lobby holding a pale fawn chamois bag. Solemnly she handed it to David. "Perhaps you should check it before you go," she said.

David felt the stones inside the bag, loosened the leather thong at the neck and peered briefly inside. Then he shrugged his shoulders and tightened the thong. "What do I know about uncut diamonds?" he asked. "If you say they're worth ten million francs, then they're worth ten million francs."

He turned to go, then turned back as a thought struck him. "Tell Herr Hurtil I'll report back to him as soon as this is over. The way the instructions read I have no way of knowing when that will be. They could keep me sitting there for twenty-four hours, but I doubt it. I think they will want to get this over and done with just as much as we do, so you should see me about closing time." David lifted the bag. "Thanks again." He went through the door and into the street.

Benninger followed him out and walked with David to the car. He was obviously nervous, and David gave him time to come to the point. "Miss Jensen called me," he began.

David thought to himself that Miss Jensen and Benninger had probably spent a good part of the night together, but he waited for Benninger to go on.

"I understand—that is, I can see why, how my clandestine meeting with her would give rise to some suspicion in your mind."

David was about to reply, but there did not seem to be anything much to say, so he shrugged his shoulders instead.

Benninger hurried on. "I can assure you, Herr Christopher, that your suspicions are groundless. Hurtilbank is my life. Whatever I do is dictated by an ambition, I hope a laudable ambition, to expand Hurtilbank into one of the world's most respected financial institutions. It is unthinkable that I would do anything to harm the bank."

"I'm glad to hear that, Herr Benninger," David said. "If it is true you have nothing to fear. I deal in facts. Where the facts lead I follow. It's as simple as that. *Au revoir.*" He shook hands with Benninger and then went around the car to get into the driver's seat. David opened the glovebox with a key, put the bag of diamonds inside and pushed the door closed. While Benninger stood on the curb watching him, David picked out the ignition key and started the Lamborghini. He waved at Benninger, slipped the car into Drive and purred away toward the Quai Bridge. Benninger, watching him go and wondering whether or not it had been right to speak about his business with Rita, was too busy with his own thoughts to be suspicious of the avocado-green Mercedes trailing David or to observe the workman in the cloth cap speaking rapidly into a two-way radio further up the Bahnhofstrasse.

The Denise of early Thursday morning was strictly business. She was wearing large diablo dark glasses, a Hermès scarf, a sea-green pants suit over a turtleneck shirt and a pair of low-heeled Florentina shoes. On her left arm was a pale-green raincoat to match her pants suit, and she carried a Louis Vuitton shoulder bag filled with items she had prepared for the trip to Neufsuzerain. The Bellevue Hotel boasted a doorman resembling a yeoman of the guard at the Tower of London, and he waved David aside as he assisted Denise into the car and shut her safely inside.

"All set?" David asked her, as he settled into the driver's seat and fastened his seatbelt. Denise turned and dropped her raincoat on the rear seat, turned back, and settled her bag beside her feet.

"When I fasten this damn seatbelt," she told him. "I can never find both ends at the same time." While David helped her into harness she asked him, "Where is Neufsuzerain anyway, and why the hell are they sending us there wherever it is?"

205

David took a folded map from the dashboard of the car and unfolded it before passing it across to Denise. "You're the navigator," he said, "so you should have this anyway." He pointed with his index finger. "We take the autobahn down the southwestern shore of the lake as far as this Wadenswil turnoff. We go away from Wadenswil toward Zug, and Neufsuzerain is up there in the mountains. I've marked the turnoff."

Denise studied the map seriously. "Could I make a suggestion?"

"It's a free country," David answered.

"Why don't we whiz up the mountain and go by the mountain road along here ... the Adliswil, is it?"

David was inclined to demur. "It will be a lot slower," he objected.

"Who cares? These dirty blackmailers are pushing us around. After all, they could have given us something easy. Like leaving the diamonds in a locker at the Hauptbahnhof. Let's take our time. All my life I've wanted to see the view from the—what's it . . . ?"

"Adliswil?"

"Right, the Adliswil. There's a cable car up there. To Felsenegg. It's supposed to have this fantastic view over the lake and the Alps. I love those aerial cars. Scary!"

"We'll compromise . . ." David began.

"I love compromising situations."

"We'll go by the mountain road. We'll come back by the autobahn and we will not stop to take the cable car to Felsenegg."

Denise grimaced. "The first moment you walked into my suite," she said sourly, "I knew you were not a nice man." They both laughed as David

206

switched on the engine, slipped the car into gear and drove around the Bellevue Platz to return over the Quai Bridge.

At the tram terminal in the center of the Bellevue Platz Heidegger watched the Lamborghini on its way and passed the information back to Frey's listening post. At a judicious interval behind the Lamborghini, the green Mercedes bearing Murdoch and Johnson followed David across the Quai Bridge. The early-morning traffic was building up, and Johnson decided it would be safe in a city of Mercedeses to move in closer to the Lamborghini.

When David looked into his rear-view mirror he saw the avocado-green 450 and the idle thought crossed his mind that if he ever had to give up the Lamborghini, he might easily switch to a Mercedes. When he saw the car again in the General Witte Strasse and once again in the Beder-Strasse his first thought was Frey.

"Bastard!" he muttered.

"What's the matter, D.?" Denise asked him.

"A car following us," David said tersely. "At least it looks like it."

"Who could it be?" Denise wanted to know.

"Probably our friend, Captain Hans Frey," David answered. He glared at the Mercedes in the mirror on his door. "If you don't mind," David said, "I think I'll try to lose him while we're still in the city. Once we're on the open road it will be more difficult, and the last thing we need up there in Neufsuzerain is Captain Hans Frey."

"If you want to lose him," Denise said coolly, "you should let me drive."

"I'll bet," David replied.

Grim, he swung off Beder into Waffenplatz and then immediately switched to Schulhaus. The 450 gave up its pretense of being just another car on the road and gave full-throttle chase. David told Denise to watch out for the Mercedes while he concentrated on a furious effort to outdistance his pursuers in the maze of streets behind Rieter-Park. Not knowing quite how he did it, he dodged sleepy early-morning drivers, children on bicycles and the occasional horse and cart. How he found his way to Brunau-Strasse was largely a matter of good luck, but he had a corner jump on the Mercedes and decided to risk a plunge toward the Allmend-Strasse, where he thought the dammed-up flood of rush-hour traffic would be his best protection.

They managed to negotiate the underpass without any further sign of the avocado-green Mercedes 450, and Denise was confident that David had shaken off his pursuers. David did not take any chances. He pushed the Lamborghini as fast as he dared go without risking an interview with the traffic police and reached the Zug–Luzern trunk road in safety.

"Whew!" Denise let out her breath. "That's my first in ten minutes."

"It's easier when you're driving," David admitted.

"You can say that again," Denise agreed. "Next time we go in my car and I'm driving."

"What do you drive?" David asked conversationally.

"Jag, when I'm at home."

"Where's home?" David asked as casually as he could.

"Who knows?" she answered him. "Wish I did. Look at that view. I told you."

Denise was right, David thought to himself. It

was magnificent, especially in the early morning with mist still on the lake and in some of the valleys. Thick green forests on the slopes of the Uetliberg and Zurich coming into view—a panorama spread out below them. Over all, the vast blue Swiss skies and snowcapped mountains appearing on the horizon.

"Don't take this the wrong way," David said, after driving for a time in silence, "but I wish you were not here."

"Nothing personal, I hope," Denise answered.

"You're a hostage," David pursued his thought. "To prevent me getting close. If I try to pull anything, it might cost your life."

"I'm not afraid," Denise said—and meant it.

"Maybe you aren't," David admitted, "but I am."

"They probably know you're a typical old male chauvinst pork chop," Denise answered, "and chose this way to tie your hands."

"Could be," David said. "On the whole, though, it seems to me we are dealing with some very smart people. Too smart to get trapped at this point anyway."

They were silent again while David guided the car smoothly past a farmer on a red tractor dragging behind him a trailer with two laughing children inside. The children waved and Denise waved back.

"You intend to pay?" Denise asked.

For answer, David put his right hand under the wheel and pointed to the key of the glovebox. "Take off that key," he told her.

Denise slipped the key from its grip. "What now?" she asked.

David pointed to the glovebox. Curious, Denise used the key to open the door. She gasped as she saw the chamois bag. "What's that?" she asked him.

"About four million bucks, they tell me. Have a look for yourself."

Denise was trembling as she took out the bag and loosened the leather tie. When the neck of the bag was free, she shook it until some of the diamonds poured into her hand. She looked at the dull stones for a space.

"They're not very pretty are they?"

David shrugged his shoulders. "They have a place in somebody's heart."

"Why?" Denise asked him. "I mean, why these?"

"Huge value in a small package," David explained. "They're easy to conceal. Easy to market. They are virtually untraceable. A very smart guy, Mr. X. Or Messrs. XYZ. I'll give them that."

Denise dribbled the dull stones back into the bag, drew the tie-thong tight and then sat the bag in the palm of her left hand. She moved her hand up and down a little, enjoying the soft heavy feel of the diamonds inside the chamois leather. There was a sound of relief in her voice as she said, half to herself, "It will be all over soon."

David glanced toward her and a wave of tenderness welled up in him as he saw her pale-gold hair, the classically lovely profile, and the weight of anxiety drooping her shoulders.

"You'll be all right," he said. "I promise."

His voice came out slightly husky, and she looked up in surprise. "Why, David, that's very sweet of you." She leaned over and her lips touched his cheek lightly, a feather-kiss that rippled through his body and increased the pressure of his foot on the accelerator just as he passed the limiting speed zone sign at the entrance to a small hamlet.

"Whoops," David laughed.

Denise laughed in response, a girlish laugh that he had not heard before. She leaned over and replaced the diamonds inside the glovebox, then returned the key to David's key ring.

"There it is," Denise exclaimed in triumph, pointing to the signpost.

"Attagirl," David answered. "That's my navigator." They were driving through Sihibrugg, negotiating sheep flocks, herds of goats, small farmers' vans, horse-drawn carts carrying steel cans of milk, and a medley of cars and people, jammed into narrow paved streets between tall, gaily painted gabled houses. It was a relief to leave the main trunk road to Baar and Zug for the less-frequented road climbing through a series of hairpin bends to the tiny mountain village of Neufsuzerain. Although the deciduous trees on the heights were still only budding, grass was already greening the fields and one enterprising herdsman was stealing a march on his rivals in the annual trek to the Alpine pastures. His string of long-horned, red-and-white Simmentals, flower-crowned, was lowing its mournful way along the edge of the roadway to the accompaniment of the clanging cowbells suspended from the neck of each animal.

Denise clapped her hands. "It was worth it just for that," she told David. He did not answer until he had inched his car ahead of the last cow. By that time Denise was already admiring a sweep of rugged valley falling sheer away from the road and ending in a tiny lake that was just beginning to light up with its first sun.

Denise drew in her breath sharply. "Do you think that's it?" she asked.

David took a quick look. Seemingly suspended on a ledge of outcropping granite was a small jumble of red-tiled roofs surrounding a steeple.

"Guess so," David answered.

He found a belvedere large enough to take the Lamborghini and ran the car off the road. Before he had switched off the engine, Denise had unfastened her seatbelt and was out of the car, drinking in deep draughts of the spring-fresh air. Slowly David followed, stretching his arms and indulging in a luxurious yawn to loosen his body.

"It's so beautiful," Denise told him.

There did not seem to be any need for an answer. The two of them stood side by side, feasting their eyes on the incredible vista from the lake below through the dark-green firs and the Norway spruce and the Arolla pines, the pale lime of the new grass, the rich red of the small hamlets, jagged outlines of bare rock, and, over all, Neufsuzerain perched on its eyrie.

"When these blackmailers get the Hurtilbank diamonds," David observed, "they must be planning to go into the tourist business. Seems like they're getting in some practice at our expense."

"I don't care," Denise answered. "Couldn't you always live in these mountains?"

David did not answer, and when Denise turned to see why she found him scanning the mountains with narrowed eyes, as if he was willing himself to peel away the disguising horizon until it revealed the blackmailers' hiding place. Her lips pouted. "I'm here too, you know," she chided David gently.

This time he heard her. He turned, affection in his eyes, and would have taken her into his arms but, womanlike, she avoided the moment she hungered for and turned away toward a narrow path

212

leading to a huge gray rock standing out dangerously over a thousand feet of empty air. "Careful," David called. Her laugh dared him to follow her and he took up the challenge, scrambling to the top of the rock just as she flopped down, breathing deeply.

David sat beside her and took her face in both his hands, turning it so that he was looking directly at her, as if trying to probe beyond the startling blue veil. She returned his look with candor.

"What is it, David?" she asked him.

His hands dropped and he turned his head away from her to look out over the rolling hills of the Middle Country. "I've been researching you," he said carefully. "Your tastes, habits, favorite colors, sports, seasons, spas. You weigh one hundred and five pounds. You're five-five, aged twenty-four. You hate avocado and love hamburgers."

"Is that all?" she asked him seriously.

"Oh, no. There's much more." He was quite cheerful. "It is generally agreed you could be Top Dog as an actress, if you wanted, or as a singer, if you also wanted, but apart from a few special assignments you stick to the modeling. Nobody seems to know why."

Her finger pursued an ant which had already come exploring the interesting new blend of scents in its habitat. "Anything else?"

"Why, yes, now that you ask. Bank drafts find their way into your account. Regularly. From London." David's chest was tight and his breathing short and he didn't know why. "Ultimately they come from an English account held by Lord Esherbridge. He is a high-ranking English peer. A political comer. Wealthy. And married."

Denise's finger crushed the ant and she watched

it struggle for life. "You have been a busy little boy, haven't you, David Christopher?" She stood up on the rock and walked to the edge, careless, uncaring.

"Watch it," David warned. "That's damn dangerous." He stood up and put his arms around her from behind, bringing her back into the protecting orbit of his own body. Something went through her, a kind of shudder that might have been a sob. David waited. At last she breathed in deeply and let her voice come through a sigh that seemed to David inexplicably full of sadness.

"I'm a secret person," she told him, thinking as she went along. "Always have been. Ever since I was a little girl. I've been trying to tell you all about myself ever since you walked through that door, damn it. And the harder I try and the more I want to tell you, the bitchier I get. Can you believe that?"

"It's about par for the course, baby," David comforted her. "But who's in a hurry. You'll tell me. When you're ready."

She turned around to hug him tight, her head against his shoulder. "Thank you, David. You're very sweet." There were tears in her eyes, wetting her lashes as she looked up at him. David was conscious that he had never held so beautiful a girl in his arms in his entire life. "If only we could start all over again," she said.

David put a finger on her lips. "Shush," he said.

Then her head lifted and his head bent and their mouths met wide open in a kiss that sent wild streams of hormones surging through their bloodstreams. When David came up for breath he said, "Christ Almighty! Do you realize we may have chosen the most dangerous spot in Switzerland to let passion rear its ugly head?"

"I don't care," Denise said happily, "I've been wanting you to kiss me like that since about one minute after we met."

"Now you tell me," David replied. "Let's go find that chalet and register like the man said. Always obey orders even when they are issued by a blackmailer."

"Especially when they're from a blackmailer," Denise corrected. "Last one back to the car is lousy," she challenged and ran down the rock to the pathway with the agility of a gazelle.

The Neufsuzerain Gasthaus was a typical Central Switzerland mountain inn. Its roof was steep so that snow would not lie on it to rot the wooden shingles. It had an outer casing of weatherboards connecting a row of windows in each of its four upper stories. The windows were enclosed with shutters hinged at the top so that they opened vertically and were propped open with pine poles. However, the inn at Neufsuzerain had made a concession to convenience by combining the raised ground floor with the semisunken basement at the main entrance that opened out to a paved courtyard surrounded with a low wall. A half a dozen tables were already in the courtyard, covered with snow-white linen tablecloths and set with sterling silver cutlery and gleaming cut-crystal Zurich glasses.

The concierge of the Gasthaus told David that he was holding reservations for two singles. David looked at Denise. "Shall we go with the flow?" he asked her.

"Why not?" she said, scribbling out her registration card and signing her name with a flourish. "Nothing like a change of scenery."

David noticed the concierge looking around curiously for luggage.

"It's just a day reservation as far as we know," he told the concierge. "We expect to return to Zurich this afternoon." The face of the concierge cleared.

"Will there be lunch?"

"Yes, indeed," David told him. "Midday O.K.?"

"Whatever you say, sir. Shall I have the maid show you to your rooms?"

"Sure," David said.

"Are the rooms on the courtyard?" Denise asked.

"Naturally, madame," replied the concierge.

"David," Denise said, turning to him. "Why don't you sit in the sun and have a beer or a coffee while I slip into something comfortable?"

David's eyebrow shot up quizzically while he looked in disbelief at Denise's shoulderbag.

"You'd be surprised at what I have in here," she told him. "I was a Girl Guide. We're like the scouts. Always prepared."

When the concierge rang a counter bell, a plump little maid appeared, dressed in a black uniform with a white collar and a white cap perched on her short-cropped black hair. Denise followed the maid while David ordered a beer from the concierge and strolled out into the sunshine of the courtyard. He had his choice of tables and took one near the parapet with a view over the village, the cleft of sunken valley, and then the rolling hills toward the peak of the Zugerheim. The waiter brought his beer, and while he sipped it he thought of the delivery of the diamonds. As David figured it, sitting there in the brisk clear mountain air, his chances of nailing the blackmailers in this setting were remote. He had to admit that the choice of site for a drop was well-planned. Like everything else the bastards had done. Talk about a clockwork-precision operation. They would have him drop off the diamonds someplace visible to them, but where they were invisible to him. All they had to do then was wait until he drove off in the Lamborghini. Through binoculars they could watch him go down the sloping wall of the mountainside and, when he was far enough on his way, pick up the stones and get the hell out in the other direction. As far as David could judge, their plan was foolproof.

"Damn!" a feminine voice said quite clearly, interrupting David's reverie. He looked up to the facing wall of the Gasthaus, and almost straight overhead, standing at a wide-open window on the third story behind a window box thick with flowering geraniums, was Denise. She had taken off her scarf and dark glasses and had shaken her hair loose. The jacket of her pants suit was also missing. Otherwise she was fully dressed.

"Got a problem?" David called up softly. Looking slightly disheveled and altogether ravishing, Denise whispered back, "Bloody zipper's stuck, if you'll excuse the French."

"I'm on my way," David told her, standing up.

"It's 306," Denise warned. "If you get lost I shall poison your lunch. Happily."

David waved and walked across the courtyard into the lobby of the hotel. He had to admit to himself that his pulse was racing in anticipation. It was a good feeling. He was starting up the dark-oak staircase when he heard a cough from the desk. He looked across.

"Excuse me, sir," the concierge apologized, "but your key is here."

David replied, "So it is." He cupped his hands and the concierge tossed the key over to him. David caught it and continued on his way up the stairs.

"It's 305, sir," the concierge yelled after him.

"Thanks," David answered.

A thin runner of carpet ran down the third floor corridor. It did not prevent the floor from creaking noisily under David's feet. On an impulse he looked into 305. It was a cheerful room with a double bed and what looked like a comfortable, high-piled feather mattress. David told himself, I know where I'm going if her room has twin beds. He shut the door behind him and knocked on 306.

"Nobody here but us stuck zippers," Denise's voice called out to him. The thought struck David that he would never have picked Denise for a girl with this bubbling undercurrent of fun in her.

When he went inside 306 and closed the door the first thing that struck him was not Denise, but a huge fireplace where a small fire was crackling cheerfully.

"Now there's a sexy setting for you," he exclaimed to Denise.

"Zippers before sex, please," Denise pleaded.

"Sorry," David said.

He looked at her as he walked across the room and she seemed to be engaged in a futile attempt to strangle herself with her own arms as she made a last effort to clear the zipper.

David released her arms, kissed her on the tip of her nose and turned her around. Denise had slipped off her shoes. She had managed to get the zipper down as far as the band of her bra, where it had caught a thread and jammed tight. David flicked it forward to give it play, then ran it down

218

the full length of the turtleneck shirt. Denise wriggled her arms free, saying, "Wow! What a relief." Then she instinctively clutched the blouse to her breasts.

"Whoops," she breathed, "there's primitive puritan instinct for you."

Then she slowly loosened her grip and the blouse fluttered to the floor.

David felt his throat go dry and his breath shorten. His chest was tight. Somehow he was aware that Denise was changing as he watched her. The whites of her eyes were growing tawny with passion. Her breasts swelled under the taut bra. Neither of them was conscious of the brain-instructions that brought their arms around each other and opened their lips to let each of their tongues probe and push and feel deep inside the mouth of the other.

"I suppose they'll be waiting lunch," Denise said.

"I suppose so," David answered. His fingers found the hooks of her bra and slipped them from their sockets.

"But then . . ." Denise went on.

"The message did say . . ." David prompted.

". . . to wait for instructions," she concluded.

Denise's hands were busy loosening David's cravat and undoing the buttons of his shirt. She helped him out of his shirt and his athletic singlet.

"Besides . . ." Denise went on.

"Besides what?" David asked.

"Get the rest of your things off," she told him. "I have a surprise for you."

David sat on a chair to remove his slip-ons and his socks while Denise pulled down the coverings from a bed that was even more roomy than the one in David's room. She stood in front of the fireplace with her hands at her waist as David undid the waistband of his trousers.

"Tra la!" Denise trilled, and with a single movement she wriggled out of her pants to reveal that she was quite naked underneath. David stood holding his trousers with his mouth open. He knew that this single moment was worth a lifetime. Her right hand was flung high, her left palm outward on her hip. Her long blond hair framed her face and dropped down until it almost screened her taut nipples. Her body curved inward to narrow at her navel and then filled out again into slim hips. Above her vagina glowed a golden triangle of pubic hair, a deeper gold than the hair on her head. Her legs from hips to ankles were slim and shapely and strong.

"You're just too beautiful for words," David told her. And he meant it.

His trousers dropped in a pool at his feet but he had difficulty removing his jockey shorts over the strong thrust of his penis. Denise ran over to help him.

"Don't hurt him," she scolded. "He's beautiful." When the shorts were gone, she dropped to one knee and fondled his organ, then began to embrace it with her mouth until it was swollen and distended to the point of explosion.

She felt his hands tugging at her shoulders and knew that it was time to slow down, but she was reluctant to leave the phallus behind and understood why once it had been a god to the goddesses who had spawned her. Then David was lifting her to her feet, carrying her and laying her down on the puffed feather mattress—crosswise so that her hips were at the edge of the bed. He spread her legs and bent over her, searching for her swollen

vulva with his distended penis. Her hands went
down to guide him inside. There was only an instant of resistance, for her lubrication was well-ad-
vanced. He drew her body to him so that he could
stand while she lay on the bed, and they pressured
against each other until her clitoris and sheath demanded more and still more and her body on the
bed was a writhing snake of voracious sexual
desire. David thought of his car and the winding
hairpin bends and the surge of power when he
demanded speed and held himself strong until her
writhing turned to a sobbing moaning shuddering
effusion of delight underneath him. Then without
breaking their union he lowered himself onto the
bed, lifting up her legs to follow him until they
were both comfortable. Gradually he moved faster
until his own tension increased to the point of explosion and he rolled over on his back and she was
straddling him. Only then did he give in to the ultimate ecstasy that left every part of his body except his thrusting penis locked in a rigidity that
was steel-like and growl his satisfaction from the
depths of his being.

Tight in each other's arms and still genitally
linked, David and Denise drifted into sleep. It
lasted only a few minutes and they awoke re-
freshed almost simultaneously. Denise separated
from David, found a comfortable position on her
back and looked at the old timbered ceiling.

"David?" she asked softly.

"Uh huh?"

"If you promise not to look at me, I'd like to tell
you about myself now."

"Too lazy to look," he assured her. "Go ahead."

Her fingers fiddled with the edge of the rough

linen sheet and she had difficulty putting her thoughts into words. "You think I am well-born, you know, born with a silver spoon in my mouth and all that sort of thing. It isn't true. My father died ... in a charity ward ... after cadging drinks from friends all over Europe. Mother got me through school. Somehow. When she died I was fifteen and penniless. The nuns said they would let me stay on in the convent. When I was eighteen I ran away . . ." Denise was reliving every minute of her unhappy youth. "I got some jobs. As a model, that is. I managed to pay for some singing and acting lessons in London. That was when I met Lord Esherbridge. He was easy to love. Handsome. Decent. I knew he was married but I didn't care ... am I shocking you?"

"No, not at all. Any girl would take the chance, seems to me."

She squeezed his arm gratefully. "Well, you could write the script from then on. The Riviera. Monte Carlo Rallyes. The Battle of the Mimosa. Sheikhs in Sardinia. Winter sports in Austria. It was the most marvelous time in my whole life."

She sat up, propped herself against her pillow and went on. "I was young, silly, ingenuous. He never said it but I actually thought he was going to divorce his wife and marry me. Then he explained it was impossible. His wife was a duchess or something and controlled the money or the castle or something—I forget which. Perhaps it was the title. Anyhow it was something vital to a man in his position who wanted to keep it."

"Tough!" David murmured sympathetically.

"Not really," she laughed. "I was only fooling myself. About getting married, I mean. Actually he was extremely generous. Insisted on giving me a settlement and an allowance through his numbered account with Hurtilbank. It was sort of supposed to be our love-nest egg against the day he could finally marry me. I had power of attorney ... Here's the worst part," she told David honestly.

"I'm unshockable," David said.

"Well, you asked for it. I was young enough to think I knew more about money than anybody else. I went to dear old Mr. Hurtil and asked him to help me invest it. You know what I thought?"

"What did you think?"

"I thought: This looks easy. I'll invest Jamey's money, double it, give him back the original and go my merry way solo. It was awful."

"How come?" David wanted to know.

"Oh, I could blame Hurtil's advice, I suppose. None of the investments were any good. I lost every penny. But it was my own fault. I never should have done it. I'm determined to pay it all back."

"Sure you are," David told her. "And you will."

"When this blackmail threat came I was terrified. Really more frightened than I have ever been in my life. You see, they threatened to reveal the account I share with Lord Esherbridge to the press in England. You can imagine what that would do to Jamey. He's in the Cabinet. Everybody says he has a fine future. There's talk he will be Prime Minister one day. You know what the stuffy English are like. They would demand his resignation from the Cabinet straight away. They'd dig up everything about us and his giving me money. I couldn't let it happen. I'd kill myself first."

"It's a very human story," David told her.

"I know—well, I don't know about human. Adolescent is more like it. I still adore Jamey—Lord Esherbridge, that is ... but just as a friend. I was a baby when it happened. Such a baby. It was over long ago. Can you ever forgive me, David, for being such a fool?" Her eyes were limpid with appeal, pleading with him for understanding.

"What's to forgive?" David answered. "If you had not been such a fool when you were young I might not have found you when you were grown up."

He reached over and kissed her on the nipple. She squealed and bounded out of bed with her hand to her mouth. She dropped her voice. "Let's eat," she begged. "I'm starved."

They ate on the terrace outside the Gasthaus. A slight afternoon breeze had sprung up, but it was not enough to make the terrace uncomfortable and neither David nor Denise wished to miss one iota of the joy of this unexpected pleasure along the way of business. They started with a light mushroom consommé and followed the soup with two enormous Berner Platte—a gluttonous serving of bacon, sausages, ham, boiled beef, Sauerkraut, potatoes and green beans, washed down with a large carafe of a heady sparkling white Colombier from Neuchâtel. By the end of the meal they were giggly with the combination of food and wine and love and altitude, and the slightest remark from one seemed to the other excruciatingly humorous and brought on a paroxysm of laughter.

Yet the inevitable had to come. Even from the first moment the waiter stepped onto the terrace with a silver coffee service on a heavy silver tray, their laughter died. Then their eyes focused on the familiar white vellum envelope. The waiter prepared the coffee while they sat in brooding silence. Then he picked up the tray and presented the envelope to David.

"*M'sieur?*"

"Must I?" David asked Denise.

"I wish ..." Denise answered. Then sighed, "I suppose you must, David."

David picked up the envelope from the tray. It was addressed in the now ominous red felt script:

MR. DAVID CHRISTOPHER
WITH COFFEE

"This letter ... who delivered it?" David asked the waiter.

"A Swiss servant, *m'sieur,*" the waiter answered him respectfully. "This morning ... with instructions to deliver it to you with your coffee."

"Thank you," David said to the waiter, slitting the envelope with a clean knife.

"Will that be all, sir?" the waiter asked.

"Uh huh," David replied, already deep in the letter.

"The instructions?" Denise asked.

"Yes, damn them," David answered angrily.

"What's the matter, darling?" Denise asked him.

"The bastards. The lousy bastards. I'm damned ..."

"What is it, David? What's wrong?"

"They insist that you must deliver the diamonds. Make the final drop, that is."

"Oh," she answered in a small voice.

"I'll see them damned first," David told her.

"I'm not afraid," Denise told him.

"I am."

"Darling, let's face it. If they mean to kill me does it make any difference whether I am waiting for you in the car or delivering the diamonds. Really?"

"I—suppose—not," David admitted grudgingly.

She patted his arm. "All right then. Now let's enjoy our coffee. Then you can pay the bill while I tidy myself up and collect my bag. Relax and enjoy it. In twenty minutes it will be all over and you and I will be on our way back to Zurich. Please?"

With Denise's blue eyes, sun-drenched hair and lovely face appealing to him, what could David do? He nodded and tried to smile, but inside himself he knew trouble when he smelt it.

The hunter was wearing a tweed coat with leather patches on the elbows and a hunting cap. Leaning against a rock beside him was his rifle. It was fitted with a telescopic sight. It looked like a deadly weapon. The hunter might have been searching for game with a pair of powerful zoom lensed Zeiss binoculars but in actual fact he was focused on a pale-gold Lamborghini leaving the Gasthaus at Neufsuzerain. The man was driving the car and the girl beside him called out instructions from a map or piece of paper she was holding in her hands. As it happened, the man was well positioned to follow the Lamborghini. He had taken a chance on its course and was relieved to find that he had guessed it correctly.

The Lamborghini turned off from the paved roadway into a lane winding toward the hunter. The lane was a dead-end track finishing in an open pasture on the edge of a valley that was almost a canyon. The valley was rimmed by broken rocky ledges and clumps of stunted firs that could have sheltered a small army. The floor of the canyon was thick with a forest of pines. When the hunter swept the valley with his binoculars he could see that a narrow pathway entered the pine forest from the pasture and emerged again in a small clearing. In the center of the clearing there was a cairn of stones.

The man and the woman got out of the car and seemed to argue for a while before the man reluctantly handed a small pouch to the woman. She turned and walked down into the pine forest. The hunter guessed her destination, but he waited to make sure. His binoculars picked up the scarfed head of the girl as she entered the small clearing. She ran to the cairn of stones, climbed until her hand could reach the top, and then she dropped the pouch into a hole at the pinnacle of the cairn. When she had done this the girl stumbled back off the heavy stones at the foot of the cairn and ran back toward the open field where the car was waiting for her.

This was all the man needed. He encased his binoculars, picked up his rifle and, at a quick, sure trot, ran through the trees toward the cairn of stones below him.

If the message had not said that Denise would be shot if she did not deliver the diamonds in person, David would have done the job himself and be damned the blackmailers. As it was he waited at the car fuming with anxiety and impatience, hoping that she would be all right. Then he remembered the binoculars in his trunk. Cursing himself as a blundering idiot, he took the keys from the ignition, opened the trunk and took out the binoculars. Slamming the trunk, he threw the keys onto the driver's seat and began to make broad sweeps of the rocky ledges with the glasses. Gradually he slowed himself down until he was really seeing the individual trees and the sharp outlines of the rocks. He was about to give up when he saw the man in the tweed coat and the hunting cap, carrying a rifle, cutting across the edge of the canyon slope on a diagonal that was obviously leading to the cairn of stones.

David was in an agony of indecision. The instructions had ordered him to stay put and then to get out, but Denise was down there and every second brought the man with the rifle closer to her. Finally he said, "The hell with it." He leaned into the car, dropped his binoculars beside the keys on the seat, took out his .38 from under the plastic pouch filled with his automobile papers and ran toward the pine forest. He met Denise at the edge of the forest, running toward him. When she saw him her face lit up with relief.

"Oh, David, it's finished. I did it."

He took hold of her arm and steered her away from him. "Run to the car," he ordered her peremptorily. "Put up the windows and keep down. If you hear shots, drive like hell for Neufsuzerain and see if you can find help. Any help."

"What's the matter? The instructions said—"

"Run," he told her savagely.

One look at his face told her not to argue. She turned and scuttled toward the car like a scared rabbit.

David turned and, with his gun ready, pushed his way down the path as quietly as he could, stopping to listen for the sounds of the hunter. His footsteps were quite audible, crackling through the underbrush on the twigs and pine needles, still obviously heading for the cairn of stones. Christopher ran as hard as he could until he came to the edge of the small clearing. If it came to a shootout, it was better to give himself time for a breather at the shooting end. He crouched low and could hear the hunter thrashing his way toward the center of the ravine. Finally he appeared, at a sharp angle to David, perhaps eight o'clock to David's six o'clock. The hunter looked around carefully. David could hear his breathing. Then he rushed into the clearing toward the cairn of stones, dropped his rifle at the base, and began to climb.

David made his run as the hunter's hand went into the hole at the brim of the mound and came out with the bag of gems. He covered the last six feet in a diving tackle, taking the man around the waist and dragging him down to the ground. The man rolled, taking David with him, but he could not shake David off until his elbow came back sharply into David's stomach. David loosened his grip enough for the man to turn. At the same time they both struggled to their feet, fists ready.

It was only then that David recognized his opponent. "Captain Hans Frey," David exclaimed bitterly. "You goddamned son-of-a-bitch fool. You've fucked up everything."

IX

Hurtilbank President Johann Hurtil could not believe what David and Denise were telling him.

"You mean the whole ransom payment was aborted?"

They nodded agreement.

"By this Captain Frey?"

"That's right," David affirmed.

Hurtil colored with anger. "Blunderer, fool, that Frey is. Or worse, the extortionist himself. Did you ever think of that?"

They were standing in Hurtil's office on each side of the president's desk. Between Hurtil beside his chair and David and Denise opposite him, lay the chamois bag of uncut diamonds. The bag was open and some of the diamonds had spilled onto the dark-blue leather of the desktop.

"The extortionist himself?" David echoed.

Hurtil took a pipe from his rack and waved it at David.

"Why not? He is in charge of the Zurich Bank

Detail. In that capacity ... by George, I think I've got it." The elderly president was excited by his thought.

"You see a solution?" David asked.

Hurtil gestured again at David and Denise with his pipe, using it like a conductor's baton. "Tell me—who knows the names that go with these numbers on the secret accounts?" Denise looked at David as he thought over the question before he replied. "You. Florelle. Benninger. That's about it." He looked up at Hurtil. The old man smiled back triumphantly.

"You've missed something. The most important of all."

"I have?" David asked. Instinctively his hand went to his chin and he searched his memory. The flash came to him from his first night in Hurtilbank. "By God," David exclaimed, "you could be right."

Hurtil nodded his head, his eyes gleaming. "You see. We all of us overlooked it."

Denise looked from one to the other in perplexity. "Somebody tell me," she demanded. "What are you talking about?"

"There is a copy of the master list of the names that go with secret numbered accounts in each bank ..." David began.

"At the Federal Treasury in Berne," Hurtil concluded. "Now tell me this, my dear. If anybody could get at that list in Berne who might it be?"

"The—I suppose—well, you mean Frey?"

"That's exactly who I mean. As head of the Zurich Police Bank Detail . . ."

"It's against the law," Denise objected.

"That's right," David agreed.

Hurtil was crestfallen. "Well . . . that may be

true . . . but . . ." Hurtil brightened up again. "Perhaps he did it unofficially. Bribed somebody in Berne. As Head of Bank Detail, Frey would surely know the people responsible."

Denise put her hand on the edge of the desk to steady herself.

"Are you O.K.?" David asked her anxiously.

"I'll be fine," she answered.

Hurtil was chagrined at his own thoughtlessness. He came around the desk to Denise. "My dear Mlle. Abbott. You must forgive my inexcusable lapse of manners. I did not even ask you to sit down. Could I give you sherry? coffee? a little whisky?"

Denise was pale, seemed not herself. "Perhaps we girls are the weaker sex after all. It's been rather a traumatic day for me. If you men will excuse me I just want to go back to my hotel, take a tub and rest for a while. You don't need me, do you?"

"Of course not," Hurtil reassured her.

"Can I drop you?" David asked.

"Don't be silly, darling," Denise answered. "I'll pick up a taxi at the door."

She kissed David lightly on the cheek, but her eyes were rich with memory and promise. Then she put her arm in Hurtil's while he showed her to the elevator.

On his way back to join David, Hurtil had a word with Anna, his secretary. Then he insisted that David sit down and fixed him a scotch on the rocks. Hurtil poured vodka for himself, straight without a mix, and while he was in the bar, told David, "I've had a thought and I asked Anna to check it out. I just don't like the way this Frey always seems to be under our feet. Did he say why he was at Neufsuzerain? What was his explanation?"

David sipped his scotch appreciatively. "He said an anonymous tip."

"Did you believe him?" Hurtil asked as he returned to his desk with his drink and sat down.

David shook his head. "Frankly, no."

"What other explanation is there?"

"I'm pretty sure he has a twenty-four-hour tail on me," David answered. He thought about that morning. "Then again I did some pretty fancy driving just before I took off—to shake off a possible tail." David clicked his fingers. "Traffic 'copter. Damn. I never thought of that. Frey could have had the traffic chopper spot me clear through to Sihibrugg. While I was waiting for instructions at the Gasthaus . . . sure, he had a couple of hours to run me down."

Hurtil's intercom buzzed and he picked up his receiver to listen to Anna. "I suspected as much," Hurtil said when he put down the phone.

"What is it?" David asked.

"Frey has a brother . . . the name was familiar and I asked Anna to check."

"Who's the brother?"

"A fellow called Armand Frey. He is a Zurich-born Swiss who lives in Paris. A dealer in international bonds . . . and other things. They say it doesn't matter what you want to buy or sell. Armand is willing to act for you—for a twenty percent commission."

David clapped his hand to his head. "Damn!" he said. "I clean forgot. That Armand Frey. He was trying to contact his brother urgently yesterday. They called my room."

"You see," Hurtil answered. "That proves it."

234

"I still don't see what the Freys stand to gain?"

"How do you mean?" Hurtil asked him. The president put down his drink and began to push the diamonds back into the chamois bag. David had only his glass to wave, so he waved it.

"Let us assume for the sake of discussion that your theory is correct—that Frey and his brother are in this together. What is the purpose of the blackmail gambit? Is it just those?" David pointed with his glass at the pouch of gems.

Hurtil drew the thong tight at the mouth of the bag, stood up and went over to his bookcase to deposit the stones in his wall safe. He did not reply until he had closed the safe and returned the section of books to its place. Turning to David, he put his thought to him. "This is probably going to sound farfetched to you, but my theory is this: If Hans Frey is half as shrewd as his brother, Armand, they're playing both ends against the middle."

"In what sense?"

"They'll take the money for a start. After all, they would already have it, if you had not acted with such dispatch this afternoon."

"And then?"

"Then the policeman Frey will expose the blackmail attempt on Hurtilbank to the press."

"That would make sense," David mused. "It would certainly be the ideal way to cover himself."

Hurtil pressed his point. "Oh, it's much more than that," he told David. "Much more. When the story reaches the public through the newspapers, our worst fears will be realized. There will be at least a short-term run on Hurtilbank. Perhaps on all Swiss banks. Swiss currency will be depressed, at least temporarily, in the world markets. Do you see the plan?"

"Frankly, no. What plan?"

Hurtil spread his hands. "I'm sorry. I'm going too fast. I'm taking it for granted . . . You know what futures are?"

"Vaguely," David told him. "Sort of buy-now-pay-later deal, isn't it?"

"In a way," Hurtil told him. "Let us suppose Armand Frey in Paris orders ten million United States dollars today, payable in ten days' time in Swiss francs. The number of Swiss francs he owes on this transaction is, say, twenty-five million, no matter what the value of the Swiss franc is, in ten days' time. You follow?"

"I'm with you now," David said. "He gambles on the market."

"Exactly. Now when the blackmail story causes the Swiss franc to plummet in value, Armand Frey is still required to pay only twenty-five million devalued Swiss francs for his ten million American dollars or Eurodollars. By that time, however, the ten million dollars are worth say thirty or thirty-five or even forty million Swiss francs."

David whistled. "A couple of telephone calls and he makes himself five or ten million Swiss francs?"

"If his gamble pays off, yes."

"And the Freys believe in hedging their bets with a little blackmail on the side," David suggested.

"Give me a better solution," Hurtil challenged. The president stood up and went to the bar. "A refill?" he asked.

David joined him at the bar. "Just a short one," he said. He handed Hurtil his glass. "Is there any way we can check this out?"

236

"How is that?" Hurtil wanted to know.

"There must be some kind of list someplace," David explained, "of people who bought big on currency futures this week. Could you check it out?"

Hurtil glanced up at a handsome electronic wall-clock. The red figures showed 6:30 P.M.

"The exchanges are closed, of course. It could take time. But let me try. There are one or two people I might call." Hurtil returned to his desk.

"While you're doing that," David told him, "let me call my assistant in Geneva. I have not checked in all day."

"Use my phone, then . . ." Hurtil began.

"Not at all," David refused. "Anna and I are old friends."

David went in to the outer office where there was a telephone on a coffee table for the convenience of clients waiting to see the president. He told Anna what he needed.

"Let me dial her for you," Anna offered. "You sit in the easy chair and I'll connect you." Anna used her switchboard dial to get through to Geneva, told Corinne Mr. Christopher was calling, and nodded to David to take the call.

"Corinne?"

Her voice came through cautious, careful. "You're at the bank?"

"That's right."

"I'll be a model of propriety," she told him. "What's cooking?"

"Sorry I couldn't get through to you earlier. It's been a helluva day. I left at dawn and just got back."

"My heart bleeds for you. O.K., you can't talk, so I will. About this Jensen dame?"

237

"That's the one."

"You caught yourself a weirdo this time."

"How come?"

"One of the assignments her father had—besides all the others, that is—was German Ambassador to Ethiopia. Abyssinia that was, you know?"

"So?"

"Apparently she got herself into bed with a handsome army officer down there—"

"Happens all the time."

"Yeah. Except that this young West Point-type grew up to be a member of the Supreme Progressive Council of Ethiopia."

"That sounds like a tidbit for the cocktail circuit, but I fail ..."

"Damn it, boss, will you shut up and let me finish?"

"O.K. I'm listening. I'm sorry."

Mollified, Corinne went on with her story. "This Rita Jensen was apparently part of the revolution all the way. She is now an Ethiopian citizen. The gossip is—hold your hat—she is a kind of ambassador-at-large for Ethiopia. She packs plenty punch with the present government . . ."

"Any special job?" David asked her.

Corinne waited before replying.

"What's the matter?" David insisted.

"Well, Chris, I don't know about this one. Freddy said it was just a wild rumor."

"Give it to me, damn it."

"The story is, her job is to run down Haile Selassie's gold and get hold of it for the new government. Sounds crazy to me. That's Arabian Nights stuff and your Rita is Scheherazade—are you still there, Chris? Say something. Speak to me, my darling."

"I'm thinking," David said.

Her voice held relief. "Thank God," she answered. "I thought Anna must have turned on the vacuum cleaner. Anything else, or may I go home to my starving husband and adorable children?"

"Go home," David said magnanimously, "but just remember when you're lounging around the apartment, being waited on by your husband and children, that some of us have to go on working."

David quietly cradled the receiver on Corinne's reply. He thought it was unfair to the switchboard at Hurtilbank to subject it to the strain. He stood up, pleased with himself, just as the door of Hurtil's office swung open. Hurtil stood there. Not the composed aristocrat familiar to David, but a man with disheveled hair and wild eyes.

"Christopher? Where are you?"

David rushed to the door and followed Hurtil inside, slamming the door on the bewildered Anna. Hurtil was standing with one hand supporting himself on his desk. He was breathing unevenly and his face was pallid and waxen.

"What's the matter, sir?" David asked him. "Here, you must sit down."

"Something terrible," Hurtil muttered. "Too terrible for words. Just too terrible to believe." He allowed David to seat him in an easy chair from which he stared blindly ahead of him.

"Whisky?" David asked. He did not really know what to do. Hurtil did not hear him.

"You were right," he said at length in a low voice.

"I was?" David replied. He did not know where or when he had been right in this senseless whirlpool of conflicting evidence.

"A large order for currency was placed today. At

a minute to five. Just before the exchanges closed."

"What sort of currency?"

"Marks and dollars. Twenty-five or thirty million dollars' worth."

"Payable in Swiss futures?"

"Yes."

David sat down or, rather, slumped into a seat. This was a topsy-turvy world to which he did not belong. "So it is the Freys?" he said.

"Not the Freys. Not the Freys," Hurtil said.

"Who then?" David asked incredulously. There was a long pause and David could hear Hurtil's labored breathing. When the answer came he could not hear it. "Speak up, Herr Hurtil, please. Who placed the order?"

"Hurtilbank." The words sounded ridiculous in the office of the president of the bank.

"Hurtilbank?" David croaked. "Hurtilbank! Who in Hurtilbank?"

Before Hurtil answered David knew what he was going to say. "Franz Benninger, my executive vice-president."

Rita Jensen walked into the restaurant at the Hauptbahnhof and looked around. The *maître d'hôtel* hurried to her side.

"For one, madame?" he asked her.

"I'm meeting a friend," Rita answered curtly. "I believe he is already here."

"Of course, madame. Why don't you look around?"

Rita thanked him and went forward into the restaurant. An arm lifted and she saw Franz Benninger in a far corner. She thought to herself that that was Franz, careful to the nth degree.

Benninger stood to greet her and a waiter hur-

ried across to seat her in a chair opposite Franz.
Then he stood by attentively waiting for her to
order.

"What will you have?" Benninger asked her.

"Oh, just a campari soda for now."

Benninger nodded to the waiter, who retired to
the bar to pick up the drink.

"I'm all ears," she said. "You have some news already?"

"I don't know about news," he said. "It was just
a conglomeration of circumstances and I decided
to take a first step." Benninger paused to let the
waiter set down Rita's drink.

"Cheers," she said.

He lifted his own vermouth in response and they
drank.

"Tell me." Rita put her hand on his arm. "I can't
tell you how grateful we all are for this . . . but I
promise I'll try. Later on, tonight."

Benninger knitted his brow. "It's been a very
busy day. You phoned me at midday to let me
know that Addis Ababa was giving us one hundred
percent support and the papers would be on their
way to Rome this afternoon for transfer to us. At
the afternoon fixing gold unexpectedly jumped almost five dollars an ounce. I seized the opportunity
to put about thirty million dollars' worth up for
sale. Your gold, I mean."

Rita clapped her hands. "Oh, Franz, that's
wonderful."

"That was only the beginning," he said. "I took
Swiss francs for the gold. Then I began to worry.
You know there is something . . . ?"

"David Christopher? The secret accounts? Did
you find them?"

"On the contrary," Benninger confided. He looked at her. "Rita . . . ?"

"Franz," she chided him. "If I let you down on this, after what you are doing for our country, I deserve to be horsewhipped. Really."

"I know," he said, "I know. It's just . . . well, to-day Christopher left with one of the people being blackmailed, to make the payment to the black-mailers . . . in a little town south of here."

"Something went wrong?" she asked anxiously.

Benninger took a mouthful of his vermouth be-fore he could reply. "Worse than that. The police were there. I don't know exactly what happened, but Christopher telephoned Hurtil from the village and said he was on his way back with the di-amonds and the full story."

"How does that affect us?" Rita wanted to know.

Benninger twisted his swizzle stick until it broke in his hands. "It probably does not affect us at all," he said, "unless our worst fears are realized. It de-pends on how much the police found out."

"I don't see . . ." Rita began.

Benninger interrupted her. "It's a long, long story. Too long to explain now. Our fear is that if the police get on to this blackmail attempt on Hur-tilbank, then it will leak to the newspapers. There will be a scandal. The net effect could be a run on the reserves in Swiss banks. People withdrawing their funds. It could mean at least a temporary de-valuation of the Swiss franc."

"I think I am beginning to get the story," Rita said, and now there was real fear in her eyes. "Is there anything we can do?"

"I have already done it," Benninger told her.

"You have? But there was no time . . ."

"If you act fast, there is time," Benninger said, a little too smugly.

"Franz, you thought of something?"

"I did something. Just before the exchanges closed I converted all your francs into marks and dollars."

"God, Franz, what can I say?"

"I don't know what you can say. What I can say is that if the worst comes to the worst and this blackmail thing does get into the newspapers with the results we fear, Ethiopia is going to make a lot of money in ten days' time."

"You gambled on futures?" she gasped.

"It isn't a gamble for you," he told her. "Just for me and for Hurtilbank and for Switzerland."

"Oh, Franz." Rita could not say any more, but the quick tears showed her feelings. She dabbed her eyes with a small lace handkerchief she took from her purse.

"Another drink?" Benninger asked her.

She shook her head. "I'll have some wine with our food." While he called the waiter and ordered another vermouth for himself, Rita stirred her drink thoughtfully. "Franz?" she asked.

"Yes?"

"I've been thinking, too. During the day. Nothing as dramatic as what you have been doing, but I'd like to make a suggestion."

"Go ahead."

"Franz, I think you have to tell this David Christopher what you are doing."

"I am afraid . . ."

"Afraid of what?"

"Oh, afraid he will misunderstand."

Rita let irritation creep into her voice. "That is so—so typically male, Franz. You're so brilliant in

243

solving my problem and so stupid when it comes to protecting yourself. Don't you see? He already misunderstands. He will go on misunderstanding until he knows the truth."

"You think so?" Benninger asked her.

"I know so," she replied in exasperation. "Look, Christopher is a clever man. He suspects you are blackmailing the bank. Suppose he builds a case against you? Suppose he concludes that you are responsible? You could be charged, go to jail . . . it could be terrible, Franz. You have to call him."

"You mean now?"

"I mean now."

"But . . ."

"Make it easy on yourself. Tell him to come to the station. To meet you here. Say at the information desk in the main lobby. As quickly as he can get here. Hurry, Franz, or it might be too late. At this very moment he could be telling Herr Hurtil that you are the one responsible for the blackmail."

Benninger did not need any further prodding. Anxiety in his eyes, he went to look for a telephone.

President Johann Hurtil looked gratefully at David Christopher. Strengthened by a shot of scotch whisky, comforted by a stream of reassuring clichés from David, their substance being that there could be some other explanation of what Benninger had done and that he might have been acting in the interests of Hurtilbank, Hurtil had pulled himself somewhat together. Now he was ready to leave the bank and return to his home believing that only David had made it possible for him to get through the evening.

The intercom buzzed.

"Yes, Anna?" Hurtil said into the phone.

"Herr Franz Benninger for David Christopher," Anna told him. Hurtil put his hand over the speaker.

"It's Benninger," he told David, "for you."

"See what I mean?" David spoke as cheerfully as he could. "That doesn't sound like a guilty man, does it?" David took the phone from Hurtil while Anna put Benninger through to him.

"Mr. Christopher?" Benninger asked.

"Speaking."

"Could I meet you? I think we should talk. It's very important."

"Where are you?" David asked him.

"I'm at the Hauptbahnhof. I could meet you at the information counter. With a mutual friend."

"Fine. I'll be there in ten minutes."

David put down the receiver. "I'm meeting him at the railroad station right away. He says it's important."

Hurtil threw his topcoat and hat onto a chair. "In that case," he said, "I'll stay on until I hear from you."

"There's no need," David began.

"I'll phone my wife," Hurtil reassured him. "I would prefer to clear this matter up if we can. I must say it has been quite a shock to me."

"Expect to hear from me in a half hour or so," David promised. "I'll call you from the Hauptbahnhof."

In the dusk on the Bahnhofstrasse Big Lug's soldiers waited patiently for David Christopher to finish his interviews in Hurtilbank. They had changed their green Mercedes for a black one that was boldly parked only three cars away from the Lamborghini. This time they were taking no

chances. Murdoch sat in the car, north of the bank.
Johnson was playing the tourist south of the bank,
where he pretended great interest in the Burkliplatz park. The bastard pig in the green Peugeot
was still floating around, but they gambled that he
was too busy watching the fink Christopher, to be
aware of them. Tonight had to be it. Big Lug was
getting nervous back in Chicago and questioning
their qualifications for this job or any other that
Luigi Valente Associates might be offering. Murdoch and Johnson knew what that meant. A one-
way trip into the central section of Lake Michigan.

When Christopher exited the bank he did so on
the run. He U-turned the Lamborghini and shot
away like he knew he was due to be burned.
Johnson got back to Murdoch as fast as he could
without being too obvious and joined him in the
Merk. Murdoch had the engine running and was
spinning the car to U-turn and follow Christopher
before Johnson had closed the door.

"Watch it," Johnson snarled. He slammed the
door. "Do you think he's on to us again?"

"Nah! Not a chance," Murdoch answered. "He's
got a meet on. Good for us, if we don't lose him.
He'll be a sitting duck."

David made the Hauptbahnhof in five and a half
minutes, leaving behind him a number of scared
pedestrians, two fuming bus drivers and five
shaken homeward-bound businessmen. Although
Murdoch and Johnson were a minute slower, a
combination of luck and desperation gave them a
glimpse of the Lamborghini disappearing into the
underground parking lot beneath the giant railroad
station.

"That place looks like the Field Museum in Chi,"

Johnson groaned. "We could lose him in there for a week."

"Maybe not," Murdoch said, easing the Mercedes into the Bahnhof Platz lane for entrance to the parking station. "People in railroad stations always make a meet under the big clock or at the information desk. It's a tradition. Any case, we lose him we wait at his car. Either way we got him."

David followed the crowd through the smart shopping plazas until he found his way to the immensity of the main concourse. He located the information desk and moved toward it, watching out for Benninger and Rita in the crowd of passengers and porters, tourists and commuters. He was a couple of minutes early, David realized, and the precise little banker would no doubt time his arrival to within seconds of the scheduled rendezvous. He picked up a folder on Zurich from the information counter and read about *"Zurich bei Nacht."* Zurich by night for the tourist seemed to consist mainly of folk music and pretty girl acrobats in fashionable nightclubs.

Glancing around again to look for Benninger, David spotted the two gunmen across the lobby. On the first sweep he did not stop, but there was something about the light topcoats, the hats drawn low over the eyes, the right hands in the topcoat pockets, and their too-casual efforts to take advantage of the screen of a passing porter with a four-wheeled cart piled high with luggage, that sounded a warning. The hairs on the back of David's neck prickled. He carefully held up the brochure with his left hand while his right hand moved inside his jacket to his shoulder holster to remove the .38. There was a mutual instant of recognition as Murdoch and Johnson knew that

David had seen them and drew their guns. In one
unbelievable action-packed second David dropped
to his knee, Benninger walked across to David with
his hand outstretched in greeting and a smile of
welcome on his face, and Murdoch and Johnson
each fired twice. Two of the bullets ploughed into
Benninger's back at chest level. Rita screamed—a
scream that froze every person in the lobby of the
Hauptbahnhof in a flash photograph of fear. The
smile of welcome on Benninger faded into perplexity and pain before he fell forward into David's
waiting arms.

Pandemonium broke loose in the Hauptbahnhof. People ran, but they did not know from what.
Others imitated Rita and began to scream, at what
they did not know. A few of the brave or foolish or
sympathetic ran toward Benninger. David did not
know what to do. He could not drop a man who
might be dying. Neither did he want the killers to
escape. In desperation he shouted in a huge voice
that momentarily squelled the babel of voices.

"Stop Killers! Stop Murderers!"

His gun pointed toward Murdoch and Johnson.
A few heads turned uncertainly. Then, as if by
miracle, from nowhere, Frey and Schwand appeared on the run, trying to get the picture. David
would have bet the chamois pouch of uncut diamonds against the idea that there could possibly
be a set of circumstances in which he would be
glad to see Frey, but now he looked up in relief.

"Frey," he roared. "Here."

Frey and Schwand pushed their way through the
growing body of curious citizens.

"What happened?" Frey asked.

"He needs an ambulance, Schwand." David
turned over the unconscious body of Benninger to

the astonished Schwand. "Come on," he urged Frey, grabbing his arm. "Do you have a gun?"

For answer Frey put his hand inside his waist to reveal a wicked-looking German handgun.

"Those two killers," David panted while they pounded across the concrete-slab floor, "went for me. Hit Benninger. Heading for the garage, I think. Must have trailed me from the bank."

While people looked at them in astonishment, Frey and David turned from the lobby into a brightly lit plaza of shops offering watches, cameras, fashionable leather goods, nuts and candy. Ahead of them they could just make out Johnson and Murdoch running for the garage stairwell.

"Stop. Police," Frey yelled.

For answer Johnson flattened himself against the wall at the head of the parking stairs and fired a quick shot back toward his pursuers. David and Frey, anticipating the shot, split toward the shop windows. The bullet hit a plate-glass window beyond them at the corridor.

"Take the stairs," Frey told David. "There's a staff elevator. I'll try to head them off."

Frey disappeared down a narrow side-corridor while David ran at full speed to the parking stairwell. He might have chanced a quick shot at the back of Johnson, but there were people using the stairs in both directions and the risk was too great. David increased his pace, taking the stairs three and four at a time. By the time the two soldiers reached the garage entrance, David was getting too close for comfort. Johnson tried to take another shot, but a bullet from David's .38 pinged into the heavy concrete wall and he pushed through the garage entrance on the heels of Murdoch.

The door swung to just as David reached it. He had a split second to make up his mind. Yelling to the stragglers on the stairs to keep back, he pulled open the door, dropped to his knees, and crawled through to the other side. A shot whistled over his head, but David was shielded by a car. Suddenly he heard the welcome voice of Frey shouting, "Throw down your guns. It's the police." The answer from Murdoch and Johnson was to shoot it out, but now they were in between their pursuers. A shot from Frey hit Murdoch in the side of the face, the heavy slug tore its way through the facial tissue and bone, taking teeth and jaw before it exited through the far side of the skull. David got Johnson in the carotid artery, and the astonished thug dropped his gun and watched his own blood spurt out his life. He dropped to the ground trying to get his hands to his throat to stop the blood-flow.

David and Frey walked slowly forward to meet each other.

"Why would they not surrender?" asked Frey in some astonishment, returning his gun to its holster.

"No point," David said. "If you didn't execute them, their boss in Chicago would."

"You seem sure of yourself, Herr Christopher, as always."

"Check out their papers, Frey, if you like. One of my employers is dying back there. I've got to get going."

David turned and ran back toward the concourse. Frey was about to stop him, but changed his mind. Instead he went to a garage office while startled attendants came out from cover and peered at where the shooting had taken place. Frey identified himself and asked for the telephone.

David was impressed with the efficiency of the Zurich police and hospital services. By the time he returned to the main concourse of the Hauptbahnhof, stretcher-bearers were already carrying the body of Benninger to a waiting vehicle they had driven right into the station itself. Shocked almost to distraction, Rita accompanied him. David tried to give her a quick word of comfort and told her he would follow her to the hospital. Then he went to the telephone to perform the gruesome task of informing Hurtil of what had happened. Hurtil, in this kind of emergency, was at his best. He promised David that he would have his own car pick up Frau Benninger and would bring her to the hospital personally. David promised to meet him there.

An eternity later Benninger was in the operating theater of the Kantonspital with a team of specialists making haste to remove the bullets and, if possible, repair the damage to his ribs, lungs and chest. His prognosis was poor. Only a miracle would save him. In a waiting room off one of the aseptic, fluorescent-lighted corridors of the hospital, David and Hurtil tried to give support to Frau Friedel Benninger and to Rita Jensen.

"It's all my fault," Rita told David tearfully.

"I doubt it," he said. "We all do what we want to do."

"No, but I insisted that he call you. We wanted to explain, you see . . ."

"Explain what?" David asked her.

Rita retained enough self-possession to look up at David, then to realize that Hurtil and Frau Benninger were in earshot even if they were not listening. She stood up and walked out into the corridor.

"It was about the blackmail."

"Uh huh!"

"You told me you suspected Franz. I persuaded him to tell you—I said it was what he had to do, even if it caused trouble."

"Tell me what?"

"That he was working for me."

"Haile Selassie's gold?" David asked her.

Rita was staggered. "You mean you knew all the time?"

"Not all the time . . . just recently. He sold Swiss futures this afternoon—for dollars and marks. What was that?"

"The same. He did it to protect our funds. In case something went wrong and the Swiss franc drops. After he heard about the police."

"What police?"

"The ones who found the diamonds."

"Holy shit!" David stuttered. "Is nothing sacred anymore?"

"Not shit, for certain," Rita replied, managing a small smile. "But your secret is with me, if mine is with you. Bargain?"

Her hazel eyes looked at David squarely. She asked no quarter, only a fair barter. She wasn't young. David guessed her to be about his own vintage. A woman of the world who knew what she wanted and used whatever was necessary to get it. But straight. You knew where you stood with a woman like this.

"One condition," David stipulated. "No, not a condition, just a piece of friendly advice. We hope Benninger lives through this, but whether he lives or dies see old Hurtil as soon as you can. He's a good man. He will understand."

Rita touched his arm gratefully and then impulsively reached up and kissed him. They walked back to the waiting room together. Hurtil stood up and came toward them.

"Pardon my intruding," he said, "but I wonder if I could have a word with you, David?"

Rita went over to Friedel Benninger, leaving David free to talk to Hurtil. They returned to the quiet of the corridor.

"My apologies, David. With this tragedy of Benninger, it completely slipped my mind. Strange how one's priorities can alter."

Hurtil reached into his pocket. David was hardly surprised to see his hand come out with a white vellum envelope addressed to Hurtil in script with a red felt pen. Hurtil handed the letter to David.

"This came," Hurtil said.

"New delivery instructions?"

"That's right. For tomorrow morning. They've raised the demand to fifteen million Swiss francs and say that if anything goes wrong this time, the three hostages will die."

"The three hostages?" David asked, puzzled. "What three hostages?"

"Oh, sorry," Hurtil apologized. "I consistently forget that you have not read it."

David opened the letter and read it quickly. "Mlle. Abbott, McGowan and Villegas as hostages. They are really playing it safe this time."

"They're certainly taking no chances," Hurtil said. He coughed. "Did you get any information on—er, the unfortunate Franz before he was—the—er, incident in the station?"

"I believe he is in the clear," David assured Hurtil. "Completely. What he did was a normal bank transaction. He genuinely believed he was safe-guarding Hurtilbank."

Hurtil lifted himself straight. A tremendous weight had gone from his shoulders. "Thank God."

The two men walked silently together, both thinking of the implications of David's statement. If it was not Benninger, then what? At the same time both began to speak.

"If not . . ."

"Did you . . ."

They laughed quietly.

"You first," David said.

"Oh, I was about to ask if Benninger is not re-sponsible, are we back to the Freys?"

"Maybe," David told him. He was not really an-swering Hurtil but looking at the letter of instruc-tions from the blackmailers. "Three hostages," David said. "I don't like it. Something smells. Where are they?"

"Where are who?" Hurtil wanted to know.

"The three victims?"

"Well, how would—that is, I don't know."

"Contact them as soon as you can," David said. "Let them know about the new instructions and please tell them to be extra careful tonight."

"You had better use my car this time," Hurtil suggested.

"Good idea," David agreed. "Have your chauf-feur pick us up—well, say, start from your villa with Villegas about eight o'clock, then pick me up at the Regina. We'll be calling for McGowan and Mlle. Abbott about eight-thirty." David pressed the but-ton of the elevator.

"You're leaving?" Hurtil asked.

"A couple of things to check out," David said

lightly, "but I'll be there in the morning. Don't worry ... and I'll keep my fingers crossed for Benninger." The doors of the elevator opened and David stepped inside. Then he remembered. "What about the diamonds?"

"Florelle is preparing the additional stones for me. My chauffeur will have the pouch for you tomorrow morning."

Hurtil bowed as the doors closed on David. David thought that Hurtil was bearing up well, considering the strain. Better than he could have expected. Although you never really knew who could take pressure until the pressure came. Speaking of pressure, a certain David Christopher was about to undergo one helluva pressured night. First a telephone call to Corinne, then some tight connections, and in between, if he was lucky, the interview that might just enlighten him on the identity of the very bright people who were trying to take Hurtilbank for a trifle of fifteen million Swiss francs or a nice round sum of six million U.S. dollars.

X

The weather forecast for Friday in French out of Geneva argued flawlessly for a dull, cloudy, over-cast day for the Zurich region east to the borders of Austria and Lichtenstein and north to the German border except for some occasional patches of sunshine. The weather forecast in German out of Zurich for the same day in the same region listed cogent reasons for sunshine following some early morning cloudiness, except for occasional overcast periods. In his room at the Regina Hotel in Zurich, David Christopher suspected the day ahead was going to be wet, cold and miserable.

This was just what he needed in the circum-stances. Apart from a couple of catnaps sitting up, he had had no sleep. The early-morning shower and shave had not wrought their usual magic. The coffee had been cold, the juice canned, and the rolls appeared to be leftovers from the day before. Definitely not his kind of day. And he was facing a blackmail drop that appeared to have been designed by the Swiss National Tourist Office. Now that he had had time to compare the blackmailers' instructions to a roadmap, David was sorry he had not made the call for 7:00 A.M. instead of 8:00. They would have to take the autobahn south to Pfaffikon, cross the lake to the north shore via the Hurden–Rappiswil bridge, then drive east to Wattwil. Ten kilometers before Wattwil they should look for a resting zone where there would be an abandoned car. In the car there would be further instructions.

Once again David found himself forced to admire the meticulous mind which had planned the crime. Wattwil. That was just great. From Wattwil you could go anyplace. You could circle back to Zurich via the Wil–Winterthur highway. You could drive northeast to St. Gallen or to the Bodensee or even to the Austrian border. Wattwil, for that matter, could also be a jumping-off point to the great Alpine cleft, the Upper Thur Valley of the Toggenburg, or it could be thought of as the foothills of the Alpstein, that series of jagged crests rising to the majestic Santis that reared its snow-capped peak over eight thousand feet above the Rhine valley. Who knew which option this crafty brain had chosen? One thing David did know for certain. The blackmailers did not intend to leave any survivors of today's payoff. David knew that when all three remaining victims were named as hostages. A nice clean operation. Remove all the evidence, including David Christopher. The only uncertainty was the setting of the last murderous act.

David jumped as his telephone buzzed harshly. It was the desk to advise him that his car was waiting. David folded his map and the instructions

and slipped them into the inside right-hand pocket
of his jacket. He patted the .38 under his left arm-
pit and took a final look at himself in the full-
length mirror on the door of his clothes closet. He
was wearing a brown suede jacket over a canary
shirt with a russet silk cravat. His form-fitting
double-knit trousers were a pale beige. His fawn
suede shoes showed a touch of gold metal loop in
the center of the cross-strap. David slipped on a
fawn Italian raincoat and drew the matching gold-
buckled belt tight. He thought he was dressed for
the part. If he won, fine. If he lost, too bad. He
thought he would like to look like this anyhow
when he was laid out.

Johann Hurtil's limousine was a black Mercedes
600. When David came down the steps of the Regina, the chauffeur was standing respectfully beside
the car, waiting to open the door. Villegas was
sitting in the back and his hand waved a welcome
at David. David waved back and turned to the
driver.

"Good morning, I'm David Christopher."

"The driver saluted. " Morning, sir. It's Stephen
Krause. Mr. Hurtil usually calls me Krause."

"Fine, Krause. You have a package for me?"

Krause reached into the front of the Mercedes
and took the familiar chamois pouch from the
glovebox. It was bigger now. By another couple of
million dollars, David thought to himself.

"Here you are, sir."

"Thanks, Krause. Wish it was ours, huh?"

"So I understand, sir. From Herr Hurtil." David
was about to step into the car, but turned back as
he remembered. "Oh, Krause?"

"Sir?"

"Did Herr Hurtil tell you where we are going?"

"Just the pickups, sir, here in Zurich. Mr. Mc-Gowan next and then Mlle. Abbott. After that he said I was to take orders from you, sir."

"Fine. Then it's Wattwil. About ten kilometers before Wattwil, let me know."

"The autobahn satisfactory to you, sir? It would be faster."

"That's how I figured it, Krause. Glad to have my opinion backed by a professional."

The broad face of Krause colored at the compliment, and his smile was warm as he let David into the car. Villegas was waiting for David. He was courteous as always, but on edge, mystified, wondering what game he was being asked to join in.

"Ah, Mr. Christopher," he said to David, "I cannot tell you how relieved I am to see you."

"After what happened to your fellow victims, Mr. Hayes and Herr Rascher," David answered grimly, "I am relieved to see you—still alive."

"That goes for both of us, señor," Villegas said. "Now what will happen today?"

"If you don't mind, Señor Villegas," David parried, "why don't we wait until we have McGowan and Mlle. Abbott with us? Saves repetition."

"Of course, Señor Christopher," Villegas apologized. "I should not even have asked, but you will forgive me if I am somewhat apprehensive."

"Aren't we all?" David agreed. "Especially if we are fond of living."

There was silence in the car until Krause negotiated the Burkliplatz and the Quai Bridge and pulled up at the Plaza. McGowan was already outside the hotel, waiting impatiently. His Stetson sat askew on his head. His eyes were bloodshot from the previous night's drinking. His topcoat was rumpled, as if he had flopped on his bed and slept in it without bothering to change. His face was flaccid, pasty. There was no trace of the false joviality he usually assumed. As soon as he settled in the back seat of the car beside David and Villegas, he began to complain.

"What's this here meetin' all about?" he demanded of David. "That damned Hurtil. He wouldn't tell me nothin'."

"We'll discuss it after Mlle. Abbott joins us," David told him shortly. For some reason McGowan irritated him. Had from the first. Perhaps it was some kind of inverted national pride—he wished a fellow American to cut a better figure.

"What's the matter with now?" McGowan asked belligerently. "Who the hell are you, Mr. Goddam Smartass Christopher? You're bein' paid by our bank, the bank that makes money out of our money, to protect us. Helluva job you're doin' of protectin'. Hayes is dead. Rascher's dead. I see by the paper Benninger's near-dead. You ain't protected nobody but your own precious skin and that million-dollar automobile you drive around in. No, sirree. You ain't protected nobody."

David would have given his fee from Hurtilbank, if he lived to enjoy it, to have been able to stop the car, get out, drag McGowan out by the shirt and beat hell out of him. It might have been fortunate for McGowan that at that very moment Krause drew up outside the Bellevue Hotel where Denise Abbott was waiting just inside the foyer. David tapped on the window and Krause came round quickly from the driver's seat to open the rear passenger door for him. David was glad to get out and give himself a moment to put the lid on his seething anger at McGowan. Denise helped. She appeared at the entrance of the hotel, underneath its façade of cornices and carvings, like some latter-day Virgin Mary revealing herself to her devotées at the portals of Notre Dame in Paris. She was dressed entirely in white—from her Balenciaga scarf to her Gucci shoes. A super-gilded paramilitary-type doorman followed carrying her small suitcase. As she walked across the esplanade between the hotel entrance and the street where the Mercedes was parked, her bottom undulated just sufficiently to draw every male eye within a hundred yards. David knew that he had never felt about any girl the way he felt about Denise.

"Hello, darling," she said in a low voice to David. She touched a finger to her lips and then placed the finger on David's lips. She was fresh and glowing and it was easy to forget that clouds were obscuring the sun. The doorman coughed and Krause took the bag from him.

"Be a dear," Denise said to Krause. "Please put that with you in front."

"Certainly, mademoiselle," Krause answered.

David slipped the doorman ten francs and then helped Denise into the car. McGowan and Villegas had moved apart to leave the center free for her.

"Where is David going to sit?" Denise asked.

"Jump seat. Get in. No problem," David told her.

When they were settled and the Mercedes had joined the Quai Bridge traffic en route to the autobahn, McGowan, sweaty, unwell, uneasy, returned to his argument.

"Maybe you can find out what this here's all about," McGowan appealed to Denise. "He won't tell us nothin'."

"David?" Denise asked. Her blue eyes looked at

him with the confidence of a woman who knows her man.

"Just waiting for you to join us," David answered. He had fought himself back to calm. "Villegas knew that. Our Texan maverick here just wanted to work off some of his anxiety on me."

"You got no right, Christopher ..." McGowan spluttered.

Then Denise put a hand on his arm. "Please, Mr. McGowan. This is difficult for all of us. We understand how you feel."

Mollified but still grumbling to himself, McGowan subsided in his corner. David took the chamois bag of uncut stones out of his pocket and, facing back to the three blackmail victims, held it up so that they could have a clear view of it.

"Mlle. Abbott knows what these are," David began.

"It looks bigger," Denise said.

"What are they?" Villegas asked.

"Uncut diamonds," David answered.

"Why is it bigger?" Denise inquired.

"Blackmailers raised their ante to fifteen million in Swiss francs."

McGowan gasped and looked even more sick and sweaty. "Who's paying'?" he asked. "I never gave no authorization for nobody to use my ninety G's. No, sir. If they used my ninety G's what they're doin' is illegal."

David was fed up with the Texan. "Listen, McGowan. I know you must have been told this thousands of times, but I'll tell you again anyway. Shut up. You're a pain in the ass."

The Texan gulped, looked as if he was going to swing a punch within the confines of the car, changed his mind, swallowed palpably, and shut up.

"This time, as before, the blackmailers have asked for the payment in uncut diamonds through a bank representative—which is me. They have also insisted that you three come along as hostages, or otherwise, no deal."

McGowan could not contain himself any longer. "After Hayes? and Rascher? and Benninger?" McGowan appealed to Denise and Villegas. "This is crazy. Where are we goin'? Where is he takin' us?"

"Where are we going, David? Can you at least tell us that much?"

"Denise, my dear. I don't know myself. We're dealing with a bright light." He took the blackmail instructions from his inner pocket and handed them across to Denise. McGowan and Villegas crowded in on her to read the red script.

McGowan leaned back, shaking his head. He popped two Gelusils and chewed away looking green-pallored, ill. Villegas also sat back, silent and dignified. Denise handed the letter back to David, concern shadowing her face. Christopher returned the letter to his pocket and turned to face front, staring through the glass panel between him and Krause. He leaned toward the door and activated the divider button. When the glass panel was down he spoke to Krause quietly. The chauffeur answered without turning his head, and his words were lost on the three uneasy rear-seat passengers. David returned the glass panel to its closed position and looked out of the side of the car to see if he could figure their position. Krause made it easy for him by slowing down to swing off the autobahn for Pfaffikon and the cut-through to Rapperswil. David was sorry that the trip was for this kind of business. The causeway and bridge across the Zurichsee were unique in Switzerland as far as he knew. Down almost on the surface of the water he had a boat's-eye angle of the low mountains rising away from the lake in slopes of green pastures and dark conifer forests.

The ferreting behind him drew his attention back from the view. He heard McGowan say, "Huntin' a bug? That's real smart, Mr. Villegas." David turned to find Villegas and McGowan searching ashtrays, lights, armrests, cushions and car ceiling.

"Everything we say is goin' through to old frosty-face up there where it's probably bein' taped. That's why he keeps lookin' straight ahead. So we won't guess it."

"Then you think I'm right?" Villegas asked McGowan.

"Damn right, I think you're right," McGowan replied. "If you mean Hurtil, my guess is it ain't no coincidence we're going on this voyage in his vehicle."

David's smile, not so much noncommittal as contemptuous, eventually stung the composed Villegas into a direct assault.

"Is it so farfetched, Mr. Christopher? Swiss banks are not compelled to publish financial statements. They have been known to fail. Suppose Hurtilbank were in trouble?"

"Hurtilbank is in trouble," David agreed. "It has to pay fifteen million francs ransom to protect you and McGowan and Mlle. Abbott."

"That's not what I mean," Villegas protested. "We could all be what they call the 'patsies.' Yes, Mr. Christopher, did you ever think that Señor Hurtil could be blackmailing himself? He seems very eager to make out that the extortion attempt is endangering the whole Swiss financial community. These repeated demands—each time for larger payments. Who knows? Perhaps the next step will be to blackmail all of the Swiss banks, and he will persuade them to pay on the grounds that they must do so to protect their own interests . . . until he has covered the millions or billions that he needs. He picks five of us he knows cannot afford to complain. Five patsies, Mr. Christopher. Two of them are already dead. Three of us remain. We wonder if we will be alive at the end of the day."

David turned full around. He looked at Villegas first. No longer the polite aristocrat but the tough partisan, cold, deadly. And then there was Denise. Her affection for David was there, true, but now colored by bewilderment brought on by the merciless logic of Villegas. And then there was McGowan, queasy, a funny smile on his face as he spoke for them all:

"You in with 'em, pal, or are you a patsy too?"

David let the question hang on the air. It was the sort of question that in the myth of the West could be solved satisfactorily with a six-gun. In the urban ghetto the teenage gangs used knives and steel rods. In the pubs of Ireland the question could start an all-in melee. In the back of a Mercedes 600 speeding toward Wattwil it produced, when David was ready, a long and luxurious yawn.

"Ever do crossword puzzles, Villegas?" David asked.

"What has that to do with it?" asked the Santacostan.

"Everything," David told him. "You're the guy who puts down a six-letter word in the center of the empty crossword and thinks it's finished."

David turned to face front again just as Krause rapped on the partition. He put up his right hand and extended the fingers twice to indicate that the ten-kilometer sign for Wattwil was coming up. Christopher lowered the glass panel and said to Krause, "Look for the first resting zone and drive in."

Krause found it and drove the big Mercedes off the highway. The resting zone was empty. "What now, sir?" Krause asked.

"Try the next one," David told him.

Krause took the Mercedes back to the road, waited for a Porsche and a Volvo to shoot past, and then swung back onto the smooth macadamized surface.

"David?" This from Denise.

"Yup?"

"Suppose—suppose there isn't anything?"

"Awfully careless of our blackmailing friends to miss out on fifteen million francs, don't you think?"

"I suppose you're right," she said doubtfully.

Krause drove carefully, in the slow lane, until a sign warned him of another resting zone. There was a semi-trailer parked, the driver sound asleep. At the far end was a sky-blue Citroën with a cream top. Krause ran the Mercedes as far as the Citroën and pulled up nearby.

"Is this what you want, sir?"

"Hang on while I look," David told him. He unlocked the door and slipped out of the Mercedes onto the gravel surface of the resting zone. It felt good to be on solid ground again. Then he walked across to the Citroën. It was empty. On the window ledge inside was a white vellum envelope addressed:

FOR THE REPRESENTATIVE OF HURTILBANK

David opened the door, leaned inside and picked

267

up the envelope. He inserted his index finger under
the flap and ripped it open, read the instructions
rapidly, and walked back to the Mercedes. He
leaned inside the car, folded the jump seat back
into position.

"All out," he said, "this is the end of the line."

David walked around to Krause, who was standing beside the passenger door on the far side of the
Mercedes to let out Villegas and Denise.

"Thanks, Krause," he said to the chauffeur.

"Does that mean you don't need me anymore,
sir?" the chauffeur asked him.

"Our orders are to take the Citroën from here on
in."

"Let us first satisfy ourselves that the Citroën is
functioning, don't you think?" Villegas asked
David. He was out of the car and giving his hand
to Denise to help her out.

"Good idea," David told him. "Why don't you
check it out?"

While Villegas walked across to the Citroën and
slipped inside with the ease of a man who is hap-
piest behind the wheel of a car, David turned back
to Krause.

"Tell Mr. Hurtil that we have been instructed to
drive to Unterwasser, wherever that is."

Krause showed concern. "That's a winter ski
resort, Mr. Christopher. I doubt if there will be
anybody there at this time."

"What happens there?" Denise asked him.

"Who knows?" David shrugged. "We wait for
fresh instructions. These babies are cagier than
Lucky Luciano. Guess they figure by giving us only
one step at a time, there is no way the police can
move in and catch them after the drop. That's
probably also the reason they're taking us so far

away from civilization. Nothing but cows up there."

The Citroën engine burst into life and the motor rose and fell as Villegas tested the accelerator.

"I'll just put Mlle. Abbott's bag in the Citroën," Krause told David. David nodded to Krause and then realized that McGowan had not moved from the Mercedes.

"Come on, McGowan," David said, leaning into the rear of the car, "I told you this is the end of the line. All out. Last station."

McGowan stirred himself, but made it only half-way to the door. One hand went down to the seat beside him. The other clung desperately to the strap above his head. He was without color. Heavy perspiration showed in his face. His breath came in short rasps.

"Not me. Not me, Davey."

Denise leaned in the far door. "Please, Mr. McGowan, you must make an effort to pull yourself together. For all our sakes."

McGowan's eyes seemed to disappear under his upper lids so that only the whites showed. His left hand came across his stomach and he dry-retched. A horrible sound. His voice came in a hoarse whisper. "Got to go back to Zurich," he said. "Sick. Can't go on."

David stood up and looked across the top of the car to Denise.

"What do you think?" she asked him.

"The way he looks," David said, "that mountain road will finish him. Krause," David ordered.

"Mr. Christopher?"

"Drop Mr. McGowan back at his hotel in Zurich. O.K.?"

"A pleasure, sir."

Krause shut the door of the Mercedes for Denise

while David closed his door on McGowan. Krause then got into the driver's seat, started his engine, and eased his car across the highway to join the Zurich-bound traffic.

David and Denise walked across to the Citroën. Villegas was revving its engine. As soon as he saw David he got out to let him into the driver's seat.

"Why don't you drive?" David asked him. "I'll map-read us in the right direction."

"In that case, let me get in back," Denise said. "Three's a crowd on these roads."

They settled into the Citroën. Villegas expertly slipped it into Reverse, backed out enough to clear the edge of the resting zone, then shot out to the edge of the highway. He drove with the sureness of a racing driver, making fast judgments of the distance and speed of the other vehicles. David was glad that he was a passenger. It would give him a chance to doze a little and refresh himself for the struggle to come.

"How do you find her?" David asked Villegas.

"There is at least one bad cylinder. The points are out of adjustment. The carburetor is dirty. It has low-grade gasoline . . ."

David laughed. "Anything else?"

"Yes. It is stolen."

"Stolen?" Denise's startled voice came from the rear seat.

"Certainly. It has no papers of any kind," Villegas assured her. "No registration. No insurance. We shall be wise not to attempt to cross any borders in this car."

"So far not on the menu," David said, "but who knows?" He stretched. David took out his roadmap, opened it up. "We're here at Wattwil," he told

Villegas. His finger pointed to the spot on the map, and Villegas picked it up.

"Where to after that?" he asked.

"South on Route 16," David told him. "Ebnat, Krumenau, Nesslau, et cetera, on through to Unterwasser. At Unterwasser we take the funicular railway. After that, new instructions. O.K.?"

"O.K.," Villegas answered.

David yawned again. "Mind if I grab five minutes' shut-eye?" he asked Villegas and Denise. "This thing's making me lose my beauty sleep."

"Me too," Denise agreed. "I'll join you."

"After this is all over, Carlos," David joked, "you can tell us about the Appenzell."

"What's the Appenzell?" Denise asked him. "I'm strictly a town girl."

"I'm glad you asked that question," David told her. "The Appenzell is where we're at. As you can see, it's strictly farm country, sloping up to the Alpstein mountains. That's where we're heading. To Unterwasser."

"What's special about it?"

"Special?" David replied. "I guess it's one of those areas you come across in Europe that don't change too much from century to century. The peasants here still wear swords at their town assemblies to show that they are citizens with the right to vote. The women and, to some degree, the men still wear the old costumes. You might have seen pictures of the coif."

"You mean that coif with the tulle wings like the nuns used to wear?"

"I couldn't have said it better myself," David told her drily. "Plus their houses are special."

"There's one now," Denise pointed out. "How

pretty. Wooden shingles. I'd love to live in one of those."

"They're supposed to maintain a very even temperature," David explained, "especially in winter at the lower levels. That is where the women do their embroidery when the farms are snowbound."

The Citroën passed through a small town.

"Let's stop and eat," Denise begged, "before I die of hunger. That could be the plan," she added seriously. "They are going to starve us to death."

"What do you say, Christopher?" Villegas asked.

"Why not?" David answered. "I could use a coffee myself."

Villegas found a parking place adjacent to the town square and they got out of the car, associates strangely brought together by the bizarre instructions of the puppeteer pulling the strings behind the clouds. They bought Appenzell cakes adorned with reliefs of cowmen in yellow breeches and scarlet waistcoats. At a stall in the market, they bought a tasty dried sausage called Alpenklubler and a strong cheese indigenous to the area. They added a loaf of warm fresh bread and sat at a table in the square where the waitress wore a richly embroidered white blouse and a full-bustled skirt under a dainty straw toque edged with velvet. She served them coffee and fresh cream and butter and two beers for the men and provided them with plates and cutlery for their bread and sausages and cheese. Denise chatted with her in German, and she returned with a honey and almond kirsch cake to eat with their coffee.

"The condemned ate a hearty brunch," Denise laughed. "Will I be glad when this is over."

"Where will you go?" David asked.

"Oh, who knows? Back on the circuit, I suppose. Modeling."

"Ever thought of trying the States?" David asked her. "They're always on the lookout for new faces over there."

"I'm afraid it's too late for that," Denise told him.

"It's never too late," David said in an odd sort of strangled voice that made her look at him questioningly. "Sorry," he apologized. "Guess something went down the wrong way." He took a mouthful of coffee.

"And you, Villegas? What about you?" David asked.

"I have my revolution," Villegas said. "That is all I live for now."

"Is it worth dying for?" David queried.

Villegas looked at David in silence, and there was a sudden tension that all three felt. "If I understand your question correctly," Villegas answered him at last, "yes."

Now the cameraderie had gone and a chill had taken its place. Each was suddenly anxious to get whatever was ahead over and done with.

The terminal for the funicular railway lay above Unterwasser. It looked over the drab weatherboard shingle-roofed houses of the village toward the highway climbing from Unterwasser to Wildhaus through the steep escarpments cutting away from the majestic folds of the Wildhuser Schafberg. An engineer was working on the motor of his train as the Citroën drove up and parked. He looked up without surprise at Villegas, David and Denise as they got out of the car, slammed the doors, and approached him. He seemed to be expecting passengers and nodded his head toward them, then climbed aboard and started his engine. Its chug-chug echoed strangely in the quiet air, bouncing back from the face of the steep wall.

The trio climbed into the railway car, Denise wedged in between David and Villegas. On his box the engineer engaged his lever and the train jolted abruptly as its drive-cogwheel started to turn. Denise let out an involuntary cry of surprise and both men, also instinctively, told her not to worry. Looking up ahead, David found it hard to accept his own confident words. The narrow-gauge tracks climbed the steep incline, almost perpendicularly it seemed, and disappeared into a tiny tunnel bored into the granite substance of the Churfirsten range rearing up ahead of them.

Neither David nor Denise nor Villegas spoke. They were awed by the sheer, stomach-churning cliffs disappearing below them into nothingness or rising up beyond sight. Then they plunged into the blackness of the small tunnel and Denise clutched David's arm as she felt the walls and ceiling of the tunnel envelop her. There were no lights in the tunnel. The darkness was total. Nothing but the magnified sound of the cogwheel biting into its track and the creaking whine of the steel outer wheels of the train scraping on the rusted iron rails. Then a tiny disc of light appeared ahead, growing larger and larger, eventually becoming the tunnel exit. When the funicular emerged the three passengers found themselves blinking in the unaccustomed daylight. The train ground to a halt in front of a ski lodge.

Villegas was first out. He gave a hand to Denise, who followed him. David stood up in the car.

"Wait for us," he called to the driver. "We won't be long."

The engineer smiled and nodded and, as soon as David joined Denise and Villegas, he reversed the train. David turned in time to see him disappearing into the tunnel.

The ski lodge was abandoned for the summer. The world around David and his two companions was empty. It seemed forlorn without the laughter and chatter and colors of the skiers, without the crisp, inviting beauty of the snow. David pointed to the flat open space that was the start of the ski tow.

"That's it, I guess."

"You must be right," Denise agreed. "It said to wait at the ski tow."

"Wait for what?" Villegas asked.

"Further instructions, I guess," David said.

They were walking toward the ski lift and the short climb in the high altitude was already making them short of breath.

"I don't see a soul," Denise panted.

"Maybe another note," David suggested.

They reached the start of the ski lift and gladly paused to catch their breath. The lower anchor of the ski lift was a sturdy concrete block carrying a pylon, a motor and a giant steel drive-wheel. Around the drive-wheel was the steel cable that powered the tow. It connected with the enclosed red ski cars stretching still and lifeless at intervals up the long hill to the peak above, suspended from their overhead cable. Without their mantle of snow, the ski slopes looked colorless, useless even as pasture for the mountain cattle.

Villegas stood wary, watchful beside the concrete parapet, his eyes sweeping the slopes and the area back toward the lodge for signs of movement. David climbed the parapet to the ski-tow machinery. Abandoned as it seemed, the tow was in good shape. A switchbox on the wall of the concrete housing for the electric motor had simple green and red press buttons to activate or stop the tow. Denise watched David and Villegas in turn and drew her spring coat more tightly around her. Although the clouds had broken and the sun was shining from an azure sky, she felt chilled. All three started as a telephone unexpectedly jangled.

"Answer it," Denise cried impatiently.

"O.K., O.K.!" David snapped back.

He found the telephone along the wall from the switchbox and wondered why he hadn't seen it before. He picked up the receiver.

"Hello. This is David Christopher."

A voice came through. It was either deliberately muffled or the antiquated phone distorted it.

"Start the ski tow. Bring the diamonds up. Tell the others to wait in plain sight or they're dead."

The phone clicked off, and David was slowly cradling the receiver as Denise and Villegas scrambled up to meet him.

"What did he say?" Denise asked anxiously.

"I have to take a ride," David told her.

"A ride? where?"

David flicked a thumb toward the head of the ski run. "Up there," he said casually. "It's payday for Mr. X."

David took the chamois bag of gems from his pocket, bounced it in his hand a little before the fascinated eyes of Denise and Villegas. Then he turned and pressed the *On* button of the switchbox. He heard the whirr of the powerful motor, and the big wheel began to grind and crank and the row of ski cars started to climb their incongruous, improbable way to the peak above. David watched the ski cars circling around the parapet for a few seconds to make sure that they were functioning correctly, then moved to the boarding platform.

Denise ran after him. She clutched his sleeve in near-panic.

"David, don't leave me here. I'm frightened."

"Better cool it, baby. Mr. X says you two stay in plain sight or you're candidates for the embalmer." David looked around the slopes. "He probably has a telescopic sight on us right now. Maybe a couple. You stay here with Villegas."

Denise, still clinging to David, began to sob. "I won't stay here to die. I'm going to be killed. I know it. As soon as you're gone, David. They'll kill me. I won't stay."

Embarrassed, David tried to disengage her hand from his arm, but she only held on more desperately. Then Villegas was standing beside him.

"May I suggest a solution?"

"Suggest away," David said. "This girl's getting hysterical."

Villegas reached over and disengaged the chamois bag of diamonds from David's hand. "Allow me," he said.

"Hold it, Villegas? No games at this point."

Villegas was not playing any games. He was tough, fearless, and determined. "What difference does it make?" he asked David. "One man delivers. One man and one woman stay here. I shall deliver. You remain here."

David protested, "I'm being paid to protect you, Villegas. If somebody has to take a chance . . ."

"Nobody is taking any chances," Villegas assured David. He put a hand inside his jacket and brought out a .45. Villegas dropped the chamois bag into his left pocket and expertly checked the chamber of the .45. Very obviously Villegas was a man who could shoot as well as he could drive.

"*Sta bien?*" he asked David.

"O.K.," David agreed, "but I don't like it."

Villegas returned the gun to a belt holster inside his jacket and took out the gems. "No problem," he assured David and Denise. "They are as good as delivered."

"Hold it, Villegas," David ordered.

Puzzled, the handsome Santacostan turned and then saw David pointing beyond the cables and the moving cars parading up the desolate slope to the soft haze at the top of the mountain. A tiny white helicopter had appeared from behind the mountain, and now it hovered above the peak, watching, waiting, seeing.

"All mod cons," David said. "Our Mr. X."

"I am ready for him." Villegas smiled.

David put his hand out and touched the arm of the Santacostan. "I hope you are, Carlos. No matter who it is. Don't trust him. Two of your friends are dead. Remember that."

The smile died on Villegas's face and he turned back to the ski cars, grabbed the door handle of the first car to move by, twisted it open, and leaped inside. It was smooth, like everything the Santacostan did. From inside the car Villegas waved.

"Adios!" he called out.

The car swung around the parapet and Villegas moved away with it, sitting up very straight, his eyes fixed ahead on the goal of the long tow journey. The bag of gems was in his lap and David hoped that Villegas's gun hand was firmly on the butt of his .45.

David took Denise by the arm—the girl had said

nothing since her hysterical outburst, but now she seemed calm—and walked to the edge of the concrete upper parapet where they were clearly visible to the helicopter. From the lower parapet behind them, the ski cars appeared, empty and lifeless, to the scrape and squeak and moan of the cable. When the car bearing Villegas was perhaps halfway up the lift, suspended high above the floor of the canyon below, the helicopter dropped toward the ground and finally sank behind the rim of the mountain.

The inactive, obedient David Christopher, standing passively on the edge of the parapet, was immediately a different person. He dropped back toward the engine housing, dragged two life-sized cutouts of skiers from the wall back to the edge of the platform, and set them up facing the skyline where he had been standing with Denise. From close-up the cutouts were painted skiers, a man and a woman, in vivid colors, advertising ski-lift prices in three currencies. David hoped that from a distance, at least to the naked eye, it would seem as if he and Denise were still standing there. Then he grabbed Denise by the arm. She resisted.

"What are you doing, David?"

"There's a rifle up there, honey, trained on us. I saw the gleam of the sun on the barrel. Quick, this way."

Denise was dubious, but she followed David down to the lower ski-car boarding platform and stood there uncertainly while David appraised the oncoming car. Without warning he grabbed Denise from behind, pushed her forward toward the car, opened the door, lifted her bodily inside, then followed her in, and slammed the door behind them. This time Denise was angry. Really angry.

"You bloody fool," she shouted, "you'll abort the payment."

David ignored her. In the distance, many cars ahead, he could make out the faint outline of Villegas, still sitting upright, still focused on the landing platform at the top of the slope.

"David, listen . . . the blackmailer said . . . you're risking everything . . ." Denise was shocked, furious.

David took a final look up ahead, but could not see any sign of either the helicopter or whomever had been in it.

"David . . . listen," Denise appealed to him once again. "For God's sake, do something. We'll all be killed. Please do something, David . . ."

This time Christopher turned back to her. There was contempt in his eyes. "You filthy bitch," he said. "Save it for the judge." If he had struck Denise with the full force of his fist she could not have been more shocked. She blanched and shrunk away from him.

Then she spoke in a voice that was choked and hoarse: "You don't know what you're saying, David," she moaned piteously. "This is us, David. I love you . . ."

"Save it, honey. I've got to the point where I'm liable to throw up."

"David—what . . . ?"

David could not bring himself to look at Denise, so he looked out instead toward the line of descending ski cars a few feet away.

"I never wanted to check up on you," he said. "I guess I really cared. I didn't want it to be you. I refused to let myself think it could be you . . . until you ordered three hostages. Then just too many things added up. Too many things. I flew to

London last night. I spent two hours there with your friend, Lord James Esherbridge."

He heard Denise suck in her breath. It was a heaving sound. Like a death rattle. In a way it was a death rattle. She was a lifeless rag doll crumpled in the corner of the ski car. There was a lump in David's throat as he remembered the golden glow they had shared together in Neufsuzerain and the way that glow turned bleak and gray in London.

He had driven to the Zurich airport from the Kantonspital like a man possessed, persuaded the multilingual blonde hostess at the ticket desk that it was a matter of life or death for her to hold the 9:15 flight to London until he was aboard, had even persuaded her in addition to let him use her phone to call Corinne at home. One thing about Corinne. When he needed action he got it. She had not only promised, she had guaranteed to trail down Lord Esherbridge for him, to make an appointment for 11:30 and to have a chauffeur waiting for him at the airport who would know exactly where to take him.

From a purely clinical viewpoint it had jelled just right. Lady Esherbridge was at the country estate with the children and Lord Esherbridge had agreed to meet David at his home in Lancaster Gate. With the light, late-night traffic and an expert driver, David was pressing a button that rang musical chimes inside Lord Esherbridge's home exactly at 11:30 P.M. Esherbridge answered the door himself, apologizing to David for the absence of his manservant, who had gone off for the evening before Mr. Christopher's secretary had reached him at his club.

Esherbridge had taken David into a den, apologizing afresh for its untidiness. The untidiness con-

sisted of a newspaper and a couple of books not in
their places in the floor-to-ceiling bookcase that
lined one of the walls of the room. They talked
over a scotch poured from a Waterford crystal de-
canter. David had warmed to Esherbridge immediately. He was one of those elegant Ascot types who
breathe the culture of Oxford and the dignity of a
man who has not known anything else. He was
younger than David had expected, barely forty,
tall, good-looking.

Although time was of the essence, David could
see that the man was concealing a pressure cooker
full of dread. So David took him quietly, showing
Esherbridge his private investigator's registration
card, speaking of his background in the United
States Department of Justice and his close relations
with M15 and M16 in the United Kingdom. He
eased into the Hurtilbank case backward. Said that
he had reason to believe a group of Hurtilbank
clients were trying to blackmail the bank. Among
the blackmailers was, unfortunately, a friend and
protégée of Lord Esherbridge called Mlle. Denise
Abbott. Even more regretfully, David went on, the
evidence seemed to show that this was not Mlle.
Abbott's first involvement with blackmail. It would
appear that for some years she had been blackmailing Lord Esherbridge himself.

Presented with the *fait accompli*, Esherbridge
was only too willing to confide in David. He had
met Miss Abbott in London when she was studying
at the Royal Academy of Dramatic Art. At least
that much was true, David thought to himself, but
he let Esherbridge talk, and once he had managed
to overcome his fears, the words gushed forth. Esherbridge made no excuses for himself. It was one of
those things. He had thought the girl knew her

way around, was taking it as it came. She gave him a thrilling affair. He gave her entrée to his circle in Europe, not to mention clothes, jewelry and an all-expenses-paid two-year extravaganza in the Continent's best hotels. It was when he told Denise the affair had to end—that it was interfering with his marriage, endangering his career and costing him far more than he could afford—that Esherbridge discovered his pretty blond kitten was a voracious maneater. She told him coolly that she had a deposit box full of evidence that she would be very happy to turn over to one of the English evening papers: hotel bills for double rooms, accounts for her clothes and furs and bracelets and necklaces, photographs of the two of them together through the entire period of their romance.

It was terrible, Esherbridge told David, just terrible. Even now he was pale at the thought. He had first tried to pay off Denise by opening a secret account with Hurtilbank and giving her power of attorney over the ten thousand pounds he had deposited in it. She had gone through that in what seemed like days and then come back after him for more. It could not go on much longer, Esherbridge confessed. He had borrowed until he could borrow no longer, mortgaging the home they were in and his estates as well. He had come to the point, in actual fact, where he would be compelled to stop paying and take his chances. If that meant the end of his political career, so be it. He hoped that it would not mean the end of his marriage, but that was a problem he could only face up to himself.

Esherbridge promised to cooperate with David in whatever way was necessary. He just hoped that David could keep the matter from the press. But

even that was preferable to a continuation of the
mental torture of the last two years. David was
able to assure Esherbridge that the blackmail attempt on Hurtilbank should remove Denise from
circulation without mention of her relationship
with Esherbridge. At the same time, the bank
would give him access to Denise's safe-deposit box.
All going well, Esherbridge could fly into Zurich to
collect the papers from the box in a couple of days.

David left behind him at Lancaster Gate one
grateful, relieved Englishman for whom life
seemed to be worth living once again. Thanks to
his efficient chauffeur he was back at Heathrow in
plenty of time to catch the 2:45 A.M. Swissair DC9
that landed him in Zurich at 5:15 A.M. There he
had picked up his car, driven back to the Regina
and waited for Hurtil's driver to come with the
Mercedes. While he waited David had plenty of
time to think. In the gloomy pessimistic wisdom of
early morning what he thought was that the best
disguise a criminal could have was to be a woman.
When it came to real crime a man automatically
assumed that another man had planned and executed it. A man never started with the assumption
that the villain might be a woman. Take this case
for example. Without Denise would there have
been a case at all? Probably not. Hayes, the two-
timing little weasel from Chicago. Rascher, the
ruthless son of a bitch from Bonn. McGowan, the
blubbery phony from Houston. Even Villegas, determined to avenge his uncle and win back his
country at no matter what cost. Take any one of
them or put them all together and ask yourself who
would have fallen for them? Not him, Christopher
hoped. Give him a few hours and he would have
put all that together. Not old Hurtil, either. A de-

cent man. Good judge of character. Not Benninger. Man to man, he would back Benninger to have come up with the solution himself.

But, and here was the great big *but*, move those male plotters into the background and bring Denise on stage: the glamorous Mademoiselle Abbott in her clinging sharkskin pants and her Pucci blouse, her jewel-rimmed diablo dark glasses and her carelessly expensive jewelry, straight from an assignment for *Vogue* or *Elle*. Right away they were blind. Fumbling their way around in the fog. Not only blind. Christ, that was the beginning only. He, David Christopher, had been so goddam predictably male-protective. "Saddle my charger, varlet. The white stallion. I'm off to slay the dragon that is threatening my princess up there in Neufsuzerain."

And all the time the princess was the dragon. That was the hell of it. A brain like a calculating machine inside a face and a body that a man didn't want to look past.

"How did you get on to it?" Denise asked David in a small remote voice.

"The common factor," he answered.

"What common factor?"

"The link between the victims and the blackmailer. There had to be something. A way to get hold of those statements, a way to know the real identities behind those account numbers, something somewhere that tied you all together."

"Only the bank could do that," she argued, some of her spirit returning.

"Right," he agreed. "That's what I thought. That's what we all thought. That's why it looked like Benninger. But even before Benninger was shot I knew I was on the wrong trail. There had to be another possibility. Some other common factor right under my nose. So close under my nose it would not even occur to me."

"And what was it, Mr. Clever Christopher?"

"It was you, honey. It was you all the time."

David looked up toward the top of the ski tow, another giant wheel etched against the skyline. The car carrying Villegas was nearing the crest. Villegas seemed not to have moved and still sat bolt upright facing ahead. There was no sign of any other figure or evidence that whoever was waiting there had realized that the tiny figures below were cardboard cutouts. Maintaining his careful lookout, David went on talking.

"Your great strength, sweetheart, was that those four had never met. They could look me or anybody else in the eye and deny knowing each other. They could defy Interpol or anybody else to find a connection because there was none except through you. You were the only connection."

Denise was biting her lip and her fingers intertwined with such force that they showed white, but she said nothing.

"My guess is that it all started with Villegas. You met him on the circuit and went after him, thinking he was rich. Then you discovered what money he had left was dedicated to a countercoup in Santacosta. Like you, he had a numbered account with Hurtilbank and a reason to keep it secret. For him it was a life-or-death reason. That gave you the combination: a secret numbered account, a life-and-death situation if the cover was blown, and a desperate need for more money. You found McGowan, in trouble with the U.S. Internal Revenue and crazy to pull off one more big deal. You found

Hayes, who had to save himself from the syndicate. And you stumbled on Rascher walking the tightrope between assassination by Africans and the chance of money to pay them off. One by one you took them to bed, extracted their secrets and persuaded them to pool their bank statements and to threaten themselves. Nobody ever broke bank secrecy. You just made it look that way."

Ahead of David and the sullenly silent Denise, the ski car carrying Villegas had nearly reached the top. David put his right hand inside his jacket, took out his .38, and tested the action. Denise's eyes were drawn to the gun and she watched it while David finished his indictment.

"Five 'victims' who were five 'extortionists' in reality. That much fairly straight ahead. One problem remains. There was a killer loose among them. Who was the killer? Not Hayes because he was the first to die. Not Rascher, either, because he died too—and poor Benninger got mashed up in the process. The question is who? You, Denise? Or Villegas? Or McGowan? Poor lily-livered, green-faced, cowardly McGowan. That was him in the helicopter, of course. He's up there now, isn't he, little one, waiting to kill Villegas?"

A single shot rang out and Denise drew in her breath with a shuddering moan. The echo of the shot seemed to hang reverberating over the mountaintop as David grabbed Denise and pushed her forward and down with him so that their heads did not show through the glass of the ski-car viewing-top. Villegas's car swung around under the massive steel terminal wheel and began its descent. David risked a quick look over the rim of the ski car, but there were no more shots and he could see nobody waiting. Villegas was coming toward him as his car began its descent. He was still sitting in the same position staring ahead and seemed unharmed. Then, as the car holding Villegas came nearer, David realized the truth. He jerked Denise up savagely by the hair, forcing her to look straight at Villegas as his ski car passed them. There was a jagged bullet hole in the side of his head where McGowan's bullet had exited. Blood and brains were dribbling down the side of his once beautiful face. His eyes stared ahead unseeing. Villegas was dead.

"There it is, my sweet, just as you planned it."

David let his fierce grip on Denise's hair relax. Still holding his gun in his right hand, he unlatched the handle of the ski car and fixed his eyes on the approaching landing parapet. Judging the distance to a nicety, he pushed open the door with his gun hand, grabbed hold of Denise's right arm, stepped out onto the parapet and dragged her after him. Still holding her arm, he looked around for McGowan, puzzled that there was no reaction from the Texan. Then he heard the motor of the helicopter starting up and realized that McGowan thought he was alone on top of the ridge.

Still holding Denise by the right arm, David jumped down from the concrete parapet of the ski-tow terminal and looked around quickly. Ahead of him was a short incline leading to a crest. The helicopter had to be on the far side of the crest. Taking Denise with him, David ran up the incline to the top. On the far side, as he had suspected, there was a small plateau where McGowan had set down the helicopter to be invisible from the ski tow. He was inside the bubble of the copter. The motor had fired, the blades were turning, and McGowan was seconds away from takeoff. David let go of Denise's hand, dropped to one knee, steadied himself, and fired. The shot missed, but McGowan heard the crack and his startled face looked out from the bubble to see Denise standing and David firing. McGowan acted fast, putting the chopper into Lift Off. It shuddered and then, as the blades gained speed, began to rise slowly. David fired a second and a third shot at the motor. One of his shots or both of them found a vital spot. The engine faltered. There was a hiss of escaping oil. The rotors slowed and the helicopter settled back down on the ground.

Inside the bubble distorting his face, McGowan seemed huge, menacing, vindictive. A .45 appeared in his hand as the hood shot back and a bullet ploughed into the earth beside David and Denise, spattering soil and gravel. David and Denise ran along the inside brow of the ridge toward the rear of the 'copter and the shelter of a clump of rocks. They were bent low to present as small a target as possible. Another bullet from the .45 followed them, missed, and whined off into space. While David and Denise scrambled for cover behind the mound of rocks, McGowan leaped from the helicopter, holding the chamois bag of diamonds in his left hand and the .45 in his right. The cowardly, sickly alcoholic had given place to a tough fighter, fierce and determined and deadly.

Facing the rocks where David was trying to take cover with Denise, McGowan went crabwise up the slope to the crest. David risked a shot and then ducked back under cover as a heavy bullet from McGowan's .45 slammed into a rock, scattering sharp splinters that bit into him and Denise. McGowan reached the crest and disappeared across it before David could take aim and fire.

Waiting a few seconds to make sure that McGowan was not using this method of enticing him out into the open, David stood up cautiously and then ran straight up to the crest from the rocks where he had been hiding with Denise. Denise looked longingly at the helicopter, knew that it was useless, and decided to take her chances with David. Ahead of her she saw David's head bob up over the crest, and immediately there was an answering shot from McGowan. David abruptly sank back down on the safe side of the ridge. As he had suspected, McGowan had taken shelter in the ski-tow terminal behind the concrete abutment supporting the foundations of the steel upright of the huge drive-wheel.

Thoughts tumbled inside David. It was a kind of standoff. If he left McGowan alone the Texan could reload and with the greater power of the .45 hold him off while he escaped down the valley to the Citroën. If he went in straight away McGowan had three chances to blast him before he reloaded. David decided to risk it. He ran, crouched down for concealment, along the slope in the direction of the helicopter, then stood up quickly and went over the top in a zigzag run. It was not a maneuver David would have recommended to his best friend. He thought his chances of survival were slim. The three shots came in turn as David ducked and weaved his way to the concrete parapet. It occurred to him after the third shot that McGowan might have risked breaking the gun and reloading the empty chambers while he waited for David to attack over the crest. If so, one very dead David Christopher was coming up. Then he realized that no fourth shot had come and he was already at the edge of the concrete parapet. He crouched down, but there was no sound except the click of a hammer on an empty chamber and a curse from McGowan.

In relief David jumped to the parapet, gun ready.

"Give up, McGowan," he yelled.

There was no answer from McGowan, and David saw the big man on the loading ramp clutching at the handle of a passing ski car. Afterward he thought he must have gone berserk for an instant because he could have let McGowan board the ski car and then stopped the lift when McGowan was suspended a hundred feet above the ground. At the time all he could think of was how to prevent McGowan from escaping. He dropped his gun, ran a few steps, and dived into the air at his target. McGowan, halfway into the car, dropped his gun and the chamois bag of gems and barely saved himself by clutching at the rim of the floor of the car. He kicked wildly, and David took the kicks in the chest and belly and dropped back to the ground with a heavy thud. McGowan hung on as the car swept away from the platform and out into space. There was a moment when he might have dropped safely, but in his desperate determination to escape he spent the moment in a futile struggle to lift his gross unathletic body into the car.

David lay on the ground for that same moment, dizzy with the fall. When he recovered sufficiently to stand up he realized in shocked horror that McGowan was now hanging on to the edge of the car floor far above the base of the canyon, his struggles becoming weaker. David turned to climb back onto the platform and stop the ski tow. He had a wild idea that McGowan might be able to hang on long enough for him to reverse the motor and bring him back to safety. Before David had even reached the platform he heard the awful agonizing shriek of terror as McGowan's clutching fingers could no longer hold him and his body fell one hundred fifty feet to the glass-sharp crags of the rocks on the canyon slope. It tumbled over and over, scattering gravel and dust, started a small landslide of rocks, and ended its fall against the base of a concrete pylon in a grotesque death pose.

David looked sadly down the canyon wall at the dead body of McGowan, expended the breath that he did not know he had been holding, and dragged himself back up onto the surface of the parapet. He was stiff and sore and not thinking too clearly, but he was glad that it was all over now. His body reacting to a command already issued, he walked over to the ski-tow control switch and pressed the Stop button. He heard the great wheel grind slowly to a creaking stop. He was conscious that the moving ski cars slowed and came to a halt. A stillness followed, such that it seemed the only person, the one human being in that vast expanse, was David Christopher.

He felt rather than saw or heard the other presence because she was quiet as death. His death. David slammed his open hands against the concrete wall above the switchbox and moaned, "Oh, no!"

"Oh, yes!" Denise said quietly.

Before he turned he knew what he would find. She was standing on the upper parapet, the loading and unloading ramp for the cars, and she was looking down at him. In the crook of her left elbow was her handbag. In her left hand was the chamois bag of diamonds. In her right hand, quite steady, was David's .38. It was not wavering at all, and it was pointed directly at David's broad chest.

"My own gun!" David exclaimed bitterly.

"I didn't really need it," Denise told him. "I have my Beretta in here." She gestured with the .38 toward her handbag.

"Quite the professional killer, aren't you?" he jibed.

"Not really. I never killed anybody." She was quite serious.

David laughed. It was not his best laugh, but a dying man can only do so much.

"A really great criminal never does," David agreed. "He—sorry, she—just arranges it."

"What did I arrange?" Denise asked him.

"For a while you had me confused," David replied. "I have to admit it. Hayes tried to kill me. Logical enough. He hated me. Big Lug's soldiers killed Hayes. Easy to explain. Hayes was cheating on Big Lug. The Africans killed Rascher. Fair enough. He was waiting for it. McGowan killed Villegas. Again logical. McGowan wanted you for himself. Villegas was the only guy who might take you away from him."

"So," she told him in triumph, "I killed nobody."

"Oh, yes you did, baby," he said. "You killed 'em all. When Hayes panicked and ran out of the bank and called you from the PTT, what little bird told him that I was staying at the Regina and that it would make it easier for everybody if he gunned me down? Who tipped off Luigi Valente that Hayes was cheating on him—and told Big Lug exactly how Hayes was cheating and how to find him in Zurich? Such superb timing—down to the very day. Oh, yes, and who but our thoughtful little Mlle. Abbott would have come up with the idea of

tipping off Captain Hans Frey of the Zurich Bank
Detail as well, so that he was waiting for Hayes on
this particular trip but not on any of the hundreds
of trips he had made before? Who set up Rascher
with the Africans—again, so that they got rid of
him just in time to reduce the partners to three and
increase your cut in the process? Along the way
you tipped off Frey to the drop at Neufsuzerain—or
McGowan did it for you, while you were making
sheep's eyes at me. Jesus!" David exclaimed,
throwing up his hands, "How could I have missed
that? You never intended to take the ten million.
This was the deal all along. And the fifteen million.
Another thing I missed. With any luck at Neufsuzerain I might have got into a shootout with the
police that would have got me out of the picture
one way or another. And poor Villegas. The only
decent human being among you. That's what you
were afraid of, I guess. He must have shown some
pangs of conscience when Hayes and Rascher died.
Maybe he began to suspect your tender little hand
in the deal and you thought it was time to send him
along to a better world. Not too difficult for a girl
like you with McGowan. A combination of playing
on his fears and his jealousy. Saying that you
would like to go back with him to Texas, but Villegas was your first love and such a noble man. So
dedicated. A little worried perhaps. A little con-
science-stricken over the crime, now that people
had been killed. But dedicated. Yes, that would
have been about the line you gave McGowan last
night. How about that?" David again broke into
hoarse laughter.

"What's so funny?" she wanted to know.

David's laughter threatened to turn into a paroxysm. "You—must—have—been—stringing along Mc-

Gowan," he gasped in between roars of mirth, "while I was in London ... getting the lowdown on you from Jim Esherbridge!"

David had calculated how much Denise could take down to the last millimeter. As she raised the gun and her finger tightened on the trigger, one of his flailing hands shoved the *On* button of the ski tow. The sudden unexpected whirr of the motor, the grinding of the cable on the big wheel and the lurching of the ski car beside her threw off her aim. The bullet went wild and, before she could fire her last shot, David dived over the edge of the concrete ramp. He heard her second and final shot strike a ski car above his head, then he bounced from the slope and lifted himself in a tremendous leap to the upper platform while Denise was frantically trying to open her handbag. David swept her against the concrete base of the wheel-upright and there was a brief struggle while he wrestled for her bag. When he wrenched the bag so hard that the leather handle snapped against her arm, he was conscious that he was causing her pain and was glad to see her grimace. He stood back from her and took out the Beretta. She was dry-retching, clutching the chamois bag of gems to her breast. He gestured with the Beretta toward the ski car.

"Let's go" he said grimly.

He saw her shudder and glanced over his shoulder. The car bearing Villegas swung by, Villegas still sitting stiff and upright inside. The car circled the parapet and Villegas started downhill on another long free death-ride.

"David?" Denise cried.

He looked back at her. She held out the bag of diamonds and her voice was soft and pressing.

"They're ours ... if we want them." She took a step closer to him. "Yours and mine, David."

David could not tell why he listened to her, standing there alone with her far away from the world on top of the mountain. Suddenly she had never seemed more desirable to him as a woman. He had spent his venom and solved his case. Now there was no more malice in him. No more will for vengeance. She stepped still closer until her face was almost touching his and he could taste the scent of her perfume.

"David, listen to me, please. I beg of you. The blackmailer got them. He killed Villegas and McGowan and got away from us ... don't you see? Nobody knows the truth except you and me."

Lack of sleep, the strain of the day, reaction to the tremendous pressure had got to David. Or perhaps it was the seduction of Denise herself. He had an overwhelming urge to accept what she said, to take her into his arms, to make fierce, sadistic love to her, right there—on the concrete platform—tearing scratching bloody love that he would remember forever.

"Who loses, David?" she pressed him. "Not the bank. A bank doesn't think or feel. It has no morals. How did Hurtilbank get rich? From the estates of people who died in the gas chambers of Auschwitz and Buchenwald, that's how. Do you think those people want the bank to keep it? Money is to live by and laugh by and make love by."

She took David's free hand and pressed the chamois bag into it. She touched his cheeks and chin and lips with her lips.

"Come with me, David—now. I will love you as

296

you have never been loved—never could be loved.
You remember, David? Yesterday? Could it have
been like that unless we love each other?"

David could sense the Lotusland her siren song
sang of. He looked at the chamois bag and felt the
weight of its compact untraceable wealth in the
palm of his hand. For Hurtilbank it was a fleabite,
covered by insurance, forgotten tomorrow morning
while the bank wrestled with the daily business of
its real concerns, like the small matter of a billion
dollars of Haile Selassie's gold. And beside him the
most desirable woman in Europe. A beautiful, appealing creature who had come up the hard way
and wanted to secure her position in life with a
little finagling against impersonal banks. If she let
nature take its course and a few people died along
the way, she was only really speeding up a process
already begun. Hurrying along the inevitable.
Even Villegas might have died much more horribly
at the hands of the military dictatorship he was
hoping to overthrow. Why he said what he eventually said, David didn't know. What he meant to
say was, "You've got a deal, baby. It's going to take
me a year or two to tame you, but I'm going to
have a helluva time doing it." What he actually
said was:

"All my life, Denise ... you'd have my guilty
secret. I'd be like all the others. And they're dead,
remember? ... Poor Denise."

This time when he stood back and pointed with
the Beretta, she knew that the play was over. She
walked past him toward the slowly revolving ski
cars.

"You were very clever," she said.

"Much less clever than you," he answered. "With

that brain of yours you could have made it any way you wanted. Why the hell . . . ?"

David's jaw dropped and his voice died in his throat. The door of a ski car swung open and Captain Hans Frey dropped smoothly to the unloading ledge. From the following car emerged Sergeant Schwand, uncoiling his big body with relief. In contrast to the ruffled and untidy figure of David, Frey was his usual impeccable self. His narrow-brimmed felt hat sat on his head at exactly the right angle, its peacock feather glinting in the rays of the sun. His smart charcoal-gray topcoat was belted over a matching charcoal suit, a white shirt and a steel-blue tie.

"You have an explanation, I presume, Mr. Christopher, for all of these dead people." Frey spoke primly as if he was already suspicious of the answer David would offer.

Before David could answer, Denise brushed past him and ran to Frey. She clung to his arm in desperation.

"Oh, Captain," she said. "Thank God you came in time. This horrible man was about to kill me. He threatened me with that gun, after he killed my friends. He said if I did not pretend that somebody else had killed them and went away with him, he would kill me. He's the real blackmailer, Officer. It was him all the time. Oh, you have saved my life."

Denise burst into tears and her beautiful face found its way to Frey's stiff chest.

"There, there," Frey said, patting her gently. Then Frey looked sternly at David.

"These are very serious charges, Christopher. And they have the ring of truth. You will place yourself in the custody of Sergeant Schwand and you will return with me to Zurich for full questioning."

David raised his eyes to the endless blue of the sky. "Jesus Christ Almighty!" he said. "Here we go again."

AVON ◆ THE BEST IN BESTSELLING ENTERTAINMENT!